"Your ex is an idiot," he assured Frannie. "His loss is my gain."

"Dante...when you say things like that, it's hard to remember that we're keeping things simple between us."

She was right. He was sending mixed signals. "I know. I'm sorry."

"It's okay—just wanted to point it out."

But without solid proof that there was no dangerous intent behind that mysterious flower delivery, he couldn't let Frannie out of his sight.

He made the mistake of assuming his uncle would never stoop so low to get what he wanted—he wouldn't make that mistake again.

Not with Frannie.

Dear Reader,

When I was asked to be a part of the new Colton continuity, I was humbled and flattered to be included in such an incredible lineup of talented authors.

I hope you enjoy *Colton's Secret Stalker* as you delve into a suspenseful story nestled within the complicated dynamics of a large family filled with secrets.

Hearing from readers is a special joy. You can always find me on social media or you can email me.

Happy reading!

Facebook: Facebook.com/Kim.VanMeter.37

Email: alexandria2772@hotmail.com

Kimberly Van Meter

COLTON'S SECRET STALKER

KIMBERLY VAN METER

Special thanks and acknowledgment are given to
Kimberly Van Meter for her contribution to
The Coltons of Owl Creek miniseries.

HARLEQUIN®
ROMANTIC SUSPENSE™

Recycling programs
for this product may
not exist in your area.

ISBN-13: 978-1-335-59398-6

Colton's Secret Stalker

Harlequin Enterprises ULC
22 Adelaide St. West, 41st Floor
Toronto, Ontario M5H 4E3, Canada
www.Harlequin.com

Printed in Lithuania

MIX
Paper | Supporting
responsible forestry
FSC® C021394

Kimberly Van Meter wrote her first book at sixteen and finally achieved publication in December 2006. She has written for the Harlequin Superromance, Blaze and Romantic Suspense lines. She and her husband of thirty years have three children, two cats, and always a houseful of friends, family and fun.

Chapter 1

Frannie Colton had a sixth sense about things. She wouldn't go so far as to call it a genuine psychic gift—but she had a feeling in her gut when a bad wind was blowing.

Today seemed to be one of those days.

A shiver tickled her spine as if the July sun wasn't doing its best to break seasonal records in Idaho. She hustled into her bookstore, Book Mark It, thankful for the air-conditioning that hit her face and cooled her skin.

Usually, Idaho had mild summers but brutal winters. However, this year, Mother Nature seemed interested in pushing boundaries. Today, the temperatures were pushing 90 degrees, which was practically like setting the state on fire.

She waved at her friend Darla, who'd held down the fort so she could make a quick run to the post office, and helped herself to an iced tea from the attached café.

Finally able to breathe, she joined Darla behind the counter. "Thanks for covering the store for me. I had to get those certified documents mailed before the end of the day."

"No problem. It's not every day something that beautiful wanders into the veritable bore factory known as Owl Creek."

Puzzled, she looked to Darla, who then covertly gestured

to the man sitting in one of the comfy high-back chairs, sipping a mocha while thumbing through a table book on ancient Greek architecture.

Frannie chuckled. He was definitely worth a second glance, but he wasn't new to the shop. In fact, he'd been in a few times, but Darla must've missed him.

"His name is Dante Sinclair and he's really nice. Don't go scaring him off," Frannie warned playfully, reminding Darla, "Also, you're about to be married. Keep your eyes in your head."

Not for nothing though, Dante was the kind of man you'd have to be blind to miss. He was tall enough to make the oversize chair appear modest, and his short, cropped hair and the beginnings of a beard were flecked with gray. She didn't know much about him, just that he was polite and courteous and enjoyed a quiet moment with a new book. He definitely wasn't from around these parts. Whether that was a good thing or not remained to be seen.

Darla pouted as if suddenly remembering her fiancé, Tom, was still in the picture. "Fine, but if I can't, you have to promise me you'll try to flirt with that incredible specimen. I'm serious, that right there, is an import. That's no corn-fed farm boy. He looks...dare I say... European?"

"Flirt? That's unprofessional," Frannie scoffed, "Just because he's not wearing mud-caked work boots doesn't mean he's from Europe. And what's wrong with a corn-fed farm boy? Honest work builds strong character."

"Mmm-hmm. Tell that to the Higgins boys. All raised on a dairy farm and all criminals at some point or another."

"The Higgins family has issues. That's not a fair comparison." She sipped her tea while surreptitiously stealing another peek at the stranger. Okay, he wasn't hard on the eyes, and there was a certain air about him that seemed more distinguished, more polished than the local men who called Owl Creek home, but he was probably married, and Frannie wasn't looking for drama.

Besides, men that handsome were trouble—they couldn't help themselves.

"He's probably just on vacation."

"Who in their right mind would vacation here?" Darla quipped.

"Why are you hating on Owl Creek?" she teased. "Blackbird Lake is a popular destination for boaters."

"Does he look like he spends a lot of time on a fishing boat?"

"I try not to judge a book by its cover," Frannie replied with a saucy grin. Darla rolled her eyes, and Frannie pointed finger guns at her playfully, adding, "See? There's a benefit to being a bookworm. Makes you delightfully witty."

"Don't quit your day job, kid." Darla popped from the stool and grabbed her purse. "If you don't need me for anything else, I need to run. I'm supposed to meet Tom at The Tides to go over the wedding details, sign contracts, pay our deposit…you know, all that fun stuff."

"It'll be beautiful," Frannie assured Darla. "And you'll be the most gorgeous bride this town has ever seen."

"We'll see about that. I'm starting to wonder if we should've eloped. I'm over all this wedding crap. What a huge headache. But Tom insists on doing it up big, so here we are. I mean, honestly, who are we trying to impress? Let's just head to the courthouse, sign documents and then spend all that wedding money on an epic honeymoon."

"Stop being a sourpuss and enjoy the moment," she told her best friend. She shooed her out the door, smiling as Darla drove away. Bless Tom for being a saint. Although she loved Darla with everything in her heart, the woman was difficult on her best days.

But she was also intensely loyal and would chew anyone to pieces if they dared to hurt someone she loved. Frannie found that level of commitment reassuring. Not that she wanted Darla to commit a felony in her honor or anything, but...it was nice to know that Darla had her back.

Her gaze strayed to the handsome newcomer. What would it hurt to be friendly and say hello again? Not flirting, of course.

Being neighborly was good business.

But she held back even as she contemplated walking up to the man and interrupting his quiet time. He probably didn't want to be disturbed. Being interrupted while reading was one of her biggest pet peeves, second only to people calling mayonnaise MAN-naise. She always argued, "You don't say, 'Hold the MAN-O,' you say, 'Hold the MAY-O.'"

Darla said Frannie needed to let that peeve die because it made her sound like a card-carrying member of the grammar police.

So be it. Words—and their proper pronunciation—mattered. Hence, her love of books.

But the man was intriguing, sitting in a small-town bookstore in the middle of the day as if he had nothing but time on his hands. He was older than her, she thought. If the gray flecks in his beard weren't enough, the subtle weathering of his skin gave him a rugged, if not sophisticated, look that she found appealing.

Frannie sipped her tea, contemplating the handsome stranger's back story as if he were a character in a novel.

People-watching was one of her favorite pastimes, mostly because she enjoyed creating narratives for her amusement.

He was safely engrossed in his reading, which gave her

the perfect opportunity to watch without being weirdly off-putting.

Maybe Darla was right. He did have a vibe that wasn't quite American.

International spy? James Bond–type right here in Owl Creek? What were the odds? Highly unlikely but not impossible.

It seemed everyone had secrets these days. A sour note threatened to ruin her good mood. The thing about painful breakups was that the pain popped up at unexpected times, even if you've convinced yourself that you're over the cheating jerk-face.

Three months was plenty enough time to move on from a bad boyfriend.

Except…there remained an emotional bruise beneath the skin that hurt like a sonofabitch when she poked at it.

Solution? Don't poke at it.

Instead, enjoy the imported eye candy and remember that books would always be better than boyfriends.

As the thought zipped through her head, the handsome stranger swiveled his gaze straight to hers and smiled.

Being sharp and observant was his bread and butter at work. The minute the cute young woman entered the shop, her cheeks flushed from the heat, her blond hair damp at the hairline, he'd been aware of her every move.

He unintentionally caught a whiff of her skin—a blend of coconut butter and citrus—and his senses prickled with interest.

He'd been coming to the bookstore for a while, but today seemed to be the first day the woman had taken more than a cursory notice of him.

He liked the quaint bookstore and café. For one, books

had a calming effect on his nerves, and two, the mocha blend with cream was nearly as good as the one at his favorite café back home in Italy.

Owl Creek was suitable for his needs—small enough to be unremarkable and big enough for him to blend into the scene without drawing too much attention. But he'd abandoned all hope of finding a coffee shop capable of making anything remotely palatable.

And then he'd stumbled on Book Mark It.

That first tentative sip had flooded his mouth with joy. He missed Italy, but not enough to go back. Not that he could.

And the woman had stunning hazel eyes that sparkled with curiosity and intelligence.

Collecting the book, he rose and approached the counter. "If I haven't said it already, you have a lovely shop," he said, pushing the book toward her. "And I'd like to purchase this."

"Oh! Yes, thank you." Was it the heat, or had he caused that fluster? She quickly rang up the purchase. "So… I have to ask, are you on vacation or something?"

He ignored her question yet extended his hand. "I'm not sure if I've formally introduced myself… I'm Dante Sinclair."

"Frannie Colton. Likewise."

Her hand had calluses on the palm like she was accustomed to working with her hands. Was she the handy sort? Lugging hardware and hammering nuts and bolts for her business? Didn't she have a man to do that for her? He had to remind himself that American men weren't like Italian men, and women here were far more independent. "Is this your shop?"

"Yep. Every nook and cranny. My love affair with books

is an obsession that will never end. I figured I ought to try and monetize it so I can at least use my book purchases as a tax write-off."

He chuckled. "We share a similar love. Whenever I travel, I always seek out the bookstores first."

"Me too! I thought I was the only person to do this anymore. It seems everyone's nose is so stuck in their phones most days that reading an actual book is a foreign concept. My friend Darla, the woman who just left, she's always saying that I was born in the wrong generation, though I don't think I would do very well in a corset with these sturdy hips."

Her self-deprecating humor made him chuckle. Although he didn't see anything wrong with her build. He liked what he saw. *Careful. You're not here to make connections.* He straightened, collecting his book with a short smile. "It was a pleasure to meet you."

"Same to you. You didn't say whether you're here on business or pleasure..."

"A little of both," he answered. "Colton...any relation to the Colton hardware store I saw earlier?"

Frannie's little bashful laugh was adorable. "Um, yeah, my family's been here for generations. There are plenty of Coltons running around this place. You can hardly walk down the street without bumping into one. Made it difficult to get away with anything when we were kids."

"I can only imagine. Probably makes it hard to date, too."

"Oh, yeah, forget about dating," she agreed, chuckling, though there seemed a strained quality to her humor. "Especially with three older brothers who think their baby sister should be kept behind glass. They were a little overprotective."

"Brothers are good for protecting sisters." He paused before asking, "Any older sisters?"

"Yep, two of those. We have a big family. You?"

"No, I'm an only child," he answered without elaborating. Talk of his family was a bad idea. Especially if he wanted to glide under the radar. He supposed no matter where he landed in the heartland of America, he was bound to draw some attention, but he'd needed a place where his family wouldn't think to look.

"So, I hope it's not offensive or anything, but my friend said you have this look about you that's…I don't know how to say…not from around here, which I think is a good thing! Don't get me wrong, you're like a breath of fresh air but was she totally off-base to guess you're from…?"

She was fishing. He ought to lie. But it seemed harmless enough to share a small truth. "Italy."

"Oh damn, she was right. She said you were European."

He smiled, reluctantly charmed, though a frisson of alarm followed. "Is it that obvious?"

"Um, well, a little bit, but I like it. We don't get many international visitors around here." Her cell chirped to life, and she grabbed it quickly, apologizing as she glanced at the message, a frown gathering on her face. "Sorry… I… have to make a call. It was nice to meet you," she said hastily before disappearing into her office.

The door was thin, but her voice was muffled enough only to catch a word or two, and it didn't seem like good news.

He was inclined to wait and see if she returned, but whatever was happening wasn't his business.

He had his own troubles, and he didn't need to add the cute bookstore owner's woes to his plate.

Dante exited the bookstore and hoped whatever had stolen Frannie's smile worked itself out eventually.

Lord only knew he held on to no such hope for himself.

Chapter 2

"I don't understand," Frannie said, still trying to wrap her brain around what her oldest sister, Ruby, was saying. "Aunt Jessie is saying *what*?"

Ruby's voice on the other line was strained as she repeated, "She's saying that…well, that she and Dad had a secret affair for decades and…that she has kids that are owed consideration in his will."

Frannie's mind was spinning. It was hard to decide which bomb to prioritize first. "Okay, give me a minute to process, this is wild. I mean, I know Mom has a twin sister, but we've never heard from or seen Aunt Jessie for pretty much our entire lives. And now she pops up out of nowhere to lay claim to Dad's assets? What does Mom say about all of this? Oh my God, she's probably devastated. Has anyone checked on her yet?"

"I thought we could go see her tonight, maybe bring her dinner or something? I don't know, Mom is so private… even if she did know about this alleged affair, I doubt she would've shared."

"Yeah, it's not like that's something you'd want to shout from the rooftops," Frannie quipped with a rare burst of understanding for her mom. She and Jenny Colton had never been terribly close, but Jenny had been reserved with most of her children. "I shouldn't even find this shocking... It's not like she and Dad had a stellar relationship."

"Well, they got along well enough to have six kids," Ruby pointed out dryly.

The thought of her parents getting biblical ruined Frannie's appetite for the foreseeable future, but Ruby had a solid point. "All I learned from our parents' relationship is that marriages are complicated." She drew a deep breath and peered out of her office to the bookstore, disappointed to see the handsome Italian had left. She returned to her conversation with Ruby. "Okay, I'll pick up a brisket family meal from Back Forty Barbecue. Mom always said food helped bad news go down easier, though I rarely find myself interested in eating when I'm already choking down something terrible."

"Can you rally the troops? I'm swamped with patients today and my break is almost over."

"Sure," Frannie agreed but secretly she didn't want that job. Her siblings were ridiculously hard to wrangle, and she didn't like chasing them down. The easiest to get to agree would be her brother Fletcher because he frequently popped into the shop to say hi, and they were fairly close. The hardest would be her oldest brother, Chase, who was now running Dad's property business. And to be honest, sometimes Chase didn't want to carve out time for family stuff because everything else under the sun was more important.

Maybe that wasn't nice or kind to say, but the truth often stung.

Family dynamics were complicated. Just like marriages.

"So, how did you hear about this?" Frannie asked.

"Dad's attorney called to let me know Aunt Jessie had marched into his office demanding a copy of Dad's will. When questioned, she dropped her little scandal bomb." Ruby groaned. "God, I hope she didn't do this in front of people we know. I can only imagine how quickly that little nugget would roll around town."

"Small towns love gossip," Frannie agreed, wincing. "Well, I guess we'll cross that bridge when we come to it. See you around six?"

"Yeah, thanks for picking up the food. I'll call Mom and make sure she's home tonight."

"Sounds good."

They clicked off, and Frannie took a minute to breathe through the chaos swirling in her head. Was it possible Aunt Jessie was lying? Maybe she and her kids were trying some desperate money grab? No one knew the woman's financial situation. Maybe there was nothing to Aunt Jessie's claims, and all of this would go away once she realized no one was buying her story. But it sure was a whopper of a tale to tell without proof.

A DNA test would immediately prove whether or not her kids were owed something from Robert Colton's assets.

Eww. Just saying that in her head made her want to vomit.

And how old were these supposed half siblings? Younger than her? It would be unsettling to discover her place as the baby of the family had been usurped by these mystery kids.

She groaned. Two more siblings? *Our family is big enough as it is.*

Frannie rubbed her rumbling belly. Her stomach had always been sensitive to drama. The conflict made her stomach yowl in protest. Imagine being the youngest in a loud, boisterous family, the only one who preferred peace and quiet with a book somewhere far away from the she-nanigans of her siblings.

Her bookstore was not only her happy place but a reminder of how books had always been her safe place growing up.

Chase had teased her mercilessly whenever he'd found

her nose in a book, and Wade, desperate to impress his big brother, had almost always chimed in. Fletcher, on the other hand, had always defended her. It was probably why they'd remained close and why Fletcher continued to be so protective. When Fletcher had discovered how dirty her boyfriend had done her, it'd taken a reminder that he wasn't cut out for prison that'd saved Bobby Newfield's worthless hide.

But Lord knew Frannie loved him for it.

Releasing a deep breath, she sent a quick group text to the gang:

Important meeting at Mom and Dad's @6 p.m. Aunt Jessie blew into town with a potential scandal. I'm bringing a brisket meal. Feel free to bring a dessert or drinks. Frannie

Texting was better than a phone call, anyway. It wasn't like anyone liked to answer the phone anymore.

As expected, Chase's response was cut, dry and impersonal.

Sorry, out of town, but I'm already aware. Handling it.

He probably didn't mean to sound that way, but he did. And, wait a minute, if he already knew, why did Ruby have to find out through Dad's lawyer? *Damn you, Chase, always acting like the gatekeeper. So annoying.*

Hannah quickly apologized.

Sorry, Lucy's got that bug going around, so I'm going to stay home with her. Let me know what's happening after you talk to Mom. Love ya, Han.

Wade didn't respond at all. *Typical.*
Fletcher's response made her smile.

I'm around the corner. Be there in five.

He knew how to make her smile and, somehow, feel less agitated.

Thankfully, it was almost closing time. She started her closing routine, and Fletcher walked in moments later, just as he'd promised.

The look on his face pulled at her heart. "What the hell is going on?" he asked, hands anchored above his law enforcement utility belt. "Is this for real? Aunt Jessie? What kind of scandal are we talking? Has a crime been committed? Is this something that should be reported?"

Frannie sent Fletcher an exasperated look, glancing meaningfully at the last straggling customers left in the store, and Fletcher caught her drift, reluctantly waiting as Frannie closed and locked the door and flipped her sign. "Sorry, your text got me all riled up," he apologized. "But what the hell? I need more details than that."

"Honestly, I don't have much to go on. Ruby said Dad's lawyer called to say that Aunt Jessie showed up in his office demanding a copy of the will. When he asked who she was and why she was entitled to the documents, she said that she and Dad had been together for decades and that she had two of his children, who, by law, are entitled to a portion of Dad's assets."

"What?" Fletcher exploded. "That's some bullshit if I ever heard any."

"Well, maybe? I guess a DNA test will clear up that mystery real quick, but what if she's telling the truth? I can only imagine how hurt Mom will be by this news. I mean, her own sister? Her *twin*? That's cold by any flick of the channel."

Fletcher softened at the mention of their mother. "Yeah, that's a crap sandwich if it's true…but do you really think Dad would—hell, I don't even like to think he was capable of being that big of an ass."

They'd long suspected their dad wasn't faithful to their mom, but no one liked to talk about the elephant in the room.

However, to cheat with Mom's sister? Frannie pushed down the wave of disappointment. Everyone thought Frannie had been their father's favorite, but Robert Colton hadn't exactly been involved in any of his kids' lives. He'd been a solid provider, but as far as emotional support went, he'd been sorely lacking.

Even so, Frannie and her dad had shared some commonalities that had created a bit of a bond, which made the current news sit uncomfortably.

"Is it bad to hope that Aunt Jessie is mentally unstable or lying through her teeth?" Frannie asked.

Fletcher sighed, shaking his head. "Hell, I don't know but I feel the same. Guess we'll find out."

"Yeah, I guess so. Do you think I should pick up a bottle of wine or something? Feels like alcohol might help settle the nerves."

"For you or for Mom?"

Frannie laughed. "Maybe just for me."

Fletcher chuckled. "All right. I've got to finish my shift. I'll see you in a bit."

Frannie nodded and followed Fletcher, pausing to lock up the shop and head to the barbecue joint.

It might've been a misplaced attempt at distracting herself from current events, but as she placed her order, Frannie thought of Dante, the Italian stranger. As Darla pointed out, Owl Creek wasn't a huge draw for international travelers. Sure, it was quaint, and it had its charm, but it was hardly a mecca of touristy attractions, no matter what the Chamber of Commerce tried to assert with their splashy local commercials.

So why would a man like Dante, who was sophisticated, well-spoken and sticking out like a sore thumb, pick a place like Owl Creek to hang out?

Maybe she'd read too many true-crime novels because she was already formulating less-than-legal reasons why.

This was one of the downsides to being a voracious bookworm—the what-ifs were endless.

"Lord knows, Francesca, your imagination is enough to fuel an entire literary career," her mother had once said to her in a moment of exasperation. And she'd used her *given* name, which always made her cringe. Not that *Frannie* was much better, but she had to deal with the hand and the name she'd been dealt.

"Order for Frannie C," a voice rang out, and Frannie snapped out of her random thoughts to scoop up the order with a brief smile.

As she climbed into her car, the aroma of fresh barbecue filling the cab, she thought ruefully that at least the food wouldn't disappoint.

But she had a feeling tonight was going to be rough.

Dante stood on the porch of his rustic rented cabin and listened to the wind whistle through the trees. The warm air caressed his cheek and ruffled his hair. The temperate summer was similar enough to his native country, but that was where the similarities ended.

There was a comforting simplicity to the ebb and flow

of Owl Creek. He'd been here almost two weeks and had begun to get a feel for the vibe. The countryside was breathtaking, and the rental was fitting for the area. The A-frame log cabin was built to withstand bitter winters with plenty of snowfall, but he didn't know where he'd be come winter.

He wasn't accustomed to the quiet.

Dante breathed in the clean air, closing his eyes as birds twittered from the branches while unseen forest floor creatures rustled from beneath the ground cover, but something was soothing about the fact that out here, nature ruled supreme.

Not his family.

Being part of the Santoro family—one of the most powerful and dangerous in Italy—was a double-edged sword. It was only a matter of time before you got cut somewhere.

It would be disingenuous to say the money and prestige didn't have its perks: the fine clothing, expensive cars and the privilege that came with the association. But nothing came without a cost.

And he was done chipping off pieces of his soul to pay the toll.

Dante straightened, rubbing his arms as an errant chill popped goose bumps along his skin. The paranoia never left him. No matter how random Owl Creek seemed on a map or how remote this cabin was, he couldn't shake the tension that eyes were on him.

His uncle Lorenzo wasn't the kind of man to let any perceived slight go unanswered.

Not even when it was family committing the offense.

His only insurance policy until he could figure out a better solution?

Something his uncle would kill to have returned.

For now, it was locked away in a safety-deposit box under a fake name.

But sometimes, he worried not even that would keep him safe from his uncle's reach.

Dante pushed away from the railing and went inside, locking the door behind him.

Chapter 3

Jenny, always calm during any crisis, was no different when faced with the possibility that her husband had fathered two children with her twin sister. Just saying the words in her head made Frannie want to sink into the floor.

Damn you, Dad.

If he wasn't already dead...

"Frannie, can you please get the plates out," Jenny said, moving on autopilot as she unpacked the brisket meal Frannie had brought. Of course, Frannie was there before any of her siblings showed up because even when she tried to drag her feet, her need to be on time took the reins.

"Mom, we don't need to use the real plates. Paper plates should be fine."

"Not for brisket, dear," Jenny replied without missing a beat. "Also, did you manage to talk to Mrs. Gershwin from the Garden Club about those dead azaleas in the planter berm in front of your store? It's such an eyesore and takes away from all the lovely work you've done for your little shop."

Dead azaleas were the least of Frannie's concerns at the moment. "Mom, I know what you're doing. It's okay to admit that you're upset. We're all here for you. What Dad did—"

"We don't know anything yet," Jenny cut in, her soft

voice with the slightest reproachful edge, as if Frannie were the one acting out of pocket for even mentioning it. "I don't believe in building bridges for rivers we don't need to cross just yet."

"But that's just it, Mom, we do have to cross that bridge, the river is here and it's about to wipe out the aforementioned bridge. We have to face this head-on."

"What's to face? If it's true…" Jenny paused, revealing a minute crack in her reserve before pushing forward "…then we deal with it. It is what it is."

Frannie hated that saying. Not only did that phrase feel like a cop-out, it also felt like defeat. "Do you think your sister could be lying?"

"I haven't seen or spoken to Jessie in decades. I haven't a clue what she might be capable of at this point in her life."

"Yeah, but you knew her as a kid. What was she like?"

Jenny blinked as if Frannie had viciously poked a bruise to see if it still hurt. It took a minute, but Jenny recovered, saying, "It was a long time ago. I hardly remember. Besides, no one is the same person they were as a child. I know I'm certainly not. Life changes people. Circumstances, choices, all those variables go into the mix, and you pop out a different version of yourself when it's all said and done. It happens to everyone. It's just the way of things, Frannie."

Frannie heard the hidden pain in that statement. As a mother, Jenny had been competent, solid and appropriately present. Even as a full-time nurse, Jenny had been the one to oversee her children's schooling, sports and home needs, though Frannie had never felt that Jenny loved being a mom. It felt contradictory to admit that truth when the woman had given birth to six kids. But Frannie always wondered if that had been some attempt to keep Robert interested in staying, not so much an interest in being a mother to a large brood.

It always hurt to stare hard truths in the eye.

But it also made her sad for her mother. "Mom…did you and Dad ever actually love each other?"

Jenny stilled, her back to Frannie. "In the beginning, very much." She slowly turned, exhaling a long breath as she admitted, "Well, at least for me, anyway. I've spent a lifetime trying to make something better than it was for the sake of my children. The truth of the matter was, Robert and I…well, maybe we were never a good fit at all."

Jenny's revelation stunned Frannie. Intensely private by nature, her mother would rather lick a dirty sidewalk than share the depth of her feelings on any particular subject. The fact that Jenny was sharing even a smidge of her business with anyone was jarring.

And Frannie didn't know how to respond.

Jenny seemed to understand and returned to unpacking the brisket meal.

But Frannie had to say something. "Mom…if it turns out to be true… I'm really sorry. You deserved better than what Dad gave you."

Jenny accepted Frannie's sentiment, sniffing back what may have been a tear or two, and then excused herself to the bathroom with a reminder that the sturdier napkins were in the pantry.

Sighing, Frannie sank into the chair at the kitchen island and mentally prodded her siblings to hurry up and get their happy asses to the house. She wasn't sure how much more she could absorb on her own. She needed the buffer of her brother and sister, or she'd end up stress-eating everything in sight.

Her gaze wandered around the home she'd grown up

in, seeing memories in a different light. It was funny how kids could be incredibly intuitive yet miss obvious clues staring them in the face.

Their home was aesthetically beautiful. Jenny had refined tastes that she used to shape Robert's rough, masculine edges into something strong yet elegant. Frannie had never known the sharp pangs of hunger or gone without anything she needed. Between Jenny and Robert, their six kids had enjoyed the privilege of an upper-middle-class upbringing. Christmas had been a favorite holiday, with the smells of holiday baking permeating the house and plenty of gifts beneath the tree.

As a kid, she remembered her dad sitting in his chair, watching the chaos with a small, satisfied smile, like the proud papa enjoying the fruits of his labor. And she remembered the hushed arguments behind closed doors and the strained smile of her mother as unspoken words between them created an invisible tension.

But even on Christmas Day, Robert only hung around for a short time, always with an excuse or reason to cut out. Now it made her wonder, had he been rushing off to spend time with his other family?

Frannie groaned, hating every syllable of that question. Even worse, had her mother known the reason he was leaving? The thought of her mother suffering such emotional agony in silence was more than she could bear.

Fresh anger at her father washed over her in a wave, and tears stung her eyes.

The front door opened, and Frannie muttered, "Thank God." She quickly wiped at her eyes, relieved that the troops had finally arrived.

Ruby lifted a brown paper bag, announcing, "I brought the wine," and Fletcher, right behind her, said, "And I brought peach pie and beer, because I don't drink wine and peach pie is good for any occasion."

"Mom's freshening up," Frannie said, motioning to Ruby. "I'll take a glass, if you don't mind."

Ruby's eyebrow rose as she reached for the wine glasses. "Already? What'd I miss?"

Frannie didn't have the words. "Just pour the wine."

"That means I'll start with the beer," Fletcher quipped with dark humor, but they all felt the heaviness in the air. How could they not? As if their dad collapsing from a stroke hadn't been a big enough shock to the family. Now this? Well, if this situation had taught Frannie anything, it was…sometimes the secrets of the dead didn't stay in the grave.

It was a dream and a memory morphing into one another to create a hellish movie that Dante couldn't escape.

"I'm not doing this anymore," Dante shouted at his uncle Lorenzo. "I'm done being the club you wield to ruin lives. I'm out."

"Who do you think you are?" Lorenzo's thick Italian accent deepened with florid anger. "I made you—I will end you. I decide when you're finished, and that time is not now."

The Santoro trust had paid for Dante's law degree, but Lorenzo acted as if the check came from his personal account. As the executor, Lorenzo knew he held a certain power over the entire Santoro family, and he wasn't shy about reminding anyone who stepped out of line.

But Dante wasn't afraid of his uncle. Maybe he should be, but Lorenzo had exhausted Dante's endurance, and if he didn't get out now, his soul would never recover. "You've gone too far. I won't be a party to this level of corruption. You'll have to find a new attorney to represent the family."

"For a smart man, you make stupid moves," Lorenzo said. "I've destroyed men for less than what you dare right now. I'll allow this one moment of insanity because I have a softness for you, nephew, but don't press your luck. My patience only stretches so far."

Dante held his uncle's stare without flinching. "I'm out."

And he left Lorenzo's office, his uncle's shouting still ringing in his ears.

One truth about Lorenzo, and perhaps why the family was obscenely wealthy—his ruthlessness was exacted with purpose.

The scene shifted, and he was at Belinda's apartment, waiting for her shift to end at the hospital. A pediatric surgeon, Belinda was at the top of her field. Hospitals worldwide courted her services, but she loved her home country and refused to relocate, no matter the offer.

Belinda made Dante realize he couldn't keep doing what he was doing at his uncle's command if he wanted a life with a woman like her. She was kind and generous and believed in the inherent goodness of people. If he married her and inevitably dragged her into his world, it would ruin everything he loved about Belinda.

And he couldn't do that to her.

Besides, he could start fresh. He didn't need the Santoro money to make his way. He'd have to start small, but he could build something he could be proud of from scratch.

Something his father would've approved of. There'd been a reason his father had moved away from his brother and the entire Santoro legacy.

If he hadn't died…maybe life would've been much different for him and his mother.

May she rest in peace.

The loud ticking of the clock reverberated in his head. Belinda was late.

The scene shifted again.

Belinda, broken and bleeding, beaten within an inch of her life, barely alive after the attack.

But the brutal destruction of her fingers made Dante realize with horror that someone had specifically targeted the very thing that made Belinda special in her field.

The tendons in her right hand had been severed, the bones in her left, crushed. The reality that she may never operate again struck his core, lodging a permanent stone in his stomach.

And then the note, delivered with a brilliant spray of flowers to Dante while he spent every hour at Belinda's beside, praying desperately for a miracle that chilled his blood.

The Family is here for you and Belinda. Arrangements are already prepared for Belinda's care when you return.

His guts twisted in agony. Lorenzo had done this. *That sick bastard.* He'd crushed an innocent woman to get Dante to return as a warning to get back in line, or else the consequences would be severe.

Dante had foolishly believed he could handle whatever Lorenzo threw at him.

He'd never imagined Belinda might be the one to pay the price for his actions.

His hands curled, shaking with impotent violence.

How could he prove it? He couldn't.

Lorenzo's strength was his ability to protect himself from legal ramifications. Dante had spent his legal career doing that for the Santoro family—enabling them to ruin people from behind the safety of legal might.

And Lorenzo had just ruined Belinda.

Belinda's eyes popped open, bloodshot, and rimmed with tears. "You did this to me!" she screeched, holding up her gnarled and broken fingers, the unnatural bend of her digits like something from a horror film. "This is all your fault, and I will never forgive you until you die!"

With Belinda's scream ringing in his mind, Dante shot up, his heart racing, staring blindly into the dark of his bedroom. *Where am I?* Sweat dampened his body and made the sheets tangled around his legs feel like cling wrap. *Idaho.* Not Italy.

Just a nightmare. No, not just a nightmare, a terrible memory. Six months later and the same nightmare chased him wherever he went.

Kicking off the sheets, he rose on unsteady feet to splash water on his face. Pale moonlight bathed the rustic bathroom, creating unsettling shadows where anyone could lurk. His heart was still beating hard against his chest.

A million apologies would never fix what Lorenzo had taken from Belinda.

What Lorenzo had taken from Dante.

And if Dante was right...that tally was far bigger than he could've imagined.

Pushing away from the sink, he returned to the bedroom and quickly dressed.

It didn't matter that it was only three in the morning. There'd be no more sleep for him tonight.

Chapter 4

Frannie would need all the coffee to keep her eyes open today at work. She tried to get Darla to come by the shop to help her do inventory, but wedding details had her busy all day. Frannie's request probably wasn't entirely based on her need for help but rather on someone to talk to about her current family situation, someone she knew she could trust.

It wasn't like she wanted to share her family's embarrassment all over town. But the news was likely circulating in hushed whispers, because the gossip hotline in Owl Creek was second to none.

The usual customers milled about, enjoying their lattes and browsing, or sitting in the big, comfy chairs while reading, which gave Frannie a chance to decompress from last night's meeting.

She supposed it went well enough, but only because Jenny Colton wasn't the type of woman to weep and wail, no matter her tragedy. If there was one thing her mother excelled at, it was internalizing emotional trauma. Marrying Robert had given her plenty of practice, if the rumors were true.

"Mom, we just want you to know we're here for you," Ruby had assured their mother, trying to get their mom to open up. But Jenny, as always, had kept her emotions in check and smiled at her daughter, suggesting that Ruby get a trim because her split ends were starting to show.

Frannie had shared a look with Ruby, feeling her sister's frustration but appreciating her restraint when she just accepted their mother's mild reproach with a tight-lipped nod. Even if she were bleeding out in the street, their mother would never admit to needing help. Maybe that was why she'd never talked about why she and her sister stopped speaking to each other. The emotional pain was private, and no one needed to know. Frannie was fairly sure her mom saved her tears for the privacy of the shower. She could recall one instance when she thought she'd heard her mom crying in the bathroom, but when Jenny emerged an hour later—dressed and ready to start the day—it was like Frannie had imagined it.

What kind of life was that?

Frannie winced as her gut cramped. She pushed away the half-eaten croissant and blew on her coffee before sipping. What she wanted to say to her dad if he were still alive to listen would make her childhood Girl Scout leader gasp.

"Frannie…a good woman minds her business," Robert had once told her when she'd dared to ask why he never bought his wife flowers on any occasion despite knowing that Jenny loved flowers of any kind.

"But Dad…"

"Your mother gets what she needs."

Even at a young age, Frannie didn't believe that. A sadness pulled on her mother, even though Jenny did a bang-up job hiding it beneath a veneer of efficiency and practicality.

But Robert Colton never made mistakes and therefore hadn't felt the need to entertain the opinions of others on the subject. Even those of his "favorite" daughter.

God, her dad had been such a prick.

And then there was her Aunt Jessie, too. What kind of woman not only slept with her twin sister's husband but then carried on a decades-long affair with the man? That was almost sociopathic.

There were also her supposed half siblings to think about, which caused an involuntary shudder.

She didn't want to be salty to innocent people—Jessie's kids didn't ask to be part of this drama—but it was hard not to feel some standoffishness when it felt like interlopers were trying to cram their way into her family.

If her Aunt Jessie was telling the truth, that meant these new cousins were her siblings—the thought gave her an instant headache. Never in a million years had she ever thought her family might have scandal lurid enough to land a guest spot on some tell-all TV show.

The front door opened, and the handsome Italian walked in. Even though she wasn't much in the mood to smile, the urge tugged at the corners of her mouth. Her heart did a little jig when he walked straight to the counter instead of perusing the shelves.

"Good morning," he said with a brief smile before going straight to business. "I'm going to be in town for a little while longer and I wondered if you'd be able to order some books for me?"

Frannie stood a little straighter. "Oh! Yes, of course. I'd be happy to. What did you have in mind?"

"Well, a combination of legal works and fiction." He slid a prepared list toward her, including his cell number. "Just call me when they come in, and I'll come and pick them up right away. I'm also happy to pay in advance."

"You don't have to do that. I trust you," she said, the words popping from her mouth before she realized she had nothing to base her assumption on. Was this her problem? Always assuming people were inherently good? Look where that had gotten her. For all she knew, he could be an incredibly attractive swindler. She hastily replied, "But if you'd feel more comfortable paying in advance, that works, too."

"I'll just go ahead and pay now," he said, smiling as if somehow privy to her mental conversation. He pulled cash from his wallet as she rang up his purchase. Hadn't she read somewhere that someone carrying a lot of cash was a red flag nowadays? Or was her overactive imagination running away with her?

"Is everything okay? I couldn't help but notice you got an upsetting call yesterday," he said.

Surprised but inordinately touched that he noticed, she answered with a smile. "Just family stuff. You know how that goes."

"Of course."

Dante had ordered legal tomes, different from the usual purchase for the average reader. Was it possible he was an attorney? She might not want to share her family drama, but Dante might have some tips on handling the situation with her Aunt Jessie. *Ten seconds ago, you questioned his moral integrity, and now you're considering asking him for legal advice?* Fair point, but what were the *actual* odds that he was a bad person? She was going to risk it. "I'm sorry if this is none of my business, but I wondered, might you be an attorney?"

He hesitated for the barest moment before confirming, "I am. Why?"

"Oh, no reason. I mean, the books you ordered suggested you might be connected to law in some way, and I could really use someone to talk to who has some understanding of certain legal things."

"Are you in trouble?" he asked with a concerned frown.

"Me? Um, no, not exactly, but my family might be."

"Do you mind sharing?"

She hesitated. Was it wise to talk to Dante about this stuff, or was she tripping headlong into a muddy puddle by asking him for advice? There was no way to explain it logically, but she felt she could trust him and needed someone to talk to.

"I should warn you, it's very 'Maury Povich' level."

His expression deepened in question. "What is… Maury Povich?"

"Sorry, it's a saying when something is scandalous and geared toward 'revealing taboo secrets.' From a daytime talk show host. Anyway, it's embarrassingly scandalous." Was that a slight smile? He must be like most people who thought nothing bad happened in small towns. *You sweet summer child.* Frannie was about to ruin his illusions. She chuckled ruefully, "No, trust me, it's next-level embarrassing. Shocking, even."

"Now you have to tell me. To leave me hanging would be cruel."

Frannie glanced around her shop. The nearest customer had left, and the only other was deep in the Self-Help aisle farthest from them. She felt safe enough to share. "I might as well just rip off the bandage. My dad died of a stroke a few months ago—it was a shock, but then again, not so much. He didn't do much to safeguard his health, so it was either going to be a heart attack or a stroke, and in the end, it was the stroke that took him out."

"I'm sorry for your loss," he murmured appropriately.

"Thank you. It's been hard but we'd started to adjust to life without Dad. Until my aunt Jessie—my mom's twin sister whom I've never met, by the way—showed up demanding a piece of my dad's assets for her children because, surprise, she and my dad were having a decades-long affair beneath my mom's nose."

Dante absorbed the information without reacting, which lawyers were trained to do, but she appreciated the mature response. It was hard enough to get the words out without having to navigate big reactions, too.

"Does this Aunt Jessie have proof of her children's paternity?"

"Not yet but that's the first thing I suggested. In this day and age, if you're going to make a claim like that, you'd better have proof."

"Yes, indeed. Your family has legal representation?"

"Um, well, we have my dad's attorney who facilitated the will and stuff like that."

"But you haven't retained him for this specific purpose?"

"No, not that I'm aware but I didn't think to ask my mom about that specifically. For all I know, maybe she already has that handled. It's hard to know the appropriate way to deal with something like this," she admitted forlornly. "Honestly, it feels like an out-of-body experience just hearing the words come out of my mouth."

Dante was kind but firm, saying, "You need to find out if you have an attorney safeguarding your father's assets. It'll be important in the future. The burden of proof is on your aunt to prove paternity. That's the first hurdle. If she fails to produce evidence that your father is in fact her children's father, then she has no case. But a good attorney will be able to smother that spark before it has a chance to cause any damage."

She didn't know if her father's attorney was good, but her brother Chase might have a good attorney on the job. Chase might be distant and preoccupied, but he wasn't stupid. He'd do whatever it took to protect the family's assets. "I appreciate the insight," she said. "My brother is probably already handling all the business side, but I can't help but worry this will unravel my family. I'm more worried about the emotional shrapnel."

"The consequence of infidelity is often destructive," he agreed with empathy. "Have you met these alleged half siblings?"

"No, my aunt and mother had some kind of falling out before we were even born. I've never met my aunt or her kids. I don't know if that's a blessing or not. I don't know how I'd feel if I found out cousins I'd known my entire life turned out to be half siblings. Blech, the whole thing is gross."

He chuckled, then apologized. "It's not funny, but I've never heard anyone characterize a family trauma as 'gross' before. I suppose you're right, though. If it's true, very gross, indeed."

I like him. Frannie smiled, biting her lip. Was she flirting? *Well, that's inappropriate as hell.* She let the smile fade, shaking off the warmth Dante's attention created. "Anyway, I don't mean to bore you with all this stuff. I'm sure it'll work out in the end, somehow."

"You're an optimist."

"Yeah, I guess so. You're not?"

"I'm a realist."

"Sounds depressing," she said with a laugh. "Reality often sucks, which is why I prefer books."

"Fair enough. Maybe that's why I prefer books, too," he agreed, flashing that million-dollar smile again. Did all Italian men have that subtle twinkle in their eye? Like a flash of banked mischief just waiting for the right opportunity to flare up?

"So, subject change, have you read the books I'm ordering for you?"

"Yes. When I left Italy, I didn't have room in my luggage, so I planned to buy new copies when I landed."

"Not that I want to talk you out of a purchase, but you know you can just download these onto your phone?"

"I prefer to hold a book in my hand. Helps me to absorb the information," he said, shrugging. "It's more of a comfort as well."

"I'm the same way," she said, tickled that they shared the same preference. She loved all access to literature but truly loved settling into a cozy chair with a printed book in her hand. Reading was more than absorbing information—it was an experience. "Well, I'll let you know when they arrive."

"Thank you," he said. If it seemed he was looking for a reason to stick around, it passed, and with a small wave, he left the shop.

Frannie wasn't looking for a date, but if she were... Dante would be at the top of a very short list.

You're playing a dangerous game, a voice warned Dante as he climbed into his car. Frannie was a sweet young woman—and he wouldn't put her in harm's way just because he found her sharp mind intriguing.

That's not the only reason you can't stop thinking about her, the voice added.

All right, there was a wholesome sweetness about Frannie that he found alluring, but that was precisely the reason he had to keep his distance.

Even though he took precautions to remain under his uncle's radar—he paid cash wherever he went and maintained a low profile—the second his diligence started to slip, he only had to remember Belinda's gnarled hands, and he snapped back to reality.

He couldn't risk Frannie falling into Lorenzo's sights.

Besides, what did he think could happen between him and Frannie Colton? If she thought the potential of her father stepping out on her mother and creating another family was scandalous, the crimes of his own family would put her into a coma.

Financial extortion, intimidation, hostile corporate takedowns...all skirting the letter of the law, but the lives ruined at the expense of his uncle's greed was nothing short of emotional bankruptcy.

What one can convince another to do with manipulative persuasion is amazing.

In the beginning, his uncle had greased the wheels with praise, pride, and familial attachments. Then it had progressed to outright bullying whenever someone pushed back.

The movies helped perpetuate the myth of the Italian mob family, but you didn't have to be toting guns and blowing up cars to intimidate people into doing your bidding.

Lorenzo wasn't a mobster, but he'd done things that should've been criminal.

And Dante had helped him.

God save my soul. It was bad enough that Dante felt he'd never be free of the stain on his soul, but after Belinda's attack, he suffered the sickening realization that maybe his uncle's crimes went farther than white-collar financial greed.

And he had to know.

Speaking of...

His cell rang with the number of the private investigator he planned to hire. The man had a reputation for having a sharp mind, discreet tactics and international contacts. Dante needed a ninja who wasn't afraid of the Santoro name.

"Dante," he answered.

"This is Nicholas Gladney, but you can call me Nick. You left a message."

"I did. I want to hire you."

"What would Dante Santoro need a private investigator for?"

The man had already done his homework. *Good.* It would be the first time verbalizing his suspicion, but after what happened to Belinda, he was done speculating.

Cutting straight to the point, he replied bluntly, "I suspect my uncle had something to do with my mother's death—and if it's true, I need proof."

Chapter 5

Frannie felt as if she were doing something wrong. She didn't know why she'd agreed to this meeting with her estranged aunt Jessie. Morbid curiosity, perhaps? Maybe she was a glutton for punishment? Who knew.

Purposefully asking for a table in the back, she chewed her cheek while waiting for the woman trying to rip her family apart. She wondered if she still had time to bail before her aunt arrived.

This was ridiculous. At the very least, she should've asked Ruby or Fletcher to come with her—safety in numbers. Not that she thought her aunt would jump over the table and stab her with a dinner fork, but she didn't know this woman from Adam. Who knew what she was capable of?

Just when Frannie's anxiety was about to hit the roof, a woman rounded the corner, and Frannie instantly knew it was her aunt Jessie.

She was the same height as her mom, but her hair was a brittle blond as opposed to her mother's dark blond with streaks of gray, and Jessie's sharpness almost seemed hawkish.

Frannie knew her mother and sister had been known around town as great beauties. Small towns loved to cling to the memory of someone's past. Whereas Jenny had aged gracefully, allowing time to soften the edges and claim its due, her sister seemed determined to cling to her youth with almost palpable desperation.

"Darling, sweet Frannie," Jessie cooed, coming straight at Frannie to fold her into a hug. The woman was so thin that Frannie could nearly count the bones in her spine. "Goodness gracious, you've grown into such a beauty."

As Frannie had never met Jessie, she didn't know how her aunt would know anything about her. Unless her mother had contacted her sister unbeknownst to anyone else, but that didn't seem likely.

Especially when Jenny had maintained that she hadn't seen or spoken to her sister since Aunt Jessie divorced Uncle Buck.

What was the etiquette for this kind of situation? She took her seat and waited for Jessie to take the lead. After all, Jessie had asked to meet.

Jessie signaled for the waitress and ordered an iced tea without sugar or lemon, which, as far as Frannie was concerned, was just bitter dark water, but that seemed appropriate given the circumstances.

"My dear, I can only imagine how confused you must be—how confused you all must be—and I want to assure you, I never wanted things to happen the way they did."

Which part? The part where she had an affair with her sister's husband or demanded some of Robert Colton's assets after he died? Frannie didn't want to be sharp but found Jessie's comment disingenuous. Frannie chose her words carefully. "Aunt Jessie... I don't want to be rude, but I can't make head or tail of anything that's happened recently. I have so many questions but don't even know where to start."

"Of course," Jessie said, flicking her napkin and placing it on her lap. "I understand. I always wanted to tell the family, but for obvious reasons, your father had adamantly opposed my ardent desire to be honest with Jenny. It was one of our more frequent disagreements."

Frannie was grateful they hadn't ordered any food. She doubted her stomach would allow for anything beyond a breadstick. "I'm not a fan of placing all the blame on a woman when infidelity is involved but I gotta say, you're coming off as real cold to do what you did with your sister's husband. You knew he was married. How could you do that?"

Jessie's smile froze, and her gaze frosted. "It's easy to stand in judgment, darling, when you're not involved."

"But I am involved, aren't I? You're my aunt, he's my dad…kinda involved by default. And now my cousins are my half siblings? It's all very Jerry Springer, you know what I mean?"

"I told your father it was best to be honest," Jessie returned, narrowing her gaze. "But your father wasn't a man who listened to any opinion above his own."

That much was true. "I'm sorry," Frannie murmured because it felt like she should, but it was hard to feel compassion for a woman who'd purposely had another life with a married man on the sly. "So what happens now?"

"Well, as distasteful as my request may seem, the ugly truth remains—Robert and I may not have been married but I was his wife in all things except on paper. My children deserve their fair share of their father's assets…as do I."

"You?"

"Yes."

"How so?"

"As I said, I was his wife as much as Jenny. The only difference—"

"The big difference was that he was *actually* married to my mother. Legally," Frannie pointed out, her temper rising at her aunt's audacity. "I fail to see how you can think that you're owed anything when you knew what you were doing was wrong."

"When is loving someone wrong?" Jessie countered. She seemed to be trying to appeal to Frannie's sense of romanticism.

"When the other person is already married to someone else," Frannie answered flatly.

"Yes, I suppose that may be true but what's done is done. Your father isn't here to bear your judgment, so that leaves only me. Whether you agree or not, legally, I'm assured I have a solid case." It didn't look like Jessie was going to go quietly.

Frannie stilled. "You have an attorney?"

"I wouldn't have stirred the pot without ample assurances that doing so would be worth the trouble."

Worth the trouble of blowing up my family's life. A blithe statement for such a terrible action.

Frannie swallowed the sudden lump in her throat. "Did you think of your sister at all? How this might hurt her? You're twins...surely you must've cared for her at some point in your life."

"I loved your father, and he loved me. It may be hard to hear but your father never truly loved Jenny."

Maybe it was the subtle shrug or the feeling that Jessie didn't actually give two figs for her sister, but Frannie saw red. "You're a piece of work. How dare you. Who do you think you are? You were my father's *mistress*, not some great love—and I hate to break it to you, but I doubt you were the only one."

Jessie's cold smile matched the chill in her eyes. "Darling, I knew your father better than anyone. Fidelity was never his strength, but he always returned to me."

"No, actually, he always returned to my mother."

Something flashed in Jessie's eyes—rage, perhaps?—and Frannie sensed this entire meeting had been a ruse to try to feel out the family's disposition about her claim. As if they were going to hand over a portion of Robert's assets with a smile and an apology for her trouble. "Your loyalty is admirable, but the law is on my side."

"And what do your kids say about all of this?" Frannie fired back, wondering if her half siblings/cousins were cut from the same cloth as their mother. "Are they okay with what you did?"

"I wouldn't dream of speaking for my children."

"Yeah, well, I can't help but wonder if they're anything like you."

Jessie drew a measured breath though the strained smile never faltered. "So full of fire and brimstone, just like my Robert."

That was a purposeful dig. Frannie rose stiffly. "I think we're done here. Please don't contact me again. I have nothing to say to you."

"No worries, dear. I'm sure the lawyers will sort the details soon enough."

With nothing left to say, Frannie left the restaurant beyond thankful she hadn't ordered anything. Sharing a meal with that woman would be enough to turn the strongest stomach.

Dante intended to keep a professional distance from Frannie, but fate seemed to have other plans.

He seemed to sense the minute Frannie entered the brewery, his pint half raised to his lips when his gaze zeroed in on the blonde woman. In an instant, the bustling chaos of a popular place faded to a low hum.

But even as he watched, privately soaking up everything about her—the way her hair lightly dusted her shoulders, the stubborn tilt of her chin—he could tell something was bothering her.

A heavy weight dampened her usually sunny disposition. Likely more of the family troubles she'd been telling him about earlier. Even though their family issues were apples to oranges, he understood the stress of familial drama.

Just mind your business, a voice inside his head warned.

And yet, he was drawn to say hello at the very least. Nothing wrong with being friendly, he argued with himself.

Making eye contact, he waved to Frannie, letting fate decide the direction. If she waved and kept on her way, that was the way of it, but if she came over to say hi, then he'd enjoy the friendly company.

Warmth spread across his chest and excitement followed when she brightened and headed his way.

"Mind if I join you?" she asked, hopping beside him at the bar.

"Not at all." He motioned for the bartender. "What'll you have?"

"I'll take a pale ale," she said, reaching for her purse, but he waved away the need. She raised a brow with an uncertain but appreciative, "Are you sure?"

For a man raised in Italy with staunchly Italian roots, it was a foreign concept for a woman to pay for her drinks in a man's company. "I'm happy to pay for your drink," he assured her.

Her smile widened, and his mouth curved in response. She had this infectious way about her that was hard to ignore. After everything he'd been through last year, he craved the sunshiny warmth Frannie radiated effortlessly. She probably didn't even realize how she lit up a room.

The bartender set down her ale, and she gratefully took a drink, instantly relieved. "God, I needed this. It's been a day."

"Everything okay?" he asked, not wanting to overstep but genuinely curious.

She drew a deep breath, shaking her head. "Honestly, I don't even know. I don't want to bore you with my family stuff, though."

"I don't mind listening," he said.

"Really?"

He gestured with a generous smile. "Please, I'm all ears."

Frannie chuckled. "Okay, well, just remember you offered."

"Go for it."

"Against my better judgment I met up with Aunt Jessie a bit ago and as you might imagine it was about as enjoyable as a poke in the eye. For one, she's a horrible human being and doesn't seem to understand that having a decades-long affair with a married man is a bad look. Two, she doesn't acknowledge how hurtful her actions were to my mom, her own sister. I was flabbergasted at how blatantly selfish she was, and I guess I was hoping that maybe there was some kind of explanation that would make sense but there's nothing that could excuse what she did. And yes, I realize it takes two to tango, but I can't help but judge her more for being such a horrible person to her sister."

"I'm curious…why did you agree to meet with her?"

"Excellent question—one I kept asking myself when it all went to crap. I'm not sure what I'd hoped for or what I thought might happen, but it surely didn't end happily. Let's just say, the word *lawyer* was used instead of a friendly goodbye."

"Always a sign that negotiations have reached a stalemate," he agreed.

She nodded. "The thing is, she seems pretty confident that she's got a legitimate claim. I get that the kids would be entitled to something if it turns out they are my dad's, but can she claim anything? They weren't married."

He didn't want to worry Frannie, but there could be grounds for compensation for the aunt if Frannie's father had been the woman's sole source of support for more than ten years. He didn't want to insert himself where it wasn't appropriate, but he hated to see her weighed down by the situation. "People can make claims. Doesn't mean they'll win in court," he said. "However, if possible, it might benefit the estate to offer a lump-sum settlement to encourage the problem to go away without dragging the family through the courts."

"I can't imagine giving that woman a dime," Frannie said with a shudder. "I don't want to be mean but she's the one who made the choice to carry on with a married man. I don't have a lot of sympathy."

"It's not so much about sympathy as it is efficiency. Settlements make problems go away."

Frannie's subtle frown as she considered his advice reminded him that they came from different worlds. She had relatively normal problems, even if they were emotionally distressing. The crises he dealt with as Lorenzo's right-hand legal muscle would turn your hair white. As if summoned by his memory, the hairs on the back of his neck prickled, making him quickly look around the brewery out of habit.

It was Frannie's turn to ask, "Everything okay?"

He forced a chuckle, shaking off the paranoia. "A goose must've walked over my grave."

"Oh, I hate when that happens," Frannie commiserated with a shudder. "Every time my grandma said that, I got the heebie-jeebies."

"The *heebie*-what?" he asked with an incredulous laugh.

"Heebie-jeebies," Frannie repeated with a grin. "You know, the creeps."

"That might be my new favorite word."

Frannie's laugh could chase away any lingering fears. It didn't feel right to enjoy this time with her, but he was selfishly unwilling to cut the night short.

He needed a mental break from the constant stress of looking over his shoulder.

And Frannie was precisely what he needed tonight.

Chapter 6

It felt good to laugh. After her disastrous meeting with Aunt Jessie, she didn't think anything could lighten her sour mood. But seeing Dante across the crowded brewery had instantly chased away the clouds.

There was something about Dante that calmed and soothed her nerves. People tended to make her fidgety, which was probably why she preferred the quiet company of books to actual people. She had a tight-knit group of friends but often kept to herself.

However, with Dante, she didn't feel fidgety or out of place.

His eyes, sharp yet compassionate, held her stare without being off-putting, and he listened when she rambled, which in her experience was rare.

Frannie often felt set apart from her peers and family, even though no one was mean. Well, her brothers used to tease that she was "weird," but that was only because she'd preferred her nose in a book than anywhere else when given a choice.

But there was something about Dante she couldn't quite put her finger on—a wariness to get too close, perhaps?—that probably should've put her off but instead intrigued her more.

Had he been hurt in the past? A harsh breakup, maybe? If so, she could relate. Also, why did he pay cash for every purchase? He walked around with a clip of money, which in this day and age seemed unusual, but to ask why felt too personal. Of course, it wasn't any of her business why he paid cash for everything, but her curious, okay, nosy mind pressed for more details.

"So, you're from Italy, and you mentioned being here for business and pleasure... What drew you to Owl Creek?" She hesitated to mention that he didn't seem the type to spend all day on a boat like most tourists who flocked to the area during the summer, but she also didn't know much about him, so it was possible he loved boating.

"I spent ten years in the States before relocating to Italy with my family. There's something wholesome about American small towns and I needed a break from my usual scene."

Frannie snorted. "Wholesome? That's a stereotype that needs to die a grisly death. We have our share of terrible stuff. I mean, I hate to be the bearer of bad news but drug use in small towns is on the rise. For some reason, the Chamber of Commerce is reluctant to put that on the brochure, though."

He grinned. "Seems like a lost opportunity."

"Absolutely." She laughed, sharing, "Oh, here's something else—last year Blackbird Lake had a red algae bloom that killed tons of fish and sections of the lake had to be cordoned off to keep people from getting sick. But no one mentioned that."

"Are you always this passionate about your lake health?"

She shrugged. "I'm not obsessed with it, but I do feel not enough attention is being put on the right things. It's a beautiful place but too many people on the water with their boats and garbage pollutes the natural ecosystem. You can't deny that there have been so many ecological disasters that have been directly attributed to human interference."

"No argument from me. Keeping the balance between

the carbon footprint and nature is a constant battle that we often lose," he admitted. "Italy faces similar issues with pollution as the rest of the world. There are always going to be people who champion the environment and those who fight any change that threatens inconvenience."

"Do you practice environmental law?"

If only. His predatory uncle was his own kind of human pollution. "No, sadly, not my area of practice but I appreciate anyone who goes into that field. It's a tough one to chase. Too much collective greed to truly affect demonstrable change. But we need warriors out there fighting the good fight."

She met his gaze, her insides warming, tingling with awareness. He had the most expressive eyes. How was he single? She wanted to ask, but it seemed so personal, and she didn't want to ruin the moment, but her mouth had other plans. "Why don't you have a girlfriend or a wife?" she blurted out.

Her abrupt question threw him off-guard—*shocker*—and he waited a minute before answering with a short yet restrained smile. "Uh, too busy, I guess. Up until recently, I was a workaholic. Never seemed to have enough time to do both."

Relief flooded her. That made sense to her. For a moment, she was secretly afraid that he had some dark secret he was protecting. Reading too many crime novels had warped her brain. "I understand," she said. "There's a comfort in the routine of work. I love my little shop, but my best friend, Darla, keeps reminding me that there's more to life than work. She's actually getting married in a few months."

"Your friend is a smart woman."

"Yeah, probably smarter than me for sure, but there's another thing about living in a small town that no one talks about…"

"Which is?"

"The dating pool is excruciatingly small." When he

chuckled, she explained with a laugh, "No, seriously! I've known everyone in this town my whole life. It's hard to see guys I went to kindergarten with in a romantic light. I know too many things about them." She glanced around the brewery, spying on someone she knew. She gestured discreetly. "See that guy over there with the ball cap talking a mad game with his buddies like he's some kind of baseball stud? That's Johnny Rogan. He peed his pants in the third grade, and when I see him acting all macho, that's all I remember."

Dante regarded Johnny. "He seems a good-looking enough adult. Has he ever asked you out?"

"Multiple times. I can't think of more creative ways to turn him down at this point. He's nice, I guess, but I literally feel nothing for him in that way. Besides, he isn't a big reader and I can't see myself tied to someone who thinks books are a waste of time."

"So a man interested in taking you out for a date...should share your love of books?"

"It's a great start," Frannie said, holding his gaze, adding, "and I wouldn't mind a foreign accent, either..."

It was bold of her—and entirely out of character—but she wanted to kiss him, and she sensed that he wouldn't make a move without her obvious interest.

Besides, being coy? Never her strength. She was either clueless or awkward, and sometimes both, when it came to approaching guys she was interested in, and that wasn't likely to change anytime soon.

Shut her down, don't encourage that kind of involvement, that infernal voice urged again, but Dante felt caught in a whirlpool dragging him ever closer to Frannie. He knew why he ought to politely set her straight, to tell her that he wasn't interested in her romantically, but it would be a lie.

He wanted her.

He thought of Frannie in ways that crossed the line, even if he knew he shouldn't. He wanted to taste her lips, touch her skin and feel her beneath him.

The smart—responsible—play would be to make some excuse, pay the tab and end the evening, but the idea of walking away was physically painful.

And he couldn't do it.

But his hesitation cost him.

"Oh, I'm sorry, I just made it weird, didn't I?" Frannie said, her cheeks flaring with pink. "I... Oh, man, this is awkward. Forget I said anything. Actually, I think I should probably go. I've taken up enough of your time whining about my problems. I'm sure you have plenty of your own, you don't need to listen to mine." And before he could say anything, she jumped from the stool and practically ran from the brewery.

Damn it. He tossed down a wad of cash and hurried after her. He couldn't stomach the thought of Frannie feeling rejected when it was a lie.

Even as he ran after her, that voice in his head countered that this was a blessing, but he couldn't let her go like that.

"Frannie! Wait!" he called after her, catching her seconds before she climbed into her car for a quick getaway.

He skidded to a stop, breathing hard. The woman could run like a track star, getting a surprising distance before he caught her. "Jesus, you're a good runner," he said, sucking in a big breath. "It's been awhile since I hit the treadmill. You reminded me that I need to return to my exercise routine."

"Sorry, I ran track in high school and the habit kinda stuck," she said, unsure of why he'd chased after her. "Are you okay?"

He wiped at the bead of sweat on his brow, admitting,

"Aside from feeling a little sheepish, yes. However, I couldn't let you go with this misunderstanding between us."

"No, it's my fault, I shouldn't have made such a forward comment. We barely know each other."

"Frannie, I like you but—"

"Oh, God, the dreaded 'I like you, but.' Thanks but I think I know where this is going and it's totally okay. We can just pretend that I never said anything, okay?"

This was going from bad to worse. "Frannie, that's not what I was going to say."

She frowned. "What were you going to say?"

"I like you, a lot. More than I should. But you deserve complete honesty. I'm not in a position to start anything real or meaningful and I respect you too much to suggest something casual, if you catch what I mean."

"You mean, sex?"

"Well, yes."

She surprised him with a chuckle. "Dante, I think you're getting ahead of yourself. I'm not looking for anything super serious either. My life is a mess right now. But we're both adults and I like you. Is that so bad?"

Frannie was giving him the green light for something casual between them. Did he want that? Was it possible to entertain a casual arrangement while he was in Owl Creek? It wasn't exactly his style, but if he couldn't offer much more, he liked the idea of spending more time with Frannie.

But was it safe?

Perhaps if they were careful…even then, it was taking a risk. He didn't know if Lorenzo had spies looking for him, but it would likely happen sooner or later. Dante had something Lorenzo wanted back. That much wouldn't change, which could put Frannie on Lorenzo's radar.

And how much should he share with Frannie about his

circumstances? He wanted to be honest but couldn't see that conversation going well. If he wasn't a red flag, he didn't know what was.

He'd underestimated his uncle's reach in the past, and he swore he wouldn't do that again. Yet, here he was, his brain clouded with desire for a woman he had no business wanting.

It was so damn selfish of him to want more with Frannie knowing that getting too close to him would put her in danger.

And yet, he still reached for her.

Was he really that much of a selfish bastard?

The answer was immediate and humbling.

Dante pulled Frannie into the cove of his arms. She nestled against him, gazing into his eyes with a shy smile. "Does this mean you're down for some casual adulting?"

"I think it does," he murmured, brushing his lips across hers, his tongue darting to taste hers. She sank against him with a sigh, and he knew he'd made a mistake immediately, but it was too late to turn back now.

She felt like a dream he didn't have any business enjoying. There was a sweetness to Frannie that felt like stolen treasure in his hands. But as before, when the voice warned him to keep his distance, he ignored every bit of good sense and tightened his hold around her waist.

"My place or yours?" she murmured against his mouth, her lips curving in a flirty smile.

"Mine," he answered, pulling away to slide his hand into hers but not before giving the parking lot a glance to check for anything that shouldn't be there.

Frannie grinned, unlocking her car. "I'll follow you."

And Dante knew there was no turning back from this decision.

He'd sealed his fate—and hers.

Chapter 7

Frannie's heart thundered in her chest as she followed Dante out to his place. Who was she? What was she doing? Listening to herself boldly offering a casual relationship with the sexy Italian when she was a serial monogamist was a surreal experience.

Darla always said she needed to put herself out there more, but this felt so far afield that she didn't know how to navigate the unfamiliar terrain.

But this was exactly what she needed. Another thing about small towns—if you weren't careful, they would keep you thinking small.

Frannie didn't want to fall into that trap.

Also, something about Dante set her blood on fire in a way she'd never experienced.

And she wanted more.

She pulled up behind Dante and exited the car, immediately recognizing the rental property. "This place used to belong to Gavin Pritchard's family. They moved away a few years ago." Frannie smiled at Dante's amusement, adding with a shrug, "Another one of those pro/con arguments for living in a small town."

"Did you and this Gavin date back in the day?" Dante asked as he unlocked the front door and waited for her to pass through before closing the door and locking it behind them.

"No," she answered, tickled by his chivalry and sense of protection. "My mom and Gavin's mom used to sell Tupperware together and would host Tupperware parties." Of course, he had a higher chance of being surprised by a bear in his kitchen than a burglar, but she liked that he cared about her safety and watched as he quickly checked doors and windows.

Satisfied they were secured, Dante asked, "Can I get you something to drink? Wine or…juice? I don't think I have beer stocked."

"Water is fine with me," she answered, taking in the surroundings. It looked different from when the Pritchard family had lived there, but she remembered the house's general layout.

Dante returned with two bottled waters, cracking hers open before handing it to her.

She smiled: there was that chivalrous nature again. "Are all Italian men as considerate as you?" Then, when he seemed puzzled, she pointed to the bottled water, adding, "And the opening of the door. It was very old-school and charming but not what I'm used to."

"Do men not open doors here?"

"In my generation? Not really. I mean, some do, but it's not common. I can't remember the last time a guy opened the door for me, much less opened my water for me."

"Would you prefer I not?" he asked, furrowing his brow.

"Oh, gosh, no, please don't stop. I like it. I'm just not used to it, that's all."

"If that's the case, American men have lost the art of appreciating women."

"It could just be here. Other states might have different traditions. All I know is Owl Creek, Idaho, though."

Dante smiled, reaching for her hand. She accepted, allowing him to pull her gently toward the bedroom. Her heart rate immediately picked up as anticipation wiped away all thoughts of anything but what was happening between them.

Dante clicked on the small bedside lamp, illuminating the room in a soft glow.

A large, rustic bed framed in rough-hewn oak and covered with a Midwestern-style comforter dominated the room. The faint aroma of Dante's cologne clung to the space—a spicy masculine scent that was both sophisticated and brawny—and Frannie immediately felt at home. But there was still the awkwardness of being in a relative stranger's bedroom after only sharing a kiss in the parking lot of the Tap Out brewery.

"Can we sit and talk for a few minutes?" she asked, hoping he didn't mind.

"Of course," Dante said, following her lead with grace. She sat gingerly on the bed, and he sat beside her. "If you've changed your mind—"

"I haven't," she assured him quickly. "I just need a few minutes to get my bearings. It's probably not very cool of me in the hookup era but I'm not in a habit of going home with someone like this. Usually, my sexual relationships happen within the framework of an actual relationship, so this is new territory for me. But I definitely haven't changed my mind."

"If it makes you feel any better, I'm not accustomed to this sort of thing either."

It did make her feel better. She smiled. "Can you tell me about your last relationship? What was she like?"

A curtain closed behind his eyes, and Frannie knew in

an instant that question was probably off-limits. She knew the signs of a painful breakup when she saw one and felt like an idiot for dragging him into the deep end of the pool before finding out if he could swim.

"Actually, that's way too personal, I'm sorry," she hastened to add, letting him off the hook with a rueful chuckle to share, "One thing about me? I have a tendency to ask all the wrong things at the absolute worst time. Either you'll find it endearing or terribly off-putting. Just let me know where you land on that score, and I'll try to adjust accordingly."

"I find you...enchanting," he admitted, gently pushing an errant strand of hair behind her ear with such tenderness she almost melted. "However, my last relationship is one I'd rather not talk about, if you don't mind."

"Of course, I understand," Frannie said quickly, her breath hitching as he leaned forward to brush his lips across hers. "We could...stop talking all together...if you like..."

"I'd like that very much," he murmured, deepening their kiss.

In an instant, Frannie forgot everything—potentially even her own name—as her senses exploded.

Beneath Dante's masterful touch, Frannie's anxiety drifted away, leaving her free to sink into the pleasure of discovering one another.

Dante pushed away all thoughts of anything before Frannie. He didn't want to contaminate the moment by allowing memories of the past to color the present.

Frannie's skin was like silk against his fingertips. Her soft moans ignited his desire like embers alighting on tinder.

She was beautiful and unfettered by an ugly past. He

didn't deserve her trust or sweetness, but his bitter soul needed it.

Dante pressed soft kisses along the column of her neck, drinking in her subtle shivers as she gave him complete access to her body.

When he came to Owl Creek, he'd never imagined meeting someone like Frannie. She was the variable he couldn't have planned for, which would probably end up being his Achilles' heel. But he couldn't stop what was happening between them.

The second he felt her body against his, something inside him shifted, and that need to protect her at all costs made the idea of something casual between them laughable.

But keeping a safe emotional distance between them was for Frannie's protection.

Even if all he wanted to do was hold her close.

"You're an incredible woman," he said, rolling onto his back, trying to catch his breath.

Frannie grinned, wiping away the sweat as she rolled to her side to regard him playfully. "No complaints on this end either."

He chuckled, grabbing his water bottle for a long swig. The pale moonlight bathed her form, giving her the glow of a reclining goddess, like something from a Renaissance painting.

Dante returned to the bed, lying on his side, facing her. He didn't have a lot of experience with "casual." He had a feeling snuggling afterward wasn't the general way of things, but he liked the idea of Frannie curling into his arms and falling asleep together.

Frannie must've had the same thoughts as she reluctantly rose and dressed. "Well, this was fun," she said, sliding on her jeans and buttoning them up quickly. "I should probably

get going. Tomorrow is inventory day. I have a big shipment of books coming in— Oh! And the books I ordered
for you might be in that shipment, too."

"You don't have to leave," he said, going against the advice in his head. "You could stay."

"The night?"

"Yeah."

She paused as if thinking over his offer but ultimately
declined because at least one of them was thinking straight.
"The thing is, I'd really enjoy sleeping over, but I'm sure
that's how lines get blurred, and if we're trying to keep it
casual, we probably shouldn't push boundaries at the very
start."

"Of course, you're right," he agreed through his disappointment. "As long as you feel okay about our arrangement."

"I mean, I don't love the idea of calling this an 'arrangement'…but yeah, it's better if we don't get too comfortable
with each other's personal space."

Solid advice. Why did it feel wrong? Maybe he wasn't
cut out for this kind of situation. Or maybe he should've
followed his good sense and buried things in the "casual
acquaintance" zone.

But now he knew the sound of her breathy moans and
had learned how her body responded to his touch. The taste
of her skin was stamped on his memory, and her throaty
laughter made his insides hum.

Yes, helluva way to keep things light and easy between
them.

Maybe it wasn't ideal, but it was necessary, he reminded
himself as he walked her to the door.

"A kiss for the road?" she asked, gazing up at him with

a playfulness in her smile that immediately made him want to scoop her up and carry her back to the bedroom.

But he obliged her request, ending the kiss when his resolve weakened.

"You are the best kisser, and I'm not just saying that to butter up your ego. Honestly, it would be better if you weren't so good," she said against his mouth, giggling at her assessment. "Would make it easier to leave if you slobbered like an enthusiastic puppy."

He laughed at her odd humor and finished with one last kiss before sending her on her way. "Drive carefully. As everyone has been fond of telling me since coming here, 'Watch for deer—and if you see one, there's more.'"

Frannie saluted with a "Will do!" and climbed into her car. He watched her drive away until he no longer saw her headlights and then returned inside the house, locking the front door as was his new habit.

Back home, he hadn't been as diligent about his safety, feeling insulated against harm because of his name and stature. Now he knew that feeling of safety had been an illusion.

And danger could lurk around any darkened corner.

Had he made a major mistake in allowing Frannie into his life, even peripherally?

His satiated body tricked his mind into thinking it might be okay. He was thousands of miles away from Lorenzo, and his trail was well covered as far as he could tell.

Maybe it was possible to enjoy his time with Frannie, even if it felt like borrowed time.

Chapter 8

Frannie had spent the day humming lightly beneath her breath, replaying her night with Dante in her head ad nauseam. It was her current favorite memory. She'd just finished her inventory toward the end of the day when Darla walked in, looking harried and the opposite of the blushing bride.

"Tell me I'm doing the right thing by marrying that man," she said as she huffed in the chair opposite Frannie. "I swear, if he lives to breathe another day, it'll be a miracle."

"What's poor Tom done now? Aside from the audacity of not wanting to elope," Frannie said with a small grin at Darla's pique.

"As my best friend and maid of honor you're obligated to be on my side," Darla warned with a glower. "And don't give me that look. Tom has crossed the line this time."

"How so?"

"He's insisting on a half chocolate cake when I specifically told the baker we would have vanilla and strawberry. It's ridiculous to have three flavors in one cake. Everyone knows that!"

Frannie shrugged. "Who doesn't like chocolate?"

"If we have a third flavor tier, people are going to get all picky about the slices and the next thing you know, we'll have a lopsided amount of leftovers and that's just wasteful. Strawberry and vanilla, people choose one or the other and that's it."

Frannie knew she ought to commiserate with Darla, but she could only giggle at how ridiculous it was. She was in too good a mood to see anything but the lighter side. However, Darla was unamused and suspicious. "Why are you in such a good mood? Isn't it inventory day? Usually, you're stressed out and grumpy on inventory day."

"No, I'm not," Frannie disagreed, wondering if that was true. She loved inventory day—*new books, what's not to love?*—but it could be a little stressful logging everything in while still running the front desk. She was a one-woman army, after all.

But before Frannie could adequately defend herself, Darla gasped, "Oh my God, I know that look!"

"What look?"

"The look that says someone got lucky last night!"

Frannie's cheeks flared with immediate heat, and she shushed Darla. "Oh my God, keep your voice down," she said, embarrassed. "And what makes you say that?"

"Because I'm your best friend and I've known you our entire lives. Since your breakup with that douche monkey, you've been depressingly celibate for reasons I can't even fathom. But you have the look of a woman who has been deliciously taken care of, if you know what I mean."

Good Lord, nothing got past Darla. "Okay, fine, yes, I had a date last night," she said, gesturing for Darla to keep it on the down-low, "but it's nothing serious. Just casual."

"You? Casual? Do you know how to do that?"

"Of course I do," Frannie lied, hating that Darla knew her that well. "I mean, I can learn. Besides, I'm not ready for anything more serious anyway."

"Okay, with *whom* did you knock boots last night?" Darla asked, needing to know all the details.

Frannie almost didn't want to say, but there was no way Darla would be satisfied with anything but the truth, and she'd get it out of Frannie at some point anyway. "You have to promise to keep this to yourself," she warned. When Darla motioned to zip her lips, Frannie shared. "Last night I ran into Dante at Tap Out. One thing led to another and the next, I was at his place."

"The hunky, mysterious Italian?" Darla exclaimed. "Oh my God, please, I need to know...was he..."

"Darla!" Frannie glared. "I'm not about to kiss and tell those kinds of details. Suffice it to say we had a nice evening."

"Nice?"

"Okay, it was amazing," Frannie corrected with a tiny swoon at the memory. "But please, we agreed to keep it casual and it's not a thing, like we're not dating or anything like that."

"And why is that?" Darla was immediately suspicious. "Is he married or something?"

"No, he's just...well, he doesn't plan on staying in Owl Creek. He's here for a short while and it doesn't make sense to start something serious when we both know he's not staying."

"Are you sure he's not married?"

"I didn't ask Fletcher to run a background check if that's what you're asking."

"Not a terrible idea, though," Darla said, believing the idea had merit. "First of all, he's not local and he could be making up any sort of story and how would you know any different?"

Frannie frowned at her best friend. "When did you become so suspicious of everyone?"

"You need to be more suspicious of people," Darla countered. "You're so accepting of everyone's motives, and I love that about you. But I worry that you're a perfect target for people who have bad intentions."

Remembering her meeting with her aunt Jessie, Frannie scowled. "Speaking of people with bad intentions... I went against my better judgment and agreed to meet with my aunt Jessie yesterday."

Darla's eyes bugged. "And why did you do that?"

"I don't know, I was hoping that maybe she was going to call the whole thing off and admit that she'd made it all up as a poor attempt at connecting with her estranged family."

Darla grimaced. "Yeah, if that were a bet in Vegas, I wouldn't take those odds."

"Yeah," she sighed, "it went about as well as you could expect."

"What did she want to talk about?" Darla asked, ignoring Dante for a moment.

"I think she was fishing for information. She's doubling down on her claim, and I have this bad feeling that she's actually telling the truth. If that's the case, I have two more siblings and I don't know how I feel about that."

Darla's expression softened. "I'm sorry, Fran. What your dad did...it's just not right. How's your mom holding up?"

"Mom is Mom. She's acting like she's fine but there are cracks in her veneer. Sadly, even if she's brokenhearted, she won't let us in. Too many years pretending like everything is fine to let the gates down now. I don't know how to help her."

"Your mom is the sweetest person I know. She doesn't deserve this."

The funny thing about Jenny Colton...to everyone else, she seemed sweet as pie, always with a smile, generous and compassionate to everyone in need. And she was that person—but there was more to the woman than met the eye.

And that was something only her children knew.

Jenny Colton was intensely private and guarded her secrets well. It was as if she prided herself on hiding her cuts and bruises from the world, no matter how she might be bleeding inside.

And Frannie could only imagine how many cuts and bruises she carried after being married to Robert for all those years.

"I do wonder if my mom knew about her sister and my dad all along but chose to ignore it because he always came home to her at some point?"

"Like the mentality of a stereotypical fifties-era housewife?" Darla suggested, pursing her lips in thought. "That generation was definitely cut from a different cloth. If I found out Tom was carrying on with another family, I'd end up in an orange jumpsuit for the rest of my life."

Frannie chuckled. "See? If you're willing to go to prison over the idea of Tom cheating, it's definitely love. Let the man have his chocolate cake," she said.

Darla huffed a short breath. "Fine. But don't say I didn't call it when I end up with an entire uneaten tier of vanilla cake."

After a beat of reflective silence, Frannie noted it was closing time. "I think I'd better go see my mom tonight. She might not want to open up to any of us, but it might be a good idea to let her know we're here for her all the same."

Darla smiled, nodding. "I think so. She needs her family, whether she wants to admit it or not." Then, as she rose, slinging her purse over her shoulder, she added, "Also, not a terrible idea for Fletcher to run lover boy's name through the system. You'd hate to find out too late that your hot, international stud muffin is a cheating bastard."

"I will do no such thing." Frannie rolled her eyes, gesturing, "Go on, get out of here."

But as she went through her closing routine, Darla's advice stuck in her brain. If Dante had nothing to hide, nothing would pop up.

There was no harm in peeking, right?

Maybe she'd talk to Fletcher about it tomorrow.

In the meantime, time to do her daughterly duty and check on her mom.

With permission from the property management, Dante spent some time installing video cameras on the front and back of the house, though it'd been a hard sell.

"Mr. Sinclair, Owl Creek is very safe," the plump lady behind the desk had assured him, regarding Dante with faint confusion at his request. "We've never had any complaints from renters in the past. Did something happen to cause concern?"

He couldn't exactly share that he needed to ensure his uncle wasn't sending henchmen to break his fingers in the dead of night, but he also couldn't set off alarm bells with the property manager.

The fat stack of cash he'd put down for the deposit when he rented the property was the only reason she was even considering his request.

"It'll be at my expense, and I can either take them down when I leave or donate them to the property, whatever the owner prefers. But I would feel more at ease if I knew there was proper surveillance around the house."

"I…that's very considerate of you, but I still don't understand the reason. Was there something that made you feel unsafe at the property?"

Yes, the fact that his unscrupulous uncle would stop at nothing to reclaim what Dante had stolen.

"In my line of work, I require a higher level of security," he'd explained with a slight, apologetic smile. "I'm truly happy with the property and I don't want to have to move but the security must be upgraded while I'm renting out the space. I'm sure you understand, and I hope my request can be accommodated."

"Oh, yes, of course." She stopped short of asking what he did for a living, but he could see the question on the tip of her tongue. When she sensed he wouldn't budge, she'd said, "I'll ask the property owners how they feel about it and let you know."

"I appreciate your attention to the matter," he'd said, adding, "The sooner the better."

Thankfully, the owners had been amenable to a free surveillance system, and within a day, Dante had purchased the system and installed it himself, not willing to trust anyone he couldn't vet with his current location.

Satisfied, he returned to the house in time to hear his cell phone ringing. Only two people had this number: Frannie and his private investigator. He would be lying if he didn't hope it was Frannie calling, but it was his private investigator.

"Hello?"

"Nick Gladney. I have some more information you might find of interest, and it's about your father."

"Go on."

"It wasn't easy, but I had a friend pull the records from your father's accident. Not a lot to go on—pretty cut-and-dried from the report—and not a big incentive to dig any deeper, if you know what I mean."

"How so?"

"You said you were a kid when your dad died, right?"

"Yes, around ten."

"Well, do you remember your dad being a drinker or anything like that?"

"My father never drank," he answered, wondering where this was going. "Why?"

"According to the records, your dad had a blood alcohol level way over the legal limit. If the report is to be believed, your dad was drunk as a skunk when his car crashed into that tree."

"That's bullshit. My father hated the smell of alcohol. Neither of my parents drank." Which made his mother's subsequent death by a drunk driver cruelly ironic. "The report has to be wrong."

"Well, through official channels, the report says your dad was drinking the night he died. I mean, you were a kid, maybe your memory is distorted of who your dad was. It happens. Kids want to believe the best of their parents."

"No—" Dante cut in sharply. "Believe me when I say, I know my father wasn't a drinker. Dig deeper. Go beyond the official channels. Find out who signed off on that report. Find out if they suddenly came into a large sum of money. Someone lied about how my father died and I want to know who."

The information nagged at his brain, deepening his suspicion of his uncle. Lorenzo had always been willing to go to great lengths to get whatever he wanted—even if it meant removing a brother who threatened his position within the family.

Dante remembered bits and pieces of conversation between his parents behind closed doors, hushed voices always coated with a sense of urgency. His father, Matteo, kept them on the move, always hyperalert and ready to hit the ground running for reasons he never shared. His sweet mother, Georgia, always tried to hide the worry in her heart by covering it with a sunny smile and pretending they were on a grand adventure.

But Dante remembered details from his childhood that most would've happily forgotten.

And he knew with certainty that his father wasn't drunk that night.

Chapter 9

Fletcher surprised Franny when he walked into the bookstore the following day.

"Aren't you supposed to be working?" Franny teased, though she was always happy to see her brother.

Fletcher smiled and kissed her on the cheek. "That's a funny way of saying, 'Hey, bro, always a pleasure to see you.'"

"I'm not saying I don't love when you drop in, I'm just saying that I'm not sure Owl Creek PD is getting their money's worth if you're constantly popping in here for a latte. Because I know that's what you're here for."

Franny and Fletcher had always enjoyed the kind of relationship where they teased one another mercilessly, but it was their closeness that enabled them to poke at each other without injury. Unlike Chase, with whom she didn't feel close enough to even enjoy small talk about the weather.

"Actually, I'm kind of glad you're here, because I need to talk to you about something."

Fletcher was intrigued. "I'm happy to listen while you whip me up that aforementioned latte. I mean, since you mentioned it."

Franny winked as she walked over to the café side of the shop. She made a quick latte, just how he liked it and handed the frothy drink to him. "Although I think it's kind of bizarre that you can drink something so hot when it's warm outside. When will you let me talk you into trying a nice herbal iced tea? They're quite good if you give them a chance."

Fletcher grimaced. "That sounds disgusting, no thank you. So, what did you want to talk to me about?"

Franny straightened, remembering. "Yeah, about that... so last night I went to drop in on Mom and see how she's doing and when I got there, Uncle Buck was there, too."

Fletcher shrugged. "And?"

"I don't know, they just seemed...there was something odd about the way they were talking to each other. I might be imagining things, but it seemed like they were *close*. I don't know how to say this without it being more than it is, but it seemed like there was a vibe between them."

"A vibe? As in a romantic vibe?"

Franny understood Fletcher's confusion because that was exactly how she'd felt when she saw it. She nodded with a grimace. "And I'm reluctant even to mention this because what if I'm wrong, but they took like two steps away from each other when they saw me walk in like they got caught or something, which seemed weird."

Fletcher seemed to mull over the information before ultimately rejecting the speculation. "Here's the thing. Uncle Buck and Mom have been close for years, but I think it's more of a brotherly/sisterly thing because Mom helped Uncle Buck when Aunt Jessie left him high and dry with the kids. We've spent how many summers out at the ranch? He's family, there's nothing more going on there."

Franny wanted to believe that, and if it weren't for the fact Aunt Jessie was currently in town telling anybody who would listen that she was Robert Colton's long-term lover, it would be easier to swallow. But the reality was that her aunt had maintained an inappropriate relationship with Robert Colton, so was it out of the question to wonder if Jenny Colton had decided to do the same with her sister's husband? *Yuck*, the whole thing made Franny want to vomit. Still, she saw what she saw. "I'm the last person who wants to think about this stuff, but I'm telling you, there was a vibe."

Fletcher grimaced at the idea as well. "They're both adults. I guess we don't really have room to say anything to them if it's true. Dad's gone, so it's not like Mom would be cheating on him. Even if it were true, it kind of feels like, maybe, payback? I don't know, the whole thing sucks to think about, and I'd rather just push it out of my brain."

"Hopefully, I'm way off base and I'm imagining things because I don't think I can take any more family surprises."

"Amen to that." Fletcher said with happiness as he sipped his latte. "You make the best lattes hands down."

Franny smiled. "Thanks, bro."

"Was there anything else you wanted to talk about? Because as much as you tease me, I do have a job to get back to."

"Actually, yes. My second reason for wanting to talk to you is a little more complicated."

"How so?"

"There's a new guy in town. His name is Dante Sinclair, and I was wondering if you would be willing to take a peek into his background."

Fletcher's demeanor changed, morphing into that of a protective brother. "Is there something I should know about this guy? Has he hurt you?"

"Good grief, no. He seems like a really great person but Darla mentioned that maybe I should ask some questions because he's not from around here. Honestly, even saying it out loud feels like I'm overreacting and makes me cringe."

"I can't run a background check on someone for no reason. That's illegal."

Franny's hopes fell. "Oh, I'm sorry I didn't know that. I wouldn't want you to do anything that compromises your job."

"I said I couldn't do it for no reason," he clarified. "Maybe this guy gave you a weird feeling? Or maybe he was asking for you to order some materials that felt a little suspect?"

Franny wanted to laugh at her brother's suggestions because they were all ludicrous. Dante seemed like the straightest arrow she'd ever met, but she also didn't want Fletcher to do anything that would get him in trouble.

She supposed a small white lie wouldn't hurt in this instance. "Maybe you could run his license because he went over the speed limit or something like that."

"What does he drive?"

"A Toyota sedan, a Camry I think? A rental."

"Color?"

"White."

"What else can you tell me about him?"

"Um, well, he's from Italy."

Fletcher's brow rose. "Italy? What's he doing here?"

"I don't know. He said it was a combination of business and pleasure."

"And you didn't ask any more questions?"

Exasperation colored her voice. "Fletcher, it was none of my business. I wasn't going to grill the poor guy when I just met him."

Guilt pinched at Franny. Why did it feel like she was selling Dante out somehow? "I don't want to make a big deal about this, okay? Just a peek. Don't go getting the FBI involved, okay?" At the mention of the FBI, Fletcher perked up, and immediately Frannie shot that idea down. "Don't you dare go bothering Max over this. He's doesn't need us pestering him with something as frivolous as this."

"No promises, sis. It all depends on what my little peek turns up. Besides, Max wouldn't mind. Hey, how about while I'm doing my little peek, you keep your distance until I can give you the all clear? Just to be on the safe side?"

She didn't like the idea of involving her cousin who worked for the FBI at all. In fact, she was looking forward to seeing Dante tonight. "I think you're going a little overboard. I'm sure Dante has no big, dark secrets. I was just curious because he's not from around here. I don't want you to get freaked out over nothing. I probably shouldn't have said anything."

"Look, not that I would ever want to find myself agreeing with Darla, of all people, but I think she's right. It's best to err on the side of caution nowadays. What is he even doing here? It's not like Owl Creek is a haven for international travelers."

Franny had had the same questions but framed in a far less suspicious manner. "You're going to feel real bad for thinking so poorly of the man when you find out Dante is a normal, friendly person."

"We'll see." Fletcher smiled, scooped up his latte and waved as he walked out the door.

Brothers.

She wasn't worried. Dante was exactly who he said he was.

At least, she hoped he was. Or else Franny would never hear the end of it.

Dante opened the front door, smiling when he saw Frannie, who was holding the books she'd ordered for him, looking like a sugary confection in a white sundress with pink accents. "Special delivery," she said, smiling up at him. "They were in the shipment that arrived this morning. I thought you wouldn't mind me bringing them to you personally."

He should mind—but he couldn't bring himself to care.

"I don't mind at all," he said, accepting the books and stepping aside so she could come in. "That's some top-tier service. Does everyone get this level of customer service or is it just me?"

Frannie's flirty smile as she shrugged nearly stole his breath. Goddamn, the woman was beautiful. "Can I get you a glass of wine or something?" he offered, trying to get his bearing before he threw her down on the sofa and devoured every inch of that smooth, succulent skin.

"I'm not much of a wine drinker but if you have something on the sweet side, I'll give it a go."

"Americans and their sweet palate," he teased, placing the books on the table before heading to the kitchen. "But I think I have something you'll enjoy. Make yourself comfortable. I'll be right back."

Dante pulled a chilled Riesling from the fridge and quickly poured two glasses. It wasn't a Moscato, but it was the sweetest wine he had to offer. He'd planned to spend a quiet evening researching, but Frannie's unexpected visit kicked those plans to the curb. He shouldn't encourage her popping in unannounced, but he'd be lying if he said he wasn't happy to see her.

She accepted the wineglass, took a delicate sniff, pretending to be a connoisseur, then sipped the wine, nodding with approval before giggling, admitting, "I have no idea if this is a good wine but it's yummy."

"That's all that matters," he said, amused at her playful nature. Frannie was unlike anyone he'd ever met. Somehow, she'd retained that sense of whimsy and wonder that most adults lost as they grew up. The part of him that needed goodness in his life soaked up her energy like a dying man. Clearing his throat, he shared, "I'll let you in on a little secret—wine snobs like to go on about a wine's properties, but at the end of the day, people like what they like, and that's what's important."

"Works with people, too," Frannie murmured, catching his gaze with a mischievous look that immediately made him forget about the wine. "I mean, from what I see... what's not to like?"

"Miss Colton, I get the impression you did not come here just to be neighborly and deliver my books."

"You might be right," she admitted, setting her glass down and climbing into his lap, straddling Dante with a boldness that ignited a fiery need between them. Her strong legs bracketed his hips, and the soft swell of her breasts caused his eyes to glaze over as he struggled to remember his name. "The thing is, I like you, Dante. I like you a lot, and I know we're doing the casual thing, but there's something about you that I can't get enough of. So, in the spirit of keeping it casual...would you like to 'casually' get naked?"

He grinned. "Right now?"

She nodded. "Right now."

He surged against her hot center. "I don't have a problem with that request," he said before she sealed her mouth to his. She tasted of sweet wine and heavenly temptation. That internal voice of reason faded to a whisper as his hands cupped her behind, drawing her close.

Their tongues tangled, and he anchored her hips against him as she ground against the hardened ridge beneath his jeans. Her little moan pushed him over the edge, and he lifted her up and onto her back, rising above her. She curled her hand around his neck, drawing his mouth back to hers.

He would lose control right then and there if he didn't

slow down, but Frannie decimated his self-control in ways that should've been a red flag.

There were many good reasons to keep a healthy distance between them, but his thoughts were hazed, and all he could focus on was the exquisite torture of Frannie writhing beneath him.

Dimly, he heard his cell phone going off. It took a minute to realize the call had to be coming from his private investigator because Frannie was the only person with the number. He hesitated, torn, but when the phone rang again, the urgency of a double call made him stop and grab his phone with a muttered apology before disappearing into his bedroom and closing the door.

He answered on the last ring before it transferred to voice mail. "Hey, Nick, this isn't a good time," he said in a low voice. "What have you got?"

"I knew you'd want to hear this right away. It's pretty significant. After you shared that your father wasn't a drinker, I did some poking around and got lucky. The investigating officer of your father's accident has since passed away, but I managed to talk to his widow. I don't have an amount, but she remembers her husband coming into a lump sum of money around twenty years ago when he still worked on the force. He bought a boat, a source of contention between him and the wife because she said it was too expensive."

"Did she say where the money came from?"

"It was hard to get specific details without coming off as suspicious for asking. I made up some story about a financial audit. She's old and trusting, so she bought it, but I couldn't dig too deep without producing some kind of documentation proving the audit."

"A boat…" he repeated, thinking over the information. "That all she said?"

"Taking into account that she was frail and nervous, she seemed real keen on protecting her old man's name. Talking about what a decorated officer he was on the force and how much pride he took in protecting his community."

"Sounds like a woman trying really hard to make sure her husband didn't sound like the kind of man to take a bribe," Dante murmured.

"Yeah, I think it's safe to assume that that boat wasn't purchased on his small-town cop salary."

When Dante's father died, they lived in a tiny town in Wisconsin. They'd only been there for two months when the accident happened. He remembered his mother's screams when the officer came to deliver the news.

Then, he remembered his mother receiving a phone call late at night, and the following morning, they were packed and on a plane for Italy. He knew Uncle Lorenzo was on the other end of that call.

His life had changed forever with that phone call.

Lorenzo had seemed the knight in shining armor at the time, swooping in at his mother's time of need, placing them under his protection, and taking Dante under his wing.

It wasn't until later that he learned nothing came without a cost.

And now? He had reason to believe someone had killed his father, making it look like an accident.

Had the same thing happened to his mother two years ago?

Was it possible his uncle had been the one behind their deaths?

Before Belinda, he never would've imagined Lorenzo to be so cruel…but now…

He couldn't deny the possibility.

Chapter 10

Frannie didn't know what to think when Dante disappeared into his bedroom. Whatever needed to be said was clearly private, but it felt wrong to stay when he didn't return.

The moment went from sensual to awkward. Now Franny wasn't sure if she should stay or go.

She could hear the muffled conversation, a low, urgent hum that felt ominous even though she couldn't exactly make out what was being said—not that she was trying.

Frannie attempted to occupy herself to avoid accidentally eavesdropping, but she couldn't do much but fidget and wait.

After another five minutes, Frannie collected her purse, preparing to quietly leave, when Dante emerged from his bedroom with an apologetic expression. But there was something about his demeanor that was far different than before.

"I'm sorry about that, a business call that couldn't wait."

"Of course, I understand," she said, feeling awkward. "Actually, it was insensitive of me to drop in on you without checking to see if you had plans for the evening. I should probably go."

She had hoped that he would ease her concerns, but her feelings were hurt when he accepted her offer.

"I think tonight I might not be the best of company. I

have a lot of work that I need to finish and we should probably just call it a night."

"Right, sure, no problem," she said, feeling foolish. "I'll just see you around, I guess."

Was this what a casual sexual relationship felt like? She had no idea. She'd never been in one before. But she didn't like this feeling, and if this was how casual was supposed to work, maybe she wasn't cut out for it.

Dante walked her to the front door, polite and considerate as always, but she could tell he was a million miles away.

The urge to ask if he was okay overrode her bruised feelings. "I know I'm probably breaking all the rules, but I can tell whatever was said on that phone call upset you. Do you want talk about it? I can be a good listener."

Dante paused as if torn between wanting to share and keeping her at arm's length. She held her breath as hope kindled in her heart, but when he ultimately shook his head, she knew that he was determined to keep private whatever was eating at him.

"I appreciate the offer. It's very kind of you, but I think I need to handle this on my own. You needn't worry. It's business and I don't want to bore you with details that aren't necessary for our relationship."

Ouch. If that wasn't a brush-off, then she didn't know what was. How could they go from nearly tearing each other's clothes off to a wall of ice suddenly going up between them?

She faked a bright smile. "I guess I'll see you whenever it's convenient. I don't know how this works but whatever. I'll see you around."

Frannie didn't mean for that to come out as sharp as it had, but Dante seemed to realize that she was wounded and tried to make amends. He reached for her hand. "I've offended you. It's not my intention to hurt your feelings. I probably should've sent you home when you first showed up, but I was really happy to see you. You aren't intruding. Due to the nature of my business, it's probably a good idea to give me a heads-up the next time you want to come out. That way, I'm fully prepared to give you all of my attention."

It was reasonable, and yet his request stung. Just one more example of how whatever was happening between them was superficial at best. He had never promised anything more, so why was she disappointed?

"Yep. Sounds good," she said, eager to get out of there before embarrassing herself further. "I will see you around. Bye."

"Frannie—"

But listening to Dante dance around the obvious would only further her excruciating humiliation for practically throwing herself at him, and that was where she drew the line.

She left so fast that she probably looked like she was running to her car. But she had to get out of there because if she had stayed a minute longer, she would've started crying, ruining the appearance of being fine with the situation.

Because she wasn't. God, she really wasn't.

See? She didn't do casual because she was terrible at it. She wasn't the kind of woman who slept around and engaged in hookups. She was the kind of girl who got invested, cared about her partner and liked feeling part of a team.

What was happening? She had to get her head back on straight and her feelings in line with the reality of the situation. Dante wasn't her forever guy. He was a man passing through town who'd been honest about his situation. So why was she hurt that he was putting up boundaries?

Because she really, *really* liked him. Damn it. That'd happened fast.

Whatever this was, it was bound to end badly—for her.

Dante swore under his breath for handling the situation like a jackass.

Frannie's feelings were plain as the nose on her face. He'd wounded her by sending her away. If the situation were different, he would've loved to spend the evening together, but that wasn't the situation he was in. The phone call from Nick had only reminded him.

Reality checks were rarely kind.

He never should've encouraged anything with Frannie because she was bound to get hurt at some point.

Like tonight.

She might think he'd rejected her, but he was trying to protect her. He'd never forgive himself if anything happened to Frannie because of him.

Still, hurting her didn't feel right.

If he left the situation as it was, Frannie would probably ghost him, which would be a blessing in disguise. Then, at least, he'd know she was safe from him. But even as his brain offered the solution, he violently rejected it.

He had to make amends.

Letting Frannie think that he wasn't interested in her, to let her marinate in that kind of emotional rejection, was more than he could stomach.

Hell, he knew the right thing to do would be to let that door close, but he couldn't bring himself to do it.

That's a problem for tomorrow.

His thoughts were a maelstrom as he processed the new information about his father's death.

He needed more information. Sitting on his hands and waiting patiently wasn't in his nature. Even though he'd hired the private investigator to do the heavy lifting, he wanted to do his own digging around. It wasn't wise, but he couldn't escape the feeling that he could be doing more.

The answers were out there—he just needed to ask the right questions.

The memory of his father's death was crystallized in his brain. Emotional trauma had a way of imprinting like no other.

Of course, experts said memories were a shaky foundation to build a case on, but sometimes a memory was a good springboard.

He remembered the bitter cold of that night. A terrible storm had blown through the state, dropping temperatures to thirty below. Weather forecasters had warned residents to prepare for dangerous conditions. Stay home, bring in your livestock and avoid the roads if possible. Of all the places they'd lived, Dante hated Wisconsin the most because of the extreme cold.

After that night, he'd had another reason to hate the place.

His cell phone chirped for an email received. His private investigator had sent a file. He opened the file to find a scanned copy of the police report.

Matteo Santoro, 32, DOA, from blunt force trauma sustained from a motor vehicle accident on Greger Road at 2200 hours. Testing revealed a Blood Alcohol Content of .30. Impaired driving and poor road conditions led Mr. Santoro to lose control of his vehicle and collide with a sugar maple tree. Mr. Santoro was ejected through the windshield and died on impact.

Report: Ulysses Weisel, Detective, Hawthorne Police Department.

In all the years since his father's death, Dante had never thought to get a copy of the police report. No one had ever told him that his father's accident had been attributed to drunk driving. Ice on the roads had been blamed, which had seemed plausible because that storm had been a doozy.

Now, as he read someone's lie in an official document that his father had been drunk, rage percolated through his veins. Why the lie? Someone had gone to great lengths to ensure that no questions were asked, that Matteo's death was written off as an unfortunate consequence of some poor sap making a bad choice.

But his father never drank. Surely his mom had to have known that was a lie? Why would she go along with something she knew to be false?

Looking back on his memory, he was willing to bet his uncle Lorenzo had somehow persuaded his mother to let him care for them. She would've been vulnerable, lost, and grieving—a perfect target for Lorenzo.

Only now did Dante realize how his mother might've been lured into a trap. She was never able to escape, which made him feel complicit in keeping her in a golden cage, unknowingly participating in what had kept her silent and cowed.

In truth, when they first arrived in Italy, his uncle had seemed a kind blessing after a lifetime of struggle and confusing instability for a young Dante.

Lorenzo had spent time cultivating a bond with him, nurturing a place in his young heart that his father should've filled.

But even in life, Matteo had seemed too preoccupied to spend time with his son. There'd been no tossing the ball back and forth in the backyard for the Santoros. At the time, Dante had resented his father's distractions, but now, he saw things differently.

Maybe Matteo had been doing his best to keep his family safe from a threat that only he understood.

Dante had only known the struggle of surviving as they'd hopped from one place to another, his dad unable to hold down a job for too long, and his mother trying to make ends meet with barely enough resources to keep them alive.

He couldn't imagine being so terrified of his brother that he kept his family far enough away to avoid all contact— walking away from a veritable fortune because of a rift that couldn't be mended.

But he now understood his father's motivation better, and it shamed him that he'd never thought to dig deeper until it personally affected him.

Even as disgrace and guilt ate at him, there was grief in the mix, too.

For all his faults, Lorenzo had become his father figure, and for a long time, Dante had trusted him implicitly.

Lorenzo had put Dante through school, seen to his needs, and put a roof over his and his mother's heads when they needed it most.

There was a time when Dante had thought the world of his uncle.

But the thing about misplaced hero worship was that the facade eventually crumbled, leaving nothing to hide the rot lurking beneath the shell.

Now he understood why his father had been adamant

that his family would have nothing to do with the Santoro name or legacy.

What had Lorenzo told his mother to convince her to leave everything behind and accept the family's help?

Had she been coerced? Or had she been tired of hiding? Struggling and too lost in a sea of grief to see the shark's shadow closing in?

Either way, it was too late now. Both his parents were gone. Lorenzo was determined to bring him back into the fold by any means necessary, and the only thing keeping Lorenzo at bay was locked in a safe-deposit box.

An old piece of paper might seem a flimsy protection against the Santoro might, but that little slip of paper had the power to go off like a bomb in his family—and Lorenzo would do anything to keep that from happening.

However, that didn't mean Lorenzo would quit. He'd get sneakier in his efforts.

Because that was Lorenzo's superpower—getting what he wanted without getting his hands dirty.

Chapter 11

Frannie tried to put the fiasco at Dante's house in a locked box and forget about it, but the feeling of being rejected remained with her, lodged in her brain like a poky sticker burrowing into her sock.

The shop door opened, and one of her favorite people, Della Winslow, walked in with her black Lab, Charlie. It was an instant mood saver.

"I need the biggest, strongest cup of sweet tea you can manage before I fall over," Della said, flopping down in the nearest chair and wiping her brow. "I cannot handle this heat wave. We're not built for this kind of torture. Give me snow and ice any day, not Satan's armpit." She gestured to her dog, who was panting. "Look at poor Charlie, he's practically hyperventilating."

Frannie laughed, setting down a bowl of water in front of the parched dog before making Della's tea. "It's not that bad. I kind of like it. I can pretend I'm living somewhere beachy and warm. Like California."

"That's a myth about California. I spent the summer with an aunt who lived in a town called Planada. Definitely no beach. Just a lonely strip of highway, some mountains off in the distance, and a 'saloon' that offered twenty-five-cent root beers. That part actually was kind of nice but other than that…zero stars, do not recommend."

"And to think you gave up a promising travel guide career for that of a dog trainer," Frannie quipped with a teasing smile.

"Um, not just any dog trainer. Charlie is one of the best cadaver dogs in the state. It's not like his factory settings defaulted with that skill."

"My apologies," Frannie said, winking. "No, you're right, Charlie is pretty amazing and you're an incredible resource to our little town. Honestly, I know you can probably get hired someplace else and make a lot more money but I'm glad you're here with us."

Della appreciated the compliment, reaching down to rub Charlie's dark head. "So, I heard a rumor yesterday—"

"If it's about my dad and my aunt…as much as I'd love for it to be trash talk, it very well could be true," Frannie said, knowing that dancing around the issue would only delay the inevitable. People were already talking. The only way to kill a fire was to deny it oxygen. "We're going to ask for a DNA test proving paternity, but I'm not holding my breath that she's lying. If it's true, we'll deal with it like adults. I mean, what choice is there?"

Della pursed her lips in commiseration, admitting, "I guess that's the only way to handle it. Still, it sucks for your family."

"Yeah, it's a crap sandwich. But clearly, Jessie isn't going away anytime soon." She paused, curious, "Where did you hear about this?"

Della exhaled a breath, embarrassed. "I overheard a conversation that I probably shouldn't have been listening to, but to be fair, the woman was being very loud."

Frannie rubbed her forehead. "Yeah, it appears my aunt Jessie has a flair for the dramatic."

"I think she was talking to her attorney, or I don't know, he was dressed nice but there was something smarmy about him. Like a used car salesman vibe. I didn't recognize him, though. I don't think he's from around here. Anyway, she was going off on how much money your dad had, and she was entitled to a piece of it. Then, she said something that was really out of line—"

"Yeah?"

"She said that she deserved more than your mom because she was his *real* wife, no matter what a piece of paper said. That's when I'd heard enough, and I left the restaurant."

Frannie tried to keep her temper in check. The amount of sheer audacity flowing through that woman's veins was nothing short of narcissistic. "She can run her mouth all she wants, doesn't change the fact that my mother deserves every penny she inherited from my dad's estate. My dad wasn't an easy man to live with and she put up with more than her share of bullshit."

An impotent well of frustration sloshed in the pit of her stomach for her father's actions, but he was dead, and even if he weren't, it wasn't as if he would've allowed himself any accountability.

"The worst part? It doesn't surprise me that Dad had a mistress—it's that he chose to carry on with his own sister-in-law. That feels particularly low."

"Were you close with your dad?" Della asked with a subtle grimace, as if she were apologizing preemptively for the question and Frannie's answer.

Frannie sighed. "For a time, yes. We got along the best, I suppose. But as I got older and started having opinions of my own, we were less close. By the time he died, we barely saw each other, and I didn't miss his company. Sounds sad to say that, though. Like, I should've felt worse when he passed. A part of me was…relieved. Just saying that out loud…makes me feel like a terrible person."

"Feelings are complicated. Sometimes they don't make sense and we have to leave it at that."

"How is that you're younger than me and so much wiser?" Frannie teased, wiping away the sudden gathering of moisture at the corner of her eyes. "Look what you've done. I'm leaking."

Della chuckled softly. "I didn't know your dad well but sometimes we have to make a mental agreement with ourselves that when it comes to family, we're going to accept them as they are, good and bad."

"That's a tall order," Frannie said, thinking of Aunt Jessie. "Some family aren't worth claiming."

Della nodded, knowing exactly whom Frannie was referencing. "My personal opinion? I think it's in really bad taste that your aunt would come into our town and start mouthing off like that for anyone to hear. It's personal business and it should stay that way."

Frannie appreciated Della's stance even though she knew plenty of people were probably eating up the fresh gossip about her family. With a family as big as hers and as connected in the town, there were bound to be people who didn't like them. Frannie tried not to dwell on the people who were eager to see the Coltons fall.

The front door opened, and Dante walked in. Before she could temper her expression, her eyes widened in surprise, and her breath caught. He was so damn handsome, and it immediately irked her how her heart rate seemed to jump a beat the minute he appeared. Why was he here? After last night, she assumed their little "casual" adventure was over.

Charlie sensed the tension and cocked his head, licking his lips as he looked to Della for direction.

Apparently, Della could feel the same energy in the room as Charlie and took that as her cue to leave. She rose from the chair, patting Charlie's head for reassurance. "Thanks for the tea and the water for Charlie. I better get going. I'll talk to you later."

"Sure thing." Frannie waved, and Della and Charlie left. Now it was just Frannie and Dante, and the awkwardness was epic. Maybe she should tackle and be done with the elephant in the room. "Dante…"

He surprised her by going first. "No, I want to apologize for last night," he said, shaking his head firmly. "I was caught off guard by the phone call and I needed to deal with a few things. I wouldn't have been good company and I didn't want you to see me like that. But I should've handled it better."

Frannie softened. "Oh…" Well, that felt different than what she had been imagining. "I'm sorry for whatever you're going through. Sounds serious. Do you…want to talk about it?" she asked.

"It's complicated and I wouldn't want to bore you. Suffice it to say I would much rather have spent the evening with you than think about what was said in that phone call."

That was cryptic. *Red flag, much?* True, but it wasn't like Dante was a criminal or anything like that. *Cue the nervous internal laughter.* Frannie didn't know what to think. All she knew was that Dante apologizing for his abrupt change in demeanor made her feel less standoffish and more willing to try again.

Was that a bad idea?

* * *

Dante had had his out, but he didn't take it. Sure, walking away without further entanglements was wise, but he couldn't bring himself to do it.

And he was about to go deeper into the realm of bad decisions.

"I'd like to make it up to you. Are you busy tonight?" he asked.

She hesitated, and he didn't blame her after last night. He was surprised she was still willing to talk to him. "What did you have in mind?"

"A nice dinner with my favorite person in Owl Creek."

"Well, that's not a great endorsement. You don't know many people."

He chuckled. "You're right. I can do better than that. How about dinner with the most *beautiful* woman in Owl Creek?"

She grinned in spite of herself. "You're definitely getting closer to success. And what would we do after dinner?"

"I would leave that up to you. But I would definitely like to take you back to my place and really make up for my poor behavior last night."

Franny's smile brightened. "Now, that sounds like a plan. How about you pick me up at my place around six?"

This time it was Dante who hesitated. He wanted to keep Frannie as safe as possible. Even though he was technically putting her in danger just by spending so much time with her, he didn't like to think that any eyes on him would follow Frannie. But he also didn't want her to think he was hesitating for the wrong reason. He finally answered, "I would be happy to pick you up," with a warm smile to chase away doubt.

"Careful, Dante, this almost sounds like a real date," she teased.

"I suppose it is," he said, fighting against the knowledge that he had no business encouraging her affection. "Text me your address and I will be there promptly at six."

"Promptly?" Her grin deepened. "A man after my own heart. I was raised to believe on time is already late, so that gives you a glimpse into my secret quirks."

It was silly, but somehow knowing that Frannie prized punctuality the same as he did only made him desire her more.

His hands itched to touch her, to wrap her in his arms and make up for all the kissing they didn't get to do last night, but he restrained the impulse. He didn't know who might be watching.

"Aren't you going to kiss me goodbye?" she asked coyly, striking with unerring accuracy at his secret desire.

"Tonight, you'll get all the kisses you can handle and then some," he promised, going to the door. "Gives us something to look forward to."

"Tease," she laughed as he left the shop to run errands.

He hadn't planned to stop at Frannie's bookstore, but he couldn't regret his choice even though it was all wrong. He couldn't deny his mood felt considerably happier than when he left the house, and he was selfish enough to enjoy it.

But now he had things to get done, such as paying the biweekly rent, which he did in cash.

Dante stepped into the property management office, expecting a quick transaction, but the property manager was feeling chatty.

"How are things with the rental?" she asked with a wide smile. "How's the heat treating you? It's not always this warm here but we're getting a real sizzler this year."

"The heat doesn't bother me, and the fans work well enough to keep the temperature down," he answered, being polite. "How about you?"

She fanned her face for emphasis. "Oh, I can't hardly handle this heat. I feel like I'm about to melt. But I'm glad to hear that you're still enjoying our little town. Do you know how much longer you'll be staying with us?"

Dante was purposefully vague. "It's hard to say. I appreciate the biweekly payments. My work is unpredictable. However, just to show I appreciate how accommodating you've been, I'll pay for the month even if I end up leaving."

"Oh, that's real considerate of you. It's not very often that we get long-term rentals like you popping into town."

"Like me? What do you mean?"

"Honey, you're practically a celebrity in this town. Seems everyone's talking about two things. The handsome Italian with the sexy accent and, of course, that terrible gossip that's going around about Robert Colton and his supposed lover who just happens to be his sister-in-law. Sordid business, that."

So, both he and Frannie's family drama were the talk of the town. Not a great combo for either of them. "I suppose all places have their secrets," he murmured, trying to downplay it for Frannie's sake.

"I feel so bad for Jenny. She doesn't deserve what her sister's done to her. Let me tell you, Jessie Robards has always been nothing but trouble all her days. It doesn't surprise me at all that she's come back just to stir up trouble."

Dante didn't like the feeling that he was participating in gossip about Frannie's business and felt mildly protective. "I'm sure it will all work out in the end. These things usually get sorted out somehow."

"I suppose so," the property manager conceded, but she

looked dubious. "All I know is that if Jessie is back in town that bodes real bad for Jenny."

"How so?"

"Oh, that woman has always wanted anything that was her sister's. It doesn't surprise me none that she went after Jenny's husband. That woman has no shame. It's hard to believe Jenny and Jessie are twins. They are night and day. Good and evil, if you ask me."

He felt terrible for Frannie. He knew something about toxic family members. "I hope it all turns out okay," he said, signaling the end to the conversation with a polite reason to leave.

Toxic people were like cancer. Sometimes it took a while to realize the insidious destruction they were doing behind the scenes. He didn't know this Jessie woman, but her intentions could hardly be good.

Stay out of Frannie's business, the voice warned. The last thing he needed was to draw unnecessary attention to himself. Engaging with a greedy woman was likely to do that.

Besides, Franny seemed capable of handling her aunt and whatever she had up her sleeve.

He might be unable to solve Frannie's family issue, but he could show her a good night.

For now, that would have to be enough.

Chapter 12

Frannie was humming under her breath the following morning as she tidied up her shelves, still thinking about last night with Dante. Dinner at The Tides—*exquisite*—followed by quality sexy time at his place—*addictive*—and she couldn't stop the giddy smile that kept curving her lips.

The man was everything she'd never realized she wanted.

Kind, considerate, funny, thoughtful—oh, and so handsome she could stare at him until the day she died. But she knew nothing about him, which was starting to bug her.

She'd begun to notice that he was skilled at dodging personal questions, but he did it so well that it wasn't until much later that she realized he never really answered anything of substance about himself.

She didn't like to create problems where there weren't any, but she also couldn't help but wonder if she was overlooking a major red flag.

People who didn't like sharing details about themselves usually had something to hide.

Like a wife or a girlfriend.

Or worse.

No, she told herself sternly, Dante was a good man who was just a little private. Clearly, he'd suffered a terrible breakup and was still healing from the emotional trauma.

That much she'd surmised when he'd admitted he didn't want to talk about his past.

Wasn't he entitled to his privacy? Of course he was.

Besides, their relationship was created within certain boundaries, which didn't encourage deeper connections, so Dante's reluctance to share details seemed to fit within those parameters.

Ugh. That level of circular justification had just made her dizzy.

Frannie already wanted to break the rules of their "relationship."

She wanted more.

It felt strange to allow someone access to her body yet receive so little of the person.

Her intrusive thoughts threatened to kill the sweet high she'd ridden all morning as the questions and insecurities started to pile up.

Grabbing her phone, she texted Fletcher.

Any luck finding anything of interest on Dante?

Even sending the text made her feel guilty, like she was doing something wrong and sneaky, but she rationalized that once Fletcher came back empty-handed, she could relax knowing that Dante was exactly who he said he was, and he wasn't hiding anything.

And if Fletcher discovered Dante was lying about something?

What then?

She pushed that thought aside. *Don't build bridges for rivers you don't have to cross yet.*

Frannie hoisted a box of books and started to walk toward the display table when the front door opened, and a deliveryman with a massive spray of flowers walked in.

"Frannie Colton?" he asked hopefully.

"Yes?"

"Delivery for you."

Frannie accepted the beautiful bouquet, flabbergasted and tickled at the same time. "Thank you!" she called out after the man as he left the shop. Dante must have some kind of telepathy. How else would he have known she was fighting her thoughts about their connection? She smiled, placing the flowers on the counter to find the card, but there was none.

"You sly dog, playing secret admirer," she murmured, gazing at the expensive blooms, approving of his choices. "This is gorgeous."

She grabbed her phone and quickly sent a text to Dante.

They're beautiful, thank you!

Her phone dinged almost immediately in response.

What is?

She giggled at the game. Sure, he had no idea what she was talking about. She liked this playful side of Dante. Frannie texted back.

How did you know I love white lilies?

Dante ditched the text and called seconds later. "Frannie, I didn't send you flowers," he said, his tone nothing like the loving and sensual man she'd spent last night with. "Whoever sent you flowers, it wasn't me."

His denial splashed water on her happiness. Then, straightening with confusion, she pressed him. "What do you mean you didn't send them? Are you being serious? You truly didn't send them?"

"No, I did not," Dante said, his tone clipped. "Who else might've sent them?"

Was he jealous? If he knew her, he'd understand how ridiculous he was being. Frannie wasn't the type to date multiple people at once. She was very much a monogamous person. She tried not to take offense, but it hurt. "I have no idea who might've sent them. I'm not seeing anyone but you."

That should've put him at ease, but if anything, he seemed more tense. "Perhaps family? A friend?"

She shook her head, baffled by his reaction and the subtle urgency in his tone. "Dante, maybe it was a mistake. There wasn't a card attached. Maybe the flowers were meant for someone else."

"Who delivered the flowers?"

"A random delivery person. I didn't pay attention."

"A local florist company?"

She paused to think. "Maybe? Like I said, I wasn't paying attention. I was so tickled by the flowers I didn't notice anything else because I thought they were from you."

Admitting this private truth felt more revealing than standing naked in the town square. She wasn't supposed to have feelings so quickly for a man who was only meant to be casual fun.

Damn it, she'd told Darla she was terrible at this stuff.

"Forget it, it's probably a mistake. I'll call the local florist and find out who the flowers actually belong to and then we can move past this awkward phone call."

The silence on the other end was unnerving. Why was he freaking out over a flower delivery likely meant for someone else? And why was she hurt that the flowers weren't from him?

"Yes, please let me know as soon as you have more information," he said as if they were discussing a business transaction that went awry.

"Yeah, sure." She blinked back stupid tears. She wasn't going to cry over this. Wiping at her eyes, she lied. "Okay, well, I have customers, so I better go," she said, hanging up so she could get off the phone and be pitiful in private.

Why did it bother her so much that Dante hadn't been the one to send her flowers? Last night had been perfect— romantic, fun, sensual—and she'd floated home on a cloud. She knew she wasn't supposed to be thinking of Dante as her boyfriend, but it was hard not to daydream about a life with him.

Too soon! Red flag! Except she was the red flag in this instance. She had no business fantasizing about a man who'd been up-front and honest about not being available for anything more than casual.

She was starting to hate that word.

Sighing, she blotted her eyes with a tissue and grabbed her phone to call the florist. The lilies were lovely, even if they weren't meant for her. Someone out there had a secret admirer with discerning tastes.

If only it had been her.

Dante stared at the phone after Frannie clicked off, his thoughts racing.

His knee-jerk reaction had been a flare of jealousy, but he could hear the sincerity in her voice when she claimed he was the only one she was dating.

Under normal circumstances, that would've been enough to calm his nerves, but more was happening behind the scenes than he could share.

If she wasn't dating anyone else, and he hadn't sent the flowers, who had?

An unexpected gift could be an ominous portent, depending on its origins.

It could be a message to Dante that no one in his life was safe—anyone could be reached.

Intimidation and manipulation were his uncle's bread and butter.

With luck, the flowers were inadvertently delivered to the wrong address.

But the warning tingle in his gut told him that the flowers weren't an innocent mix-up.

Dante started to pace while he waited for Frannie's call. It was hard not to jump in the car and start asking questions himself, but that would only make him look like a jealous jackass or a paranoid fool, and he wasn't keen to embrace either look.

Especially not with Frannie.

He knew it was too soon, but he had feelings for her. The way she laughed, her quirky sense of humor, her sense of compassion, and her levelheaded demeanor—everything about Frannie lit up his insides like a carnival.

Which was why he had to know where those damn flowers came from.

He'd never forgive himself if he'd selfishly put Frannie in danger.

He'd made the mistake of underestimating his uncle's ruthlessness once, and he couldn't afford to do it again.

Not with Frannie's life.

Maybe he ought to level with her, share with her why he was in Owl Creek, hiding from the man who'd essentially raised him after his father died.

The man he was afraid had something to do with both his parents' deaths, years apart.

He shoved shaking hands through his hair, willing the

phone to ring with good news, but staring at the phone only ramped up his anxiety as silence followed.

Finally, Frannie called back.

"Hi, it's me." She sounded standoffish, but she went on to say, "So, I'm officially confused. I haven't a clue who might've sent these flowers. The florist said they were commissioned through one of those internet companies and don't have access to any booking information. The order just shows up on the computer with proof of payment. Then, the florist fulfills the order. The only information provided on the order was my name and the shop's address."

Dante felt a cold chill dance on his spine. An internet commission could come from anywhere—even another country. "You should close up early today."

"Why?" Frannie asked, confused.

"Because your location is compromised."

"Compromised?" She forced a chuckle as if he were being ludicrous. "You sound like a spy or something. I'm sure there's a logical explanation for this, and I won't get worked up over a flower delivery. Besides, they're quite pretty and dress up the shop nicely."

Dante wanted Frannie to throw them in the trash, but he knew asking her would only create more questions and an even bigger gap between them.

"I'm sorry...maybe you're right," he conceded, forcing himself to sound less anxious than he felt. "I apologize if my reaction was inappropriate."

"Well, it hurt my feelings," she admitted. "But maybe that's the cultural differences between us. I keep forgetting you're from another country."

"Yes, perhaps."

"So...were you a teensy bit jealous?" she asked.

It was easier to admit to jealousy than to admit he had a

murderous uncle on his tail who could be targeting anyone Dante got close to. "Yes, it's possible."

"I mean, that's not so bad to be jealous… Sometimes it means you really care for someone."

"I do care about you," he said without hesitation. *More than I should.*

"I care about you, too."

He couldn't let his suspicions go, though. "There's no one that you can think of who might've sent them? Not even your ex? Perhaps he is trying to win back your affections."

"No. My ex didn't believe in sending flowers or doing anything remotely romantic. He once told me flowers were only for men who craved validation from the women in their lives. Just saying that out loud makes me embarrassed I ever thought he was The One. He was an insensitive asshole with zero emotional intelligence. So, no, I don't think he sent them."

"Yes, but manipulative men often use methods that previously would've been uncharacteristic of them, to seem changed."

She paused before admitting, "Well, that might be true, but I know he didn't send them. He's engaged to someone else and it's unlikely that he gives me a second thought."

Dante heard the quiet hurt in Frannie's voice. It was irrational, but he felt the urge to punch this ex in the face for stupidly losing an incredible woman, even though the only reason Dante had the opportunity to know her was because of this jackass's actions.

"He's an idiot," he assured Frannie. "His loss is my gain."

"Dante…when you say things like that, it's hard to remember that we're keeping things simple between us."

She was right. He was sending mixed signals. "I know. I'm sorry."

"It's okay. Just wanted to point it out."

But without solid proof that there was no dangerous intent behind that mysterious flower delivery, there was no way he'd let Frannie out of sight now.

He'd made the mistake of assuming his uncle would never stoop so low to get what he wanted—he couldn't afford to make that mistake again.

Not with Frannie.

"How about I cook you some authentic Italian tonight?" he offered.

"Are you sure that's a good idea? Somehow dinner always ends with us naked in bed."

"I'm not complaining."

She chuckled. "I'm not either, but maybe we need to put the brakes on what we're doing for a while."

Absolutely not. "Do you prefer Tagliatelle al Ragù or Rigatoni alla Carbonara?"

"I don't know what either of those are, but it sounds like pasta, and if that's the case, I love all pasta. I'm lactose intolerant, though, so nothing with dairy."

"Trofie al Pesto it is then. Bring a beverage of your choice."

She laughed in spite of the seriousness between them. "I haven't said I'll come."

"You will always come with me, that's a promise," he said in a sultry tone.

Frannie's breathy "I'll bring the wine" was all the confirmation he needed. At least when Frannie was with him, he felt secure in his ability to protect her.

If anything happened to Frannie—he'd tear his uncle apart.

And that was a different kind of promise.

Chapter 13

Frannie planned to meet with her mom for lunch at a small park within walking distance from one of Jenny Colton's private nursing clients. Despite having enough of a nest egg to retire comfortably, Jenny preferred to work part-time to keep her mind sharp and her body in shape.

Frannie thought her mom kept working because the idea of being stuck in the house with the ghosts of the past was too much to bear. But on the more practical side, Jenny prided herself on being helpful and needed, and nursing fit the bill.

She waved as her mom walked toward her. After that disastrous meeting with her aunt Jessie, Frannie couldn't help but compare the two women.

Jessie was thinner but brittle, as if she punished herself by restricting her calorie intake, whereas her mom was thin but fit. Jenny Colton didn't have a problem indulging in a slice of cake or a glass of wine, but she also stayed active at the local gym, enjoying her water aerobics and yoga classes.

"Hi, Mom," she said, kissing Jenny's cheek in welcome. "I brought sandwiches from the brewery. I hope that's okay."

Jenny approved, "I love a good sandwich." She slid onto the picnic bench opposite Frannie. "This is nice. What's the occasion?"

"Do I need a special occasion to spend time with my mom?" Frannie teased, although there was some truth to Jenny's inquiry, and that stung a bit. The recent passing of her dad was a stark reminder that her parents weren't getting any younger, and sometimes past squabbles needed to be put to rest to enjoy what time you had left.

Of course, easier said than done when the past showed up barking about wanting a piece of your inheritance.

"I love the garlic aioli they put on their sandwiches," Jenny said with an ecstatic appreciation of her bite. "I tell you, the main chef at the brewery can put a five-star restaurant to shame. It's like a little pocket of high-end cuisine hiding in an unassuming brewery."

Frannie agreed. They just enjoyed their sandwiches for a moment, soaking up the sunshine and scenery. The park was mostly empty today, which was nice because sometimes the youth soccer teams used the grassy fields for practice. Frannie had made plenty of memories in this park, some of which would remain private. She smothered a small smile and took another bite.

Jenny broke the silence first. "I heard your aunt Jessie is creating a stir in town."

Frannie was grateful her mom had brought up the topic first, but it still made her cringe. Going straight to it, Frannie nodded. "Yes, she's saying all sorts of things, and I wish she'd just shut her trap."

Jenny chuckled ruefully. "One thing Jessie does not do is silence herself for the sake of others' convenience or comfort. I used to be envious of her ability to do and say whatever she wanted regardless of how others felt. Now it seems less of a positive quality."

"Yeah, especially with what she's saying about our family."

Jenny sighed, wiping her mouth with a paper napkin.

The sadness in her mother's eyes made Frannie want to march up to her aunt and punch her in the mouth, or at the very least give her a scathing piece of her mind.

"Are you okay?" Frannie ventured, hating the position her mother was in. "It would be totally understandable if you weren't."

"Oh, I'm fine," Jenny answered with a quick smile that seemed rehearsed. "It's one of those things that you just have to accept and move on. No sense in crying about spilled milk."

She disagreed. "No, Mom, this isn't something you have to accept, and you don't have to pretend to be okay with it. How could your sister do this to you? I hate to put too fine of a point on it but aren't twins supposed to be ultra close?"

"I'm sure she had her reasons."

Frannie couldn't stop the aggravation from creeping into her voice, even though she tried to be compassionate. "Mom, please stop being so accommodating. She stole your husband and now she's trying to steal our money. It's not like Dad was an oil tycoon. Sure, he did pretty well for himself with investments and whatnot but he wasn't a billionaire. The piece of the pie is already being split seven ways, and now we have to figure out how to include three more people? It's not fair."

Jenny tried to use logic instead of emotion. "According to Chase, nothing will change until the DNA tests on the two adult children are completed. As far as Jessie is concerned—" she lifted her hands, unsure "—it's a bit more complicated, legally."

"Yeah, I heard. I will puke if she's awarded one red cent."

Jenny's small laugh reminded Frannie of when she was a kid, and she'd said something outlandish.

Frannie didn't want to laugh, but a reluctant chuckle escaped. "It would be awesome if I could manage to time that so it landed right in her greedy lap."

"Jessie can't stand bodily fluids, so that would be a perfect way to ruin her day," Jenny shared. "She couldn't even handle her own. Once she threw up when she got a bloody nose. That was a mess."

It was hard to imagine that brittle woman as anything other than the hard woman trying to ruin their family. "What was she like as a kid? I mean, what happened between you two? Weren't you ever close?"

Jenny swallowed as if pushing down a sudden lump in her throat. "Yes, we were close at one time. And I don't know what happened," she answered sadly. "Or maybe, I do know and I don't want to say because I would never want you to feel differently about your father. For all his faults, he was a good father."

Eh, that's being generous. "Mom, I love how you want to create a positive memory out of something that was crap, but he doesn't deserve that kindness right now. I loved my dad, but I'm not sure how I can forgive him for this."

Jenny accepted Frannie's frank admission and didn't try to change her perspective. How could she? The facts were hard to rearrange. "In high school your dad was quite the catch. Very popular, charming, and an incredible athlete. When you ask what happened between me and Jessie? Well, the answer is your dad. We were close until we both fell for Robert—and we both dated him."

"Ew. Gross." Frannie made a face. "I definitely feel sick to my stomach. Hadn't you two ever heard of the term 'sloppy seconds'?"

"Francesca," Jenny admonished with a grimace. "Should I continue or stop?"

"No, go ahead. Might as well hear the whole sordid story so at least I'll know the backstory of this reality TV episode."

Jenny exhaled a short breath as if praying for patience, then continued. "Yes, he dated us both but at the time, I never really thought Jessie was in love with Robert. We'd always been competitive with each other, but never maliciously, until after Robert. In the end, he chose me, and it created a deep rift between my sister and me. Your father and I got married shortly after graduation, and soon after, Jessie married Buck and I thought we'd moved past the hurts from high school. But our relationship was never the same, strained at best. Then, when Jessie divorced Buck, she took off, leaving the kids for Buck to raise alone."

Jenny's kids were close to Uncle Buck's, having spent countless summers at the Colton ranch, but Jessie had bailed on her first family while Frannie was still a baby, so she had no memory of her aunt until that horrid meeting the other day.

Speaking of, might as well share that information, too.

"I need to tell you something... The other day, against my better judgment, I agreed to meet with Aunt Jessie."

"Why on earth would you do that?" Jenny asked with a mild frown.

"Because...morbid curiosity, perhaps?" Frannie admitted, cringing. "I'm sorry. I shouldn't have met up with her. It was stupid and all she did was make me mad. Now she's running her mouth all over town saying how she deserves a portion of Dad's estate because she was more of a wife to him than you and I'm just about at my limit of patience with her. I mean, I guess there's nothing we can do about it if her kids turn out to be Dad's, but I'll be damned if that piranha should get any of Dad's estate."

"Well, we'll just have to put our faith in our lawyer's expertise," Jenny said, gathering their trash just like she would at home, as if on autopilot. "The sandwiches were delicious, darling. Really hit the spot, but I need to get going. I have a hair appointment in an hour."

Frannie nodded, mildly disappointed. Her mom was intensely private, and that wasn't likely to change, but for once, she wanted her mom to feel safe enough to be open and vulnerable with her kids. Even if she were devastated by the revelation about her sister, she wouldn't dare show the true depth of her pain.

Not even to her grown children.

One of the worst parts about being a nomad in a strange land was the lack of creature comforts, and the lack of creature comforts inevitably led to too much downtime with nothing but the thoughts in his head to keep him company.

And that was a scary place to be.

With the troubling mystery of the recent flower delivery, the tension in his body was enough to break bone. He couldn't seem overly anxious without seeming off to Frannie, who was already ready to dismiss the mystery, but he also couldn't let it ride, knowing the real threat out there.

After Belinda's attack, Dante had moved quickly to get her to safety. Once she could travel, he had arranged for Belinda to be transported to a private rehab facility in Switzerland. He didn't want Lorenzo to have easy access to Belinda in any way as she recovered, but moving her out of the country had been the only way to keep her profile low.

It hadn't been easy.

But he'd convinced her of the danger she would be in if she remained in Italy, and she'd agreed to go.

She'd left behind everything she'd built for an unknown

future in another country. That kind of bravery made him feel weak in comparison, but it also pushed him to be stronger.

In his nightmares, Belinda blamed him for her injuries, but in real life, her kind heart had never placed the weight on his shoulders.

But she should have—he was to blame.

His hubris, his smug belief that Lorenzo couldn't leverage his compliance, had cost Belinda her future in surgery.

And yet, she never blamed Dante.

Dante carried a different kind of guilt; sometimes, he didn't think he'd ever be free of its weight.

He'd decided that his penance would be to hear her voice when he checked on her progress until the day she managed to recover her hands like before.

But the doctors had been honest about the slim chance of that happening, which meant his reprieve would likely never be granted.

Grabbing his cell, he dialed the secret number, knowing it would be close to bedtime in Switzerland.

Belinda picked up on the second ring. "Dante?"

Her voice, soft and soothing, remained the same, despite her situation. "I'm sorry to call so late. I wanted to check in before time got away from me. How are you feeling? How's your therapy?"

"I'm fine, therapy is progressing. You needn't worry. I'm safe."

He didn't know that. He would never make that assumption again. "Do you need anything?"

"My needs are well cared for," she assured him. "How are you? Are you sleeping?"

Always thinking of others...some things didn't change. It was now six months since the attack. "How do the doctors feel about your progress?"

"Dante, you need to stop blaming yourself," she admonished gently. "I will be fine. And even if I never operate again, there are plenty more things I can do with my expertise. I am safe and that's what matters—because of you."

No, he was why her life was unrecognizable from before the attack. "If I could go back in time—"

"Stop. Thoughts like that are a useless expenditure of energy. You cannot change what happened, only what happens as we go forward. I refuse to look at my life as cut short. It's simply going to be different. You need to get to that place as well."

"He won't stop until I return to the fold, and I refuse to do that."

"You will find a way to beat him at his game and when you do, you must promise me that you'll get on with your life."

Her belief in him only stung more. Their romantic relationship had died in the attack, but he would never forget what they'd once had.

Still, even at their happiest, Dante had never felt with Belinda the way he felt with Frannie, which only deepened his fear of losing her.

"I've met someone," Belinda shared, surprising Dante with her admission. "I think you would like him."

"Who?"

"My physical therapist. His name is Sven. He's kind and compassionate but very funny. I like how he makes me laugh."

Belinda deserved all the laughter in the world, and if this Sven could give it to her, he had Dante's blessing.

"You don't need to call and check up on me anymore," Belinda said warmly. "I'm well cared for. I will be safe. All I need to know is that you're safe, too."

He couldn't make that promise, and he didn't want to burden her with the information he was struggling with.

"I'm happy for you, Bel," he said, his voice thick with emotion, "I really am. You deserve the best life has to offer."

"So do you."

He wished he could believe that.

"Good night," he murmured.

"Good night, *dolcezza.*"

They clicked off, and Dante spent a good minute staring at his phone, wondering how this all ended.

Did it end with him finally free of his uncle's grip, able to live as he chose?

Or did it end with Lorenzo dragging him back into the fold, yoked to the Santoro family until he died?

He didn't have the answer.

He only knew one thing for sure. He'd do anything to keep Frannie safe—even if it meant walking away from her forever.

Chapter 14

Frannie's gaze strayed to the lovely lilies, only a little bothered by the mystery. She liked to believe that sometimes nice things happened for no reason. Her brother Fletcher might say that was naive, but she preferred to look at the world with hope in her heart rather than a sour expectation that everyone was out to screw each other.

Although her aunt Jessie was challenging that worldview at the moment.

No, not going to waste the energy on that woman today, she vowed, drawing a deep breath, determined to shake off the dark thoughts, but it wasn't easy.

After lunch with her mom, she couldn't stop thinking about what it must've been like for her, knowing her sister had coveted her husband even before discovering this level of betrayal.

What happened to the "girl code"? She couldn't imagine even looking cross-eyed at Darla's soon-to-be husband or, for that matter, her sister's husband (RIP to that amazing man). Even thinking of such a thing made her physically ill.

Was Aunt Jessie a sociopath? Was that genetic? Did it run in families, lurking in the genetic code to pop out when you least expected it, like daisies in a field?

Maybe she ought to read a few books on sociopathy.

Darla blew in like a tornado, sucking up all the oxygen

in the room as usual, her cheeks flushed from the heat and whatever crisis she was running from.

"Please tell me you've started serving liquor from your little café because Lord help me, I need a margarita, heavy pour on the tequila, please!"

It probably wasn't funny, but Darla's theatrics were always amusing. "Sorry, still no liquor license and I don't know that I'll add that to my list of things to do."

"I think you're missing out on an untapped revenue stream. Wine and books always go together. Who doesn't sip on their chardonnay while reading a spicy book at the end of a long day?" Darla quipped as she flopped into a chair with a long-suffering exhalation. She opened her mouth to start again but saw the flowers and stopped, straightening abruptly to gesture at them. "And what the hell is that?"

"Last I checked, flowers," Frannie answered.

"I see that. And from whom? A certain Italian stallion, perhaps?" she asked coyly.

"Um, funny story about that…no. I have no idea who sent them but they sure are pretty. My favorite, too."

Darla's smile faded with confusion. "What do you mean you don't know who sent them? That bouquet looks expensive. People don't just send pricey flowers to strangers out of the goodness of their heart."

Frannie disagreed. "That's not true. I read the other day of someone who received an anonymous donation of $500 to their GoFundMe for medical expenses to help cover cancer treatments."

"That's not apples to apples," Darla said. "Did you post a GoFundMe for flower deliveries to the shop?"

"Of course not," Frannie said with a chuckle. "But someone wanted to do something nice, and I think it's lovely. I mean, maybe it's a condolence for losing my father? Who knows. The universe works in mysterious ways."

"And so do murderers," Darla warned.

"You watch too much true crime."

"So do you, which is why I'm baffled why you aren't freaked out by this. Honestly, it's weird. I think you should throw them away."

Frannie balked. "No way. They're gorgeous and they add a certain something to the lobby. Makes it more inviting."

"Yeah, they're beautiful but honestly, it's kinda creepy if you ask me."

"You worry too much," Frannie said, waving off Darla's paranoia. "So, what's the crisis for today? I'm assuming it's wedding-related?"

Darla scowled, not ready to let it go. "What does Fletcher or Max think about these mystery flowers? Or Dante for that matter?"

"I didn't tell Max or Fletcher. They have busy lives doing their actual jobs. I'm not going to clutter up their head-space with something as silly as this. That'd be like calling 911 because you got a sliver. It's just flowers. No big deal. As for Dante, well, he was a little jealous, actually. It was kinda hot to see him get all riled up but then, once he realized the flowers weren't from another date, he got kinda quiet, maybe even a little protective? It was really sweet."

"Yeah, because he knows it's weird, too."

Frannie shrugged, ready to be finished with this conversation. Why everyone wanted to make a federal case out of a rogue delivery was beyond her. The world had bigger problems."

"So you're really not going to chase this down and figure out who sent them?"

"I tried. It was called in using an internet web service

for flower delivery but there was no way to trace who made the purchase unless I wanted to have a forensic accountant come in and request the company's purchase logs. Which, honestly, isn't going to happen with the very little information I have. It's not like there was a threatening note or anything attached to the delivery. It was just the flowers and I love them, whether they were mistakenly sent to me or sent to me by someone who just thought I'd benefit from a little cheer in my life."

At that, Darla softened. "Your family has been served up a terrible hand as of late. I'm sorry. My head's been so full of wedding stuff that I haven't been a great friend when you need it. Is there anything I can do?"

Frannie appreciated Darla's offer, but there was nothing anyone could do but ride out the storm. "No, everything's in the lawyer's hands right now. I talked with my mom yesterday, and that's pretty much her attitude and while it sucks, she's right. My aunt isn't going to suddenly grow a conscience overnight, so we'll have to trust our lawyers know their stuff. Can you believe she's going around town saying she was more of a wife to my dad than my mother, his *wife*?"

Darla grimaced. "She's got a brass set of balls on her, that's for sure. Your mom is practically a saint."

"I wouldn't go that far but compared to my aunt Jessie, yeah, she's definitely leagues ahead on the 'decent person' track." Frannie sighed, hating the entire mess. "But it is what it is, I guess."

"You're a better person than me. I would be tearing every strand of hair from the woman's head before we even stepped foot in court. That reminds me, I ought to make sure Tom knows that if he cheats on me, I'll turn him from a rooster to a hen real quick and then I'll redecorate his prized truck with my keys."

"All of that is illegal," Frannie reminded Darla with barely suppressed laughter, "but I approve."

Darla jumped to her feet, helping herself to a bottled water from the fridge. "Okay, so enough about that, tell me about your man."

"He's not my man," Frannie corrected her with a subtle blush. "We're keeping it casual."

"Ha! You don't do casual."

"Well, I'm trying something new."

"Good luck with that. Well, how's it working out?"

Frannie pursed her lips, admitting, "Confusing."

"Go on."

"Well, I really want to ask him to go to the lake with me, but I don't know if that's overstepping our boundaries in this whole casual setup because when I'm with him, it doesn't feel casual at all."

"What does it feel like?"

Dreamy. Perfect. Exciting. Passionate. "Um, well, it's good."

"Good?"

"Better than good, amazing."

"And he feels the same?"

"I think so?"

Darla frowned. "You don't know?"

"He's hard to read. Sometimes I feel like we're totally on the same page and then the next, I feel he's shutting me out and keeping me at a distance."

"The dreaded hot/cold dance. Hate to break it to you but that's not a good sign."

"What do you mean?"

Darla's expression didn't bode well as she explained, "That's guy code for, 'I'm just not that into you, but you'll do for now.' I should've known he would be a player. He's international, for crying out loud. Too sophisticated, too handsome, too 'not Owl Creek' material, you know what I'm saying?"

Those were precisely the reasons Frannie adored him. "I think he's been hurt in the past. He doesn't like to talk about his past relationship."

"Another red flag."

"Darla, people can have things they aren't comfortable talking about. Doesn't make them red flags."

"You've had sex, right?"

Frannie blushed. "Yeah." *Multiple times—and each time was better than the last.*

"If he's truly not a player, by this point, he should be able to share some intimate details about his life before you. It's not asking too much. If anything, you're not asking enough."

Frannie digested that advice. Was it true? Was she being too accommodating and ignoring her own needs? She wanted to know more about Dante, even if he wasn't interested or available to stick around; she wanted to learn more about him as a person.

"So I should ask him to the lake this weekend?"

"Hell yeah, and his answer will go a long way toward showing you who he is as a man."

What if he turned her down? Was she ready to walk away from Dante if it turned out he was exactly as Darla feared?

Better to know now than later.

Because at this rate? She was going to fall head over heels in love with the man.

If she hadn't already.

Frannie was coming over tonight. She'd called about an hour ago, asking if he wouldn't mind some company, and while he should've made some excuse and declined, he couldn't stop his mouth from saying yes.

He rationalized that she was safer in his house with him than anywhere else, but it was a flimsy attempt at justifying his actions.

Just say it, a voice taunted. *You can't stop thinking about her, and you'll take any opportunity to be with her.*

Even if doing so put her in danger.

He growled under his breath, irritated at the useless circular nature of his thoughts. Striding to the kitchen as if he could outrun the guilt on his heels, he turned his attention to putting together a quick dinner.

He enjoyed cooking for Frannie. For one, she was open to trying anything—even though she was lactose intolerant and should avoid dairy—and truly loved his efforts. It was as if everything they did together fit like they were made for each other. He didn't consider himself a great romantic, but since meeting Frannie, he understood why poets created sonnets, even if he'd never have that level of talent.

Plus, there was something sensual about cooking for someone he cared for—the level of intimacy was something he'd never experienced before.

Belinda had been too busy with her work to spend too much time in the kitchen. They'd always eaten separately or ordered in, but at least their kitchen was always immaculate.

Mainly because they were rarely home at the same time.

Looking back, it was easy to see how they'd become affectionate roommates who'd occasionally passed each other in the night, enjoyed a smooch or two, and then went about their routine as usual.

It'd been a comfortable routine but lacking a certain level of passion that he hadn't realized he needed.

Until Frannie.

The attack had irrevocably changed their relationship, but now he realized their romantic life had died long before.

A knock at the front door told him Frannie had arrived. He wiped his hands and put the eggplant lasagna into the oven. He'd even made it with dairy-free cheese, though they'd have to wait and see if it turned out as good as the original recipe.

If it bombed, he had a mini dairy-free charcuterie board waiting in the refrigerator.

When he opened the door, Frannie smiled, holding up a bottle of wine. "I brought the beverage," she announced, lifting on her tiptoes to kiss him as if he were her favorite person.

His chest warmed and his groin tightened, and he was immediately tempted to scoop her into his arms and carry her to the bedroom for a little loving before dinner, but he restrained himself and accepted the wine with an appraising smile. "Ahhh, let's get this chilled so it's ready by dinner."

"You're the chef," Frannie said as she sank into the sofa with a happy sigh. "Have I mentioned how I love this sofa? I'm having sofa envy. It's so much better than the one I have. But to be fair, I did purchase it at a thrift store, and it may have enjoyed a full life in a frat house prior to moving in with me. Not that you would know that because you've never actually been to my house."

"Well, now that you've revealed that your sofa might've been involved in college adventures, I'm not sure that's a glowing endorsement."

"It does kinda smell, too," she grimaced. "But think of the character it has. The stories it could tell."

He grinned. "You're unlike anyone I've ever known."

"You're not the first person to say that," she said with cheek. God, she was beautiful.

He drew in a short breath, feeling as if his chest were being compressed, resisting the urge to tell her everything about his past, his family, and the trouble that was no doubt following him, but he bit down on his tongue and went to the kitchen to chill the wine.

When he returned, she patted the seat beside her. She didn't need to—it wasn't as if there were any other place he'd rather be. Dante slid in next to her, catching a whiff of her shampoo and the lingering scent of her coconut lotion, and he almost forgot why it was wise to keep things casual between them.

"So, I was thinking…how'd you like to spend a day on the lake with me this weekend? I could pack a picnic and show you some of the secret spots that the locals enjoy. We could rent a canoe and paddle to a secluded beach to each lunch."

A secluded beach? On the surface, the offer sounded terrific, but immediately he thought of all the ways that would make them vulnerable to attack if, by some chance, his uncle's men were watching and waiting for the best moment to strike, and his enthusiasm faded.

Make an excuse, say you already have plans.

It was the smart play, but he saw something in her eyes that told him saying yes was far more important than following his good sense, and he didn't dare risk turning her down.

The stakes felt so much higher than a simple outing together.

As if their future somehow rode on what fell from his mouth at that moment.

"Sounds like a perfect day," he finally answered, unprepared for how she squealed and climbed into his arms as if he'd just agreed to cosign a loan for her. "Whoa! Wild girl," he chuckled, holding her close.

"I'm so glad you said yes," she admitted, sealing her mouth to his. "We're going to have a great day on the lake!"

"Any day with you is already the best," he murmured against her lips.

He just hoped no nasty surprises were waiting for them.

Chapter 15

Frannie's heart was filled with sunshine as they slid the rented canoe into the water at the launch point. The weather was incredible, the skies blue without a cloud in sight, and she was excited to show Dante a piece of her hometown that felt personal.

"Summer days spent on Blackbird Lake were an important part of my childhood growing up in Owl Creek," she shared, hopping into the canoe and dipping her paddle in, encouraging Dante to do the same. "We're going to paddle away from the congested areas and head over to my favorite beach. You're going to love it."

"Are you trying to get me in a private place so you can have your way with me?" he teased.

She tossed him a mischievous look from behind her shoulder. "You should be so lucky."

He laughed at her sass, and they continued paddling. Soon enough, they were away from the tourist-friendly areas and heading down a calm channel where the water was barely waist-deep but crystal clear.

"So, this stretch of the river goes on for about three miles and because of the gentle current, it's great for canoeing or paddle boards. During the summer my mom and Uncle Buck used to rent paddle boards for all of us and we'd spend the entire day on the water. Some of my best memories were made on this lake. Sometimes we even got to see a moose on the shore. Of course, we left the moose alone because we valued our lives but one time my brother Fletcher got the bright idea to try and get closer. Thankfully, Uncle Buck didn't let him follow through with that idea. Otherwise, I might've been less one brother."

Dante chuckled. "Young boys often need someone smarter than them to keep them alive." But he realized she'd mentioned an uncle and not her father. "Your father didn't accompany you on these lake days?"

"My dad was always too busy. I don't think he enjoyed all the ruckus created by the kids. He was happy to let my uncle Buck handle the heavy lifting. Plus, now that I look back on the memories, I think my mom and Uncle Buck got along a lot better. I don't remember them bickering at all."

"They were close?"

"Yeah, they became close after my aunt Jessie bailed on the family and left Uncle Buck with the kids to raise." Frannie frowned. "I don't know my new alleged siblings but I kinda feel bad for them having to grow up with Aunt Jessie. At least with my other cousins, they were raised by Uncle Buck, and they had pretty good childhoods."

"Your aunt Jessie is unkind?"

Frannie lifted her shoulders, admitting, "I don't know her, but first impressions go a long way. She's kinda awful. I mean, maybe I'm biased because of what she's doing to my family right now, but she has this hard, jaded way about her that doesn't seem real conducive to being a loving parent."

"And your father was the same?"

"Um, he wasn't hard, per se, more like, disinterested. He always had other things to occupy his time. My dad was like a stereotypical fifties-era man—he expected his wife to keep the house and children while he made the money.

I don't think I ever saw my father lift a finger to clean the house, ever, and he sure as hell never cooked a meal for us. My mom did all of that and worked a full-time job. God, the more I think about it, she must've been exhausted. I need to cut my mom some slack."

"It's similar in Italy in many ways. Many traditionalists. For the record, I don't feel that way. I don't agree that the work of a household should be so unevenly split. My father and mother often cooked together. It's one of my favorite memories of when he was alive. They cooked with joy and love and perhaps it's in my head, but I always remember it tasting amazing."

"I think that's a beautiful thing to remember," Frannie said. "So, no brothers or sisters for you?"

"No, it was just me. My mother never remarried after my father's death. So it remained she and I."

"I can't even imagine being an only child, although sometimes I think I wished for it when things were total chaos around my house."

"I always wanted a sibling. Being an only child can be lonely."

"Makes sense. *Lonely* was never a word in my vocabulary. *Irritated, annoyed, frustrated*—definitely in the lexicon—but *lonely*? Nope."

His low rumble of laughter felt like sunshine on her soul.

"Oh! Look over there!" Frannie pointed to the shore on their left. "There's a deer. I know it's common, but I still get excited when I see them. My brothers used to make fun of me every time I got excited to see a deer. They said it was like getting excited to see a potato at the grocery store."

He laughed. "Depending on how hungry you are, the sight of a potato would be very exciting," he said.

"Ha! That's true. I wish I'd had the wherewithal to think of that comeback when I was a kid."

"I'm fairly certain I have the cutest tour guide in all of Idaho," he said, earning a blush from Frannie. "I love that you get excited about things that most people would take for granted. That's a gift."

She didn't know about that, but she felt warm whenever Dante complimented her over random stuff that most people never noticed about her. Dante made her feel seen, as if she'd been overlooked by those who should've been paying attention her entire life.

Girl, you're falling in love with him.

Frannie swallowed, knowing it was true. She couldn't seem to help herself. Everything about Dante was addictive. His smile, his touch, his voice—she couldn't picture anyone else as intoxicating.

Stop. You don't know anything about him. He could be an international felon.

That was why this day was so important. Today, she'd get to know more about the man.

And he agreed to come, right? That was a good sign. Besides, she wouldn't let anything ruin their beautiful day, not when it was already so amazing. It was possible Dante was very private and didn't enjoy oversharing. Once he realized his past was safe with her, he'd open up—she just knew it.

She saw her favorite beach coming up and gestured for him to paddle in that direction. Within minutes the bottom of their boat dragged through sand, and they hopped out to pull it further from the water so that the lazy waves didn't send the boat floating downstream. Swimming after a retreating boat was an experience she didn't want to repeat from her childhood.

Dante grabbed the picnic basket Frannie had prepared

while she scooped up the blanket and walked up the beach to a shady spot.

"It's not the Italian coast but I think it's pretty damn spectacular," Frannie said with pride as she carefully laid out the blanket and sat down to kick off her water shoes so her toes could dig in the warm sand. Golden sunlight glistened off the water's surface, glinting as if winking to the sky, and the gentle lap of the waves along the shoreline was a soothing sound that never failed to make her smile. If a happy place existed, it was here.

Dante sat beside her, agreeing heartily. "You do not disappoint. It's stunning."

His joy made her happy. She wished she could bottle up this feeling and moment to enjoy it forever.

A flicker of sadness threatened to dampen her joy as her mother inexplicably popped into her head. Knowing what she knew now about Jenny's past made Frannie wonder if there was ever a moment when Jenny experienced that giddy kind of love.

Somehow, she doubted Jenny and Robert had ever been madly in love. Small towns had a way of pushing people together for whatever reasons, but when those reasons expired or lost their luster, circumstances and reasons less than love kept them together. In some situations, obligation, expectation and habit were iron chains around people's necks.

With a frown, Dante caught her subtle shift and asked, "Is everything okay?"

"Oh, I'm fine." She waved away his concern, a little embarrassed to be a Debbie Downer when everything thus far had been perfect. Opening the picnic basket, she said, "I hope you like ham and turkey because that's what I packed. I even packed a few cheeses for you."

"I like whatever you thought to make."

"Stop being so perfect," she teased, leaning over for a quick kiss.

"I hate to disappoint but I'm far from perfect," he warned with a rueful chuckle.

"Hard to tell from this angle," she said, popping open the basket and pulling out the wrapped sandwiches. "Seriously, I think I'm going to need you to share some of your less desirable traits so I know you're human."

The subtle quirk of a grin was adorable, but it didn't escape her notice that he deliberately shied away from the topic. She tried a little harder. "I mean, you can't be perfect, no one is, but at least tell me something that makes you less intimidating. You're devastatingly handsome, an attentive lover, you can cook like a master chef, and you love books. I've never had self-esteem issues, but when I look at you, suddenly, insecurities start popping up like daisies in a field. Help a girl out."

"You're amazing in every way. You should never question your value, no matter who you're seeing."

"Of course, I'm just…okay, so I guess I'll stop beating around the bush and trying to be clever… I want to know more about you. What I can see is nothing short of amazing, but I need to know more. More than just the surface stuff." She traced her finger along his jaw, gazing into his eyes to ask in a throaty murmur, "Who is Dante Sinclair? Who is the real you?"

Dante froze. The urge to pull away nearly ruined everything good about his day. He wanted to be honest, but he couldn't. She wasn't asking anything out of the ordinary. She had every right to know whom she was sleeping next to, but it was the very thing he couldn't give her.

For her own good.

Swallowing, he forced a smile, gently grasping her hand and pressing a kiss to her palm, prepared to lie through his teeth. "Sweet Frannie, you make me sound more interesting than I really am. I'm just a regular guy who got tired of the same scenery and wanted a change. I didn't want to go to the usual touristy places like New York or California. I wanted something off the beaten path so I could rest and recharge. Owl Creek has been exactly as I hoped it would be—even better, I found you—making the trip unforgettable. What more could I ask for?"

Frannie smiled at the praise, but he could see that she wasn't entirely satisfied. The woman was smart. She sensed he was holding back, and the longer he danced around simple questions about his life, the more suspicious she would become.

He'd have to give her something to chew on, or she'd keep digging—and he couldn't afford her curiosity.

"Okay, you want something material…something personal…" At her small nod, Dante straightened and shared. "Well, the reason I needed a change in scenery is a little cliché. I'm a little embarrassed to admit that my last breakup was a bit intense, and it threw me for a loop. I couldn't function without bumping into memories from the past, and I thought the best way to heal and regroup would be to go on an extended vacation. My work is such that I can telecommute for most of it, so I decided to pack up and go find myself."

The way Frannie melted at his admission made him feel like a toad. He supposed it wasn't entirely a lie—he and Belinda had broken up—but after he'd had to spirit her out of the country for her own safety, they decided it would be best for them to go their separate ways. *Being attacked and left for dead by your boyfriend's uncle tended to destroy the romance in a relationship.*

"I had a bad breakup, too, so I totally understand the desire to pack up and run away. If I hadn't had the shop, I probably would've skipped town, too," Frannie conceded. "In the end, I didn't want him to have the satisfaction of seeing me break, so I toughed it out. But I feel like there's no wrong way to heal from emotional pain. We need to give ourselves permission to do what our minds and bodies need without feeling judged by everyone else."

God love this woman for her kindness and compassion. Even if he didn't deserve it. "Are you healed now?"

"I'm definitely on the right path. Relationships, good or bad, always leave a mark. I think that's what people mean by 'baggage' from previous relationships because we take a little piece of that relationship and bring it with us when we meet someone new."

"Was he a good man, this past boyfriend?" he asked, curious. "He wasn't abusive or anything like that?"

"Bobby? Oh gosh, no, just a cheater. I mean, that's pretty bad but in the grand scheme of things, not something I can't get over. Shortly after it all went down, I read something that helped put things in perspective. It was a book on healing emotional trauma. I read this part that said, 'People's actions say more about themselves than what they say about you,' and I realized Bobby's decision to cheat on me was a defect in his character, not mine."

"Very wise."

"Well, it resonated, and it really did help put things in their proper place."

"I'm sorry he hurt you."

Frannie sighed, remembering. "Yeah, I was heartbroken when I found out. Embarrassed, too. Felt like the whole town knew and was whispering about it behind my back.

Small towns are big on gossip and when someone's running around on another person, it's just too juicy to pass up."

"How did you discover he was unfaithful?"

Frannie drew a deep breath, wincing as if it hurt to remember. "I found text messages. And pictures. The evidence was pretty incriminating. He didn't try to deny it, and I was glad. I can't say I wouldn't have punched him in the mouth for lying. Growing up with a big family taught me how to throw a good hook. But, like I said, he didn't deny it. I think he was relieved, actually."

"Relieved?"

"Living a lie takes a lot of energy. Once the cat was out of the bag, he didn't have to pretend anymore."

Dante identified with that statement far more than he would've liked. The burden of a sustained lie was heavier than most people realized. Still, he felt no sympathy for this Bobby character. "He lost you. He got what he deserved."

Frannie smiled, seeming to appreciate his compliment. He'd shower her with sweetness every day if it were up to him because she deserved nothing less. She cozied up to him. "Well, sounds like whoever broke your heart got the worst end of the deal because you're amazing, and I don't like to share."

If only that were true. He'd do anything to go back in time and make a different choice, to believe how dangerous his uncle was instead of blowing off his threats. Belinda had deserved far better than she had received. *You deserve to be happy, too.* Belinda's words echoed in his head, but he couldn't take them to heart, just like when Belinda said them. He shook off the dark thoughts and directed attention to their lunch. "All that paddling worked up an appetite… Let's eat."

"Oh, right!" Frannie laughed, good mood returning.

"You'll love this bread. I buy it from the local bakery, and they make it fresh every day. It's my guilty pleasure."

Dante took a bite, appreciating the flavors. "Reminds me of home," he admitted. "In Italy, most everyone buys their bread, fruits and vegetables at the outdoor market for the day. Fresh bread should never be a guilty pleasure, *dolcezza.*"

"*Dolcezza*, what does it mean?"

"It's a term of endearment, such as sweetheart," he explained.

"I like it," she said, leaning toward him. "I like it a lot."

Lunch temporarily forgotten, Dante curled his hand behind her neck and drew her in, sealing their mouths together. She tasted like the promise of a new day with a sweetness no chocolate could ever hope to possess. He didn't deserve any of her love, her compassion or her goodness, but he selfishly craved it.

The kiss deepened, Dante needing to feel Frannie all around him. He didn't care that they were in broad daylight, that anyone could happen upon them and gawk. When he touched Frannie, the world melted away, and it was only the two of them in a tight, safe cocoon.

In those precious moments, he was far from the reality that his uncle would stop at nothing to bring him back to the family. That he held a ticking time bomb in a safe-deposit box and that his uncle would do anything to prevent the ruin of the family.

Nowhere was truly safe. His uncle had the money to chase Dante around the globe, and eventually, he would find him.

But in this stolen moment—it was only he and Frannie.

And he greedily enjoyed every second as if it were his last.

Because it very well could be.

Chapter 16

Frannie was floating on a cloud. The day couldn't have been more perfect if she'd dreamed it up with the power of a fairy godmother. She'd convinced Dante to come to her place for dinner, which was a massive win because he usually talked her into going to his place.

"You have to promise me that you won't judge my collection of knickknacks," she said, unlocking the front door. "I have a thing for collectible plates. I blame my grandmother for the obsession. She bought my first collectible plate when she vacationed in the Netherlands and the tradition stuck."

Dante smiled. "Have you ever been to the Netherlands?"

"Nope. I've never been outside of the United States, but I do have my passport just in case the opportunity presents itself."

Frannie had always wanted to travel, but she was embarrassed to admit that she was intimidated by the idea of traveling too far from home. It was a fear she hoped to conquer at some point in her life, but when she purchased the shop, her opportunities became limited.

Too limited to traipse along the countryside.

So, she purchased plates instead.

Frannie deposited her keys in the ceramic bowl by the door. "Have you been to the Netherlands?" she asked Dante.

"Not yet."

His answer sent shivers tripping down her back like he'd said he would take her to the Netherlands if she wanted to go. It was silly to think that because he hadn't said anything, but she'd felt like he had.

She was overthinking things.

"How about a quick tour?" she asked, shaking off the dizzying thoughts that served no purpose. Her mother had always said she had her head in the clouds most days and lived in a fantasyland. Probably why she loved books. "Again, no comments on the choice. I call it 'boho chic with a touch of French gothic' but my sister Ruby calls it 'thrift store chaos.'"

Afterward, Dante laughed but nodded, saying, "It suits you—and it's perfect."

"I don't know if I should be flattered or insulted," she said as he pulled her into his arms. "But I'll go with flattered for the sake of my ego."

"What's not to love? It's carefree, cozy and inviting—all good things in my book," he said, walking her backward to her bedroom, which was a short walk from the living room because her house was the size of a postage stamp. He brushed a kiss across her lips. "You know what's the best part about your place?"

She gazed up at him. "The antique claw-foot tub?"

"It's nice but no."

"What then? The suspense is killing me."

The back of her legs bumped against her bed. Dante gave her a tiny push, sending her falling back to land on the soft comforter as he followed, towering over her. "It smells like you—and I love the way you smell," he finally answered before descending for another kiss, searing her lips with the passion that bubbled between them.

Frannie wound her arms around his neck, drawing him closer, loving the way he devoured her from head to toe. When Dante made love, he made her pleasure his sole purpose. She'd never known a man so utterly consumed with his goal, and she was completely addicted.

Dante's weight pressed against her as his big hands cupped her face tenderly as if she were precious to him. *Don't you dare fall in love with him*, the voice warned, but she knew it was a pointless demand because she was falling fast.

Like being dropped from the moon and free-falling to the earth.

What they were doing felt the opposite of casual, but what did she know about being in a "situationship," as her younger cousins called it? Nothing. She was a one-guy kind of girl. And she wanted to be Dante's girl.

Don't ruin the moment, go with the flow.

"Dante...are you hungry?" she asked breathlessly as Dante lifted her shirt up and off, wasting no time nibbling along her shoulder blade, traveling up her neck. "I could... make some...pancakes."

"All I want is you," he said, pulling his shirt off and tossing it to the floor. He started to unbuckle her pants, but his gaze caught on something, and he stopped to stare with a subtle frown.

Frannie, her lips still tingling, propped herself up on her elbows, confused by his sudden change in demeanor. *Was it the mention of pancakes?* "Are you okay? What's wrong?"

He reached past her to pluck a single lily from the opposite pillow. The same type of lily that'd been delivered to her shop.

Frannie startled, staring as she scrambled to sit up, more confused than ever. "Where'd that come from?"

"It was on your pillow. Who put it there?" he asked.

"I don't know," she answered, biting her lip, bewildered. "I...honestly have no clue."

This felt different than a random delivery to her shop. She hated to admit it, but it gave her a creepy vibe. Someone had entered her house while she was gone and deliberately placed that lily on her pillow. She swallowed, feeling very exposed.

"You are positive no one you know could've left this flower for you?" he asked in a quiet yet hard tone.

She swallowed. "Dante, I swear I have no idea where that lily came from."

Dante swung away and scooped up his shirt, dressing quickly as he went to the window to check for signs of entry. Frannie grabbed her shirt, unsure of his reaction. Was this jealousy? Mistrust? Or was he concerned that someone was stalking her? "You're not staying here," he decided, pointing to her closet. "Gather your things. We're leaving."

Frannie needed a minute to think. Her heart was thundering in her chest, but she refused to be chased out of her home over something that might have a logical explanation. "I don't want to sound like the dumb girl in the movie that gets killed, but I don't want to rush to conclusions either. Let's calm down and think for a minute."

"There's nothing to think about. You're not staying."

That authoritative tone reminded her too much of her father, and she bristled. "No, I need a minute to think. I'm sure there's a logical reason... I need to find it."

Dante was about ready to ignore Frannie's protests, toss her over his shoulder and physically carry her to the car, but he restrained himself, realizing that the harder he pushed, the more she'd dig her heels in.

She didn't know how much danger she could be in, and he couldn't tell her.

How could he convince her to leave when he couldn't be honest about his circumstances?

Sweat beaded his brow. *Okay, think.* Frannie wanted logic. He'd give it to her. Throttling down his fear, he tried a different tactic. "It could be something innocent, but don't you think it's better to err on the side of caution than assuming it's nothing? What if you're wrong? What's one night? How about this…come back to my place for the night, we'll order a pizza, watch some TV, and tomorrow you can run it by your brother to see how he feels about it. If he feels it's nothing to worry about…well, maybe you're right."

"Fletcher is a cop, so maybe that's not a terrible idea, if only to create a paper trail," Frannie conceded, thinking it through. Still, she seemed undecided. "But on the surface, a pretty flower doesn't seem all that threatening. It's not like it was a bloody horse head or anything like that."

Dante wanted to shake her head off her shoulders. Her place felt compromised, and every moment they remained felt like a minute closer to his uncle's hired men showing up for an unpleasant interaction. He tried again, using a different tactic.

"Someone entered your house when you weren't home and left that flower on your pillow. An anonymous person paid for the flowers to be delivered to your shop, which was suspicious enough, but now the flower in your home? You can't see how that's something to be concerned about?"

He was pressing a little harder, desperate to get her to a safe place. Not that he knew his place was any safer, but he doubted Frannie would let him put her on a plane to Switzerland to hang out with his ex-girlfriend, the last victim of his uncle's revenge.

Frannie wavered. "It's weird," she admitted.

"Yes," he agreed, holding his breath with the hope that she was close to seeing his way of things. "If you're wrong, and someone left you this flower as a warning, I can't fathom not doing something about it. Frannie, please. I care about you."

"I know you do, and I appreciate the concern. I'm just worried about making a big deal about nothing. My family has enough to worry about without me crying wolf over strange flower deliveries. Even saying it out loud makes me cringe. Who gets scared over a beautiful flower?"

"If the message, 'I'm going to kill you,' is delivered in calligraphy does it make it any less threatening?"

Frannie blinked at the change in perspective, biting her lip with apprehension. "Oh, that's a good point. I hadn't thought of it that way. When you put it like that, it's very creepy."

Relief flooded him when he sensed he was finally winning the argument. "Can I help you pack?"

Frannie chuckled with discomfort. "It's just overnight, Dante. I'm not moving in."

He smiled, acknowledging her point. "Good. Five minutes? We can pick up the pizza on the way."

He pretended to be switching gears, excited about pizza, but he knew everything would taste like cardboard. His head was swimming with upsetting possibilities, and he felt pressed on all sides by potential danger.

Frannie reappeared with a small overnight bag, and he relieved her of the burden as he walked to the front door. He tossed her bag into the back seat and opened her door, his gaze scanning the surrounding area, looking for anything unusual. Frannie's tiny house wasn't tucked away in the mountains like his place, but the older neighborhood wasn't heavily populated either. A lot of For Sale signs in yards, which he hadn't noticed before. Vacant houses were excellent places to hide for people who didn't want to be seen.

"I didn't realize there were so many empty houses on your street," he said.

She sighed, looking out the window as they drove by. "Yeah, the economy isn't what it used to be and if you're not in the tourist trade, there isn't a lot of opportunity. I wish the city would come up with some kind of incentive to keep locals here, but I suppose their hands are tied, too. The piece of the pie is only so big."

Dante nodded, pretending to be invested in the plight of the local economy, but his mind was elsewhere, moving at the speed of light, processing possibilities, second-guessing every little thing.

God, he wanted to tell Frannie the damn truth!

If he could level with Frannie, she might understand why he was agitated about a seemingly odd but maybe innocent flower mishap.

But c'mon, a flower deliberately placed on her pillow? That screamed malice.

"You know what? I just thought of a wild idea," he said, catching her attention. "What if we got out of town for a few days? Maybe find a cozy cabin near the lake or even head to the city, get dressed up and hit the town? I'd love a chance to pamper the prettiest woman in Owl Creek. Hell, possibly prettiest in the whole state."

"You're laying it on a little thick, but I like it," Frannie teased. But she shook her head, saying, "As much as I love that idea, I can't leave the shop."

"You're the owner, you can make the rules, *dolcezza*," he reminded her.

"Yeah, but not sticking to my own rules...that's how a

business fails. I know my dad wasn't great at the whole father gig, but he was a solid businessman. One of the things
he shared with me when I opened the shop was not to fall
into the trap of thinking I'm above the rules just because
I pay the mortgage."

It was solid advice—but Dante didn't care about that. He
wanted Frannie somewhere safe and getting out of town for
a few days would give him time to determine if his uncle
had people in town. "Sure, that's excellent advice, and I
agree. But there's also something to be said for knowing
when to enjoy the fruits of your labor. I've seen how hard
you work. You deserve a little pampering."

Frannie laughed but otherwise let the offer die, and he
took the hint. If he kept pushing, it would cease to be romantic and turn into something weird, which would only
backfire.

"All right, I can see you're not on board, I understand,"
he said with a short smile. "Should we order the pizza to
go, or do you want to eat in the restaurant?"

"Oh, to go. I'll go ahead and order so it's ready when we
get there," she said, grabbing her cell phone from her purse.

As Dante listened to her order while he drove, sneaking
covert looks her way, he could tell she'd already written
the flower incident off as weird but harmless, which worried him. He couldn't blame her, though. Before Belinda's
attack, he'd been confident he could handle whatever his
uncle threw at him, but he'd been wrong.

Fifteen minutes later, they were pulling into the parking lot. "My treat," she told him when he started to exit the
vehicle. "I was going to make dinner tonight, remember?"

He grinned, accepting the offer only because it seemed
he'd have a moment of privacy while she grabbed the pizza.
Frannie smiled and left, giving him a lovely view of her

perfect backside that, if he hadn't been riddled with anxiety, he would've appropriately appreciated.

Once she was inside, he picked up his cell phone and dialed his private investigator. When it went straight to voice mail, he left a message. "I have reason to believe my uncle's associates have followed me to Owl Creek. I need you to find out if my location has been compromised. ASAP. No matter the hour, let me know what you find out."

He clicked off just as Frannie reappeared carrying the pizza. He smiled as she climbed into the car. "Smells amazing," he said.

"Tonight, I'm going to splurge," she announced. "I have special lactase enzymes in my purse and I'm going to enjoy a slice or two of this gooey, cheesy pizza. There's only one thing…"

"Which is?"

"Sometimes they make me gassy," she admitted with a short, embarrassed laugh, shrugging as she added, "You know what they say…gorgeous, gorgeous girls have stomach issues."

He laughed, momentarily forgetting about the looming danger. He leaned over to plant a hearty kiss on her perfect lips. "If that's the deal, I think I can handle the terms."

At that, Frannie barked another laugh as if he didn't know what he'd just agreed to, and he realized that she was the kind of woman he'd be lucky to call his.

Except he had no business dreaming of a future with Frannie…or anyone.

Chapter 17

Even as Frannie had been determined to downplay the flower incident, her private thoughts were in turmoil. She didn't want anyone to worry unnecessarily over something that seemed silly, but Dante had planted a seed of doubt that was quickly germinating.

As she lay beside Dante, her head resting on his chest, it should've been easy to push aside anything unpleasant, but tonight her anxiety was determined to needle her brain, making restful sleep—or sleep at all—impossible.

Usually, when she had difficulty sleeping, a little fresh air helped. Careful not to disturb Dante, she rose from the bed, grabbed a bottled water from the kitchen, and quietly stepped outside to the front porch.

Sighing, Frannie sank into one of the two porch chairs and enjoyed the starry sky with the night sounds all around her. Owl Creek might not be a mecca of modern convenience—no fast-food places or chain restaurants— but there was something special about being nestled in the heart of nature.

Drawing a deep breath, she closed her eyes and let the cool night air caress her nude skin. The best part about Dante's place was that no one was around for miles, so only the wildlife saw her naked on the front porch.

Hannah always accused her of being a closet nudist because she'd always been running around the house with as little clothing as possible, and if they all went swimming in the creek in the middle of the night, Frannie was the first to shuck all her clothes and jump in naked as the day she was born.

The memory curved her lips in a smile.

Then, there were her wild college days, of course. But that was what college was for—making a few mistakes, poor judgment calls, and memories.

Well, that and getting an education.

A subtle frown pulled her brows as she recalled a name she hadn't thought of in a long while. *Allen Burns.* He'd had a mad crush on her, but she'd only seen him as a friend. That'd been an awkward conversation when she'd had to set him straight.

She winced at the memory.

Poor Allen. So shy with the girls. Had he ever figured out the social dance steps required to find a partner?

Frannie always found it interesting that even as evolved as humans were, they were still animals and programmed to respond to certain mating rituals.

Allen hadn't been very good at discerning social cues, which made people shy away from him, but that was why Frannie had gone out of her way to befriend him.

Why had Allen popped into her head when she hadn't seen him in years?

The door opened, startling her. When she saw it was Dante, and he was holding a blanket, she smiled. "Sorry, did I wake you?"

"It's not your fault. I'm a light sleeper," he said, draping the blanket around her shoulders. His constant chivalry tickled her, but the fact that he did things out of concern for her comfort struck a chord deep inside. "Are you okay?" he asked.

"When I can't sleep, I like to go outside for some fresh air and the fact that I can come outside naked is a huge plus. I can't exactly do that at my place."

"Yes, even with all of the empty houses, it probably isn't a good idea," he said, amused.

"Thank you for the blanket," she said, patting the seat beside her. "Sit with me a minute?"

"Sure," he said, settling into the chair. "Why can't you sleep? Is there anything I can do?"

The subtle suggestion in his tone made her blush, but she playfully tapped him on the thigh. "Dante, you dirty boy," she admonished with a laugh. "No, I just needed Mother Nature, and you have the best view."

He agreed. "I was lucky to find this place. It's been exactly what I was looking for. It'll be hard to leave."

Frannie fell quiet, hating any mention of Dante leaving, but she supposed it was healthy to acknowledge that he wasn't planning to relocate to Owl Creek soon. "Do you miss home?"

Dante considered her question, finally answering, "Italy is a beautiful place but lately, I've been asking myself if I want to stay there."

Hope dared to flicker in her heart. "You're open to relocating?"

He hesitated, as if realizing he'd stumbled onto a subject he wasn't ready to talk about, but he offered a noncommittal "Well, I suppose anything is possible," before dropping it.

Frannie took the hint, but she'd be a liar if it didn't hurt. She wanted an open and honest conversation about their feelings for each other, but she was afraid of pushing against an established boundary and losing him altogether.

She winced internally—that sounded pathetic even in the confines of her head. She should be able to be honest. Without honesty, there was nothing. Why shouldn't she be able to come out and say, 'Dante, I have feelings for you. No, actually, I think I'm falling in love with you. And I need to know if you feel the same.'

But she couldn't get the words out of her mouth. Instead, she grabbed her bottled water and took a long swig before sharing, "So, a name popped into my head while I was sitting out here that I haven't thought of in years—a guy who had a crush on me back in college."

"Why'd you think of him?"

"I think because of the flowers."

Dante frowned. "What's the connection?"

"Maybe nothing but I remember he used to work part-time in the horticulture department. I think he was an Ag major. Sometimes he would bring me fresh flower clippings from the greenhouse. A lot of times, they were lilies. It was sweet."

"Did you date?"

"No, just friends. But he did like me a little more than a friend should," she admitted. "However, I set him straight, telling him that I only felt friendship for him. I didn't want to lead him on."

"How'd he take the news?"

"Um, well, he was hurt, of course, but he didn't freak out or anything," she said.

"Does he live here in Owl Creek?"

"No, we met at Boise State. I don't remember where he originally came from, and we didn't keep in touch," Frannie said with a shrug. "I don't even know why he popped into my head. Probably because he was into flowers. Anyway, random stuff goes through my head at three in the morning." A sudden, welcome yawn cracked her jaw, and she said, "See? Mother Nature is better than any sleeping pill. Ready to go back inside?"

Dante nodded and followed her into the house. Climbing back into bed, she cuddled up to Dante, sighing happily until she realized there was no turning back. She was in love with Dante, and she wanted him to stay.

But did he feel the same?

The following morning Dante rose early to make the coffee and prepare bacon and eggs for breakfast. When he'd woken in the middle of the night and found Frannie gone, his heart had nearly stopped.

When he realized she was sitting outside—naked—on the porch, he'd immediately wanted to drag her back inside. A wave of possessiveness washed over him at the thought of anyone else seeing Frannie's beautiful body, and he realized he had to stop thinking of Frannie as his girlfriend.

Even so, he'd brought her the blanket, though she looked like a wild goddess in the moonlight with her hair loose and the pale light kissing her bare skin.

Frannie appeared, wrapped in his robe, and shuffled to the kitchen, her bleary gaze going straight to the coffee. He quickly poured her a cup and pushed the oat milk toward her that he'd purchased specifically for her in deference to her tummy issues with dairy.

For himself, he enjoyed real cream, which he poured liberally into his morning coffee. "Good morning, beautiful," he said, kissing her cheek as she doctored her coffee. "How'd you sleep?"

"Good," she said, sipping her coffee with a pleased smile. "Perfect."

He chuckled, enjoying how expressive she was about

everything in life. She made a sip of coffee seem like time had stopped, and nothing else mattered but that sip. He loved that about her. He didn't blame her college friend for falling for her—how could anyone resist Frannie Colton?

But given everything behind the scenes, he'd feel better if he looked into the guy.

"I was thinking, just to be on the safe side, I should look into this college guy and see if there's anything to be concerned about."

Frannie waved off his suggestion. "Oh, goodness, Dante, surely you have better things to do than do background checks on guys I haven't seen in ages? Besides, Allen was harmless."

"You're right, it's probably nothing. But I'd feel better if I confirmed that fact."

She seemed to realize he was serious, and sobered. "Dante, are you really that worried?"

"About your friend? I don't know. But I am worried about someone breaking into your house and leaving flowers that you didn't ask for."

"I didn't want it to get into my head because it's nothing serious, but I'm a little unnerved about it."

"As you should be," he agreed, relieved she finally saw things from his point of view. "Look, I know it might seem an overreaction but it's always better to be safe than sorry. And when it comes to your safety, I don't want to take any chances."

She smiled up at him, a vision of sunshine and light, and his heart threatened to jump from his chest and land in her lap. Did she have any idea of the effect she had on him? Never in his life had he ever felt this way about a woman. He was out of his depth. The best he could do was make sure she was safe.

"If it makes you feel better about it, sure, go ahead and look into him. Although, I could probably just have my brother Fletcher look into it."

"I want to do it," he said, fighting that wave of possessiveness again. He wanted to be the one to keep Frannie safe. Ironic, seeing as he was the one putting her in danger.

"Okay," she said easily, taking another sip of her coffee. "Plans for today?"

He was waiting on word from his private investigator, but he couldn't mention that. Instead, he smiled and kissed her forehead, saying, "I'm playing detective today. Enjoy your coffee. There's a plate of bacon and eggs in the microwave. I'm going to jump in the shower. Feel free to join me if you like."

"That's not a fair choice. You know I love food, but I'd also like to be naked with you in the shower."

He shrugged. "You could always reheat the eggs and bacon after..."

Frannie considered the option, then hurried after him, taking a final sip of her coffee. "Water conservation is far more important than the inconvenience of reheating breakfast," she rationalized.

Dante couldn't say he was disappointed. She shrugged out of his robe, and he scooped her up, carrying her to the bed first.

"Hey! You said shower..." she said, playfully accusatory. "What are you doing?"

"Making a mess of you, darling," he answered with a dark grin as he pressed kisses down her belly. "Might as well make sure we're making proper use of the shower."

Her delightful giggle switched to moans, and Dante knew he could happily drown in the sound of her pleasure for the rest of his life.

He needed to find a solution to this situation with his uncle, or he'd lose out on any chance of happiness with Frannie.

He'd always known running wasn't a permanent solution, but he hadn't figured out how to keep his uncle off his back for good.

What kind of life was he offering Frannie if they took things to the next level?

He wanted her in his bed every night, not just here and there, like some meaningless hookup with a casual stranger.

Casual—that word couldn't possibly describe what he and Frannie shared, but it was what they'd agreed to.

But how could he offer anything else?

He couldn't.

Not yet, anyway.

Maybe never.

All they had was now.

Chapter 18

Frannie closed the shop and headed for the grocery store, still thinking about the exciting new shipment of books that had arrived that morning. Dante was so good about taking care of the food she wanted to show him that she could throw something together that was not only edible but delicious, too.

She wasn't Emeril but could hold her own in the kitchen. Jenny had taught all her children how to find their way around the kitchen, and it was a small point of pride that even though she had a modest menu of dishes she could prepare, she made them well.

The farmers' market was only a short walk from the shop, so she grabbed her canvas shopping bag and headed toward her favorite fruit and vegetable vendor.

"Frannie! There you are! I knew I'd find you here, sniffing mushrooms and talking about how a mushroom could be a good substitute for meat," Darla said, rolling her eyes. "As if that was actually a thing. I know you're not a vegetarian, but you do a pretty good imitation of one, always pushing those vegetables."

"Technically, a mushroom is a fungus," Frannie reminded Darla, to which Darla grimaced. "I'm just saying…if you want to be accurate. But yes, it all depends on how you sea-son and cook it." She held up a beautiful portobello mushroom. "See? Doesn't that look delicious?"

"No, it smells like dirt and looks like something I wouldn't ever put in my mouth. I'll stick with a porterhouse."

Frannie shrugged with a grin as she put the mushroom in a baggie to be weighed. "Each to their own. What are you doing here tonight? You barely cook, and you don't like crowds." She paid for her purchase, and they walked on.

Darla sighed, nodding in agreement with everything Frannie had said, but she gestured across the street, "I blame him," and Frannie saw her fiancé admiring a handmade wind chime. "He loves the farmers' market. He says it makes him feel good to support local artisans. I didn't have the heart to tell him that most of this stuff is purchased from China and passed off as homemade."

"That's not true," Frannie said, laughing at Darla's sour attitude. "I happen to know for a fact that Stacy Spencer makes her tie-dyed T-shirts in her bathtub—and they're really cute. I might just buy one today."

"You hate tie-dye," Darla drawled, calling her bluff. "You once said tie-dye is the clothing trend that refuses to die and has worn out its welcome."

She had said that—but to be fair, she'd been in a bad mood that day. "A woman has the prerogative to change her mind."

The hairs suddenly stood on the back of her neck, and she shuddered, glancing around to see why she felt like someone had been staring a hole into her back.

"You okay?" Darla asked, noticing her sudden shiver. "You look like a goose walked over your grave."

"Yeah, it was weird. It felt like someone was standing right behind me, staring."

"I didn't see anyone," Darla said, scanning the crowd.

"But I hate when that happens. Maybe a ghost was standing right next to you."

Frannie didn't like that thought at all. "Hey, don't be putting those kinds of thoughts in my head. I sleep alone, you know."

"You big fat liar. I know you're not sleeping alone these days."

Frannie blushed, clarifying, "Okay, maybe not but it's not an everyday thing. It's a casual arrangement, not a relationship and…" Her voice trailed. Why was she even trying to lie when Darla knew her like the back of her hand? *Pointless.* She met Darla's knowing smirk and gave it up. "I think I'm falling in love with him, Darla. How did this happen?"

Darla shook her head as if to say, 'You poor summer child,' and put her arm around her shoulders. "First, there are worse men to fall for—he seems pretty top-shelf. Second, would it be so bad if you were falling for him?"

"Um, yeah, we agreed to keep things casual because he's not planning to stay in Owl Creek, and I have no plans to move to Italy…or wherever he's going next. Also, I don't actually know much about him. Each time I try to get a little deeper, he switches things up and deftly changes the subject. It's a little 'red-flaggy.'"

"Yeah, you mentioned something about that. How'd the day on the lake go?"

"Amazing! Best day of my life. The lake was beautiful, I packed a picnic lunch for the beach, and we…well, we made good use of the privacy, let's just put it that way."

"Mmm, I love lake days like that," Darla said with a wistful expression. "And then what happened?"

"Well, we went back to my place and…do you remember those random flowers that showed up at the shop?"

"The lilies?"

Frannie nodded. "Well, Dante and I were messing around and just as we were about to get serious, Dante saw a single lily—the same kind as the delivery—on my pillow."

Darla's eyes bugged. "Excuse me? On your pillow? How'd it get there?"

"I don't know."

"That's some creepy shit, Fran. Did you report it to Fletcher?"

"No, it seems silly to report something so small."

"Small? No, someone broke into your house and left something there to let you know they'd been there. It's creepy and potentially dangerous. You need to tell Fletcher."

"So, Dante wants to do a little checking on a guy I went to school with at Boise State. Do you remember my friend Allen Burns?"

"The horticulture nerd who always brought you dead weeds?"

"They weren't weeds, they were clippings, and most of the time they were gorgeous lilies."

Darla's gaze widened. "Do you think it was that guy who left the flower?"

"I mean, it seems unlikely, but he popped into my thoughts at three in the morning. It's funny, I hadn't thought of him in years until I couldn't sleep and then, there he was, in my head."

"I remember him being a little on the weird side," Darla said. "Are you sure it wasn't him?"

"He wasn't weird," Frannie protested. "He was just a little on the shy side and maybe awkward but I'm awkward, too, so we got along."

"Frannie, you're quirky, which, paired with your face, is adorable. Pretty privilege goes a long way to smoothing the road for those with unusual personality quirks. If I'm remembering correctly, he didn't have that luxury."

"He wasn't traditionally handsome, but he was very sweet."

"Did you keep in touch after graduation?"

Frannie shook her head, feeling bad about that. "No, we went our separate ways. We really only had a few college experiences to draw us together. After that, our connection wasn't organic but that's the way of college, right? Everyone goes their separate ways after graduation to pursue their careers."

"I'm still not clear why you haven't told Fletcher?"

"Because it seems silly and Dante is looking into it."

"I thought Dante was a lawyer?"

"He is."

"And he moonlights as a private investigator?" Darla's incredulous expression was pretty damning. "Seriously, Fran, props to your guy for wanting to be your knight in shining armor but sometimes we have to leave certain jobs to the professionals. Dante can pitch legal advice about your family situation if he wants to feel useful."

"It's likely nothing and that's why I didn't mind Dante asking around," Frannie said, defending Dante. "Plus, with everything my family is dealing with, I don't want to add some frivolous nonsense to their plate. Whatever this is, I'm sure I can handle it with Dante's help."

"I love your loyalty to a man you barely know. I'm just saying, I wouldn't trust Tom to know what to do in this situation and I'm crazy about the guy."

"You should be," Frannie said. "Clearly Tom hasn't figured out that you're a double shot of irrational and bossy, and for your sake, I hope he doesn't figure it out until after the wedding."

"Ha! You think I don't have the same concern? That's why I wanted to lock that man down sooner rather than later. We could've eloped, and I would've had a ring on my finger by now." They shared a laugh, but Darla saw Tom waving her over, and she had to cut their conversation short, but not before she made Frannie promise to tell Fletcher. "I don't want to find out on the morning news that my best friend—and maid of honor—was abducted in the middle of the night by some stalker that no one took seriously."

Frannie rolled her eyes and waved Darla on her way. "You worry too much. Go catch up with Tom before he buys that wind chime that will definitely keep you up all night with its bing-bonging in the wind."

Darla's expression of horror as she hustled toward her fiancé made Frannie laugh, but a sliver of doubt remained even as her mood had lightened.

Was it possible she'd made a mistake in not telling Fletcher about the flower on her pillow? What were the chances that she had a real stalker? *Here in Owl Creek?* Seemed far-fetched…but not impossible.

She couldn't help another glance over her shoulder as that feeling remained that someone was watching her.

Stop freaking yourself out. You're surrounded by people you know.

No one is watching.

But just the same, she hurried with her shopping and quickly headed home.

His cell rang as Dante was getting ready to leave his place to go to Frannie's.

Seeing that it was his PI, he clicked over immediately. "Dante," he answered.

"Hey, it's Nick. I had a contact with the Wisconsin State

Coroners Association pull some strings to send me the confidential autopsy report on your father. It was relatively easy to get the information—probably too easy, they need to really improve their security systems—but I found something I thought you'd like to know."

Dante's stomach muscles clenched with tension, but he was ready. "Go ahead."

"So, I already told you there was alcohol in your father's system when he was killed but there was something else wasn't part of the public record that definitely seems suspicious."

"Which is?"

"Fentanyl—enough to kill him. Someone wanted to make sure your father didn't survive that night. My guess is that your father was dead before his car even hit the tree."

Dante took a minute to digest this bombshell. His father had been murdered. Alcohol might've been easy enough to explain, but fentanyl? If he knew his father hadn't been a drinker, he knew beyond a shadow of a doubt he never did drugs of any kind—much less a drug as dangerous as fentanyl.

"Any chance the coroner shared how the fentanyl had gotten into his system?" Dante asked.

"No, it's anyone's guess. The coroner didn't do a real extensive report. He probably assumed your dad was a drunk and a drug addict and his vices finally caught up to him. I'm sorry."

Dante accepted the man's condolences, fighting the lump in his throat. His memories of Matteo were dim and hazy, but it hurt in ways he couldn't describe knowing that it hadn't been a cruel but impartial twist of fate that'd taken his father from him but a deliberate act by another person.

"Damn it," he muttered, rubbing the moisture from his eyes, trying to regroup. "Anything else?"

There was a brief pause, then Nick shared, "The widow of the cop who wrote your father's accident report? She died yesterday."

A frisson of alarm spiked his blood. "Natural causes?"

"It appears that way, but I'll know more in a few days. It seems real suspicious that days after I spoke to the woman and she told me about the money her husband received around the same time your father was killed, she ends up dying. I was born at night, but it wasn't last night. Could be natural causes—but then, it doesn't take much to silence an old lady either."

Dante felt sick. Had he inadvertently caused that woman's death by asking questions?

"Send me her obituary so I can see if she left donation wishes."

"It's a nice thought but I'd advise against it."

"Why?"

"Because the old lady didn't have any natural ties to you. If you go and offer some pricey donation to this random lady's cause, it could alert your uncle's men as to your whereabouts. Say a prayer in your head and let God decide whether it's enough. For now, my advice to you is to continue to lay low."

It was solid advice. He wasn't thinking straight. Refocusing, he conceded with a low murmur, "You're right. I've got reasonable evidence that my father was murdered but still nothing tying it to my uncle." Not that he'd likely find any, either. Lorenzo wasn't sloppy—he was exact and precise, calculated. He didn't do anything without multiple fail-safes in place in case plan A went awry.

He used to think his uncle was a genius, which he might

be, but now Dante saw him for what he truly was—a murderer with a limitless bank account.

"Keep looking for possible ties. In the meantime, I have something else I need you to look into that's unrelated to my family."

"Yeah?"

"I want you to check out a guy named Allen Burns, attended Boise State University in 2019, possibly an agriculture or horticulture major."

"What am I looking for?"

"Anything. If the man so much as sneezed the wrong way I want to know."

"Sure."

Dante clicked off and sat for a long moment, thinking about his past, present and future. How would he feel if he never found his uncle's ties to Matteo's death? Unfulfilled? Unable to let the past go?

He didn't want that—not for himself and not for Frannie.

He knew he loved her. It was foolish to pretend otherwise. She was the light in his life, the laughter in his soul that made everything else fall away and seem less important.

But how could he drag her into his life knowing that ghosts might chase him without a chance of peace?

He didn't have the answers. All he knew was that he had to keep her safe. Right now, that meant finding out who was sending her flowers—and if they meant her harm.

Chapter 19

Frannie was still unsettled by the time she reached home. She'd planned to make a summer salad, but her thoughts were anywhere but with her food prep. Before she realized the time, Dante was at her door with a bottle of wine and that adoring smile she'd come to crave at the end of a long day.

After a sweet kiss, she admitted she was behind in making dinner, but he wouldn't let her carry any burden, much less that of sole dinner prep. "What do you still need done? I'm happy to help. You know how I love being in the kitchen. Especially with you as my sous-chef."

"Sous-chef? No, you're *my* sous-chef, you silly goose." She said it with a playful smile but was glad to have his help. She enjoyed cooking with him. Together, they were a seamless team that made light work of any task they set out to do.

Wasn't that the hallmark of most successful relationships? Embracing the concept of "many hands make for light work," as her grandmother used to preach to her grandchildren, as they groaned at having to haul wood, pick blackberries for summer jam, and peel apples to jar as applesauce for the winter.

He chuckled, seemingly accepting her statement as fact without a single protest. The man was nearly perfect. "I don't want to be casual anymore," she blurted, shocking herself and Dante with her outburst. Her cheeks flared with heat, but she couldn't take it back—not that she wanted to—and it was out there, floating between them like a giant ethereal question mark.

She held her breath, afraid of what he might say, afraid of her feelings getting squashed, but she lifted her chin and stood by her declaration, waiting for his response.

Was that fear? Disappointment? Anger? Or was he embarrassed that the young bookstore owner had gone and done the one thing he'd warned her against, ruining an otherwise great thing between them?

"Please say something."

Dante cleared his throat, apparently realizing his silence was becoming heavier by the moment. He reached for her hand and pulled her close. "You're trembling," he said softly.

"Because I think I might've just ruined what you liked most about us," she admitted in a shaky voice.

"That's not what I like best," he assured her. His throaty voice that never failed to send shivers dancing down her spine.

Was it all about the sex? Granted, the passion between them was out of this world, but she'd be a liar if she didn't say that she wanted it to be about more than something physical.

"Frannie…"

No, she couldn't do this. She couldn't hear him try to let her down gently. Her pride wouldn't suffer such a blow. She tried to pull away, but he held her close. "Dante, you don't have to do this. I get what you're not saying… It's my fault for pushing against the boundary we both set."

"It's not that," he said, furrowing his brow with frustration. "It's…complicated."

"How?"

"I—I don't really want to get into it right now, but I need you to trust me when I say that it's better to keep things as they are between us," he said, though he looked pained just saying the words, which confused her more.

"Dante, I can't—that's not good enough—I need more from you. I hardly know a thing about you. It was okay in the beginning, before feelings got involved, but now? I crave more than you're willing to give. Maybe it's not fair but I'm honest to a fault, and I can't hide what I'm feeling."

"And I love that about you," he assured her and kissed her passionately, framing her face with both hands. She could feel the love between them, yet he continued to keep her at arm's length emotionally. It was maddening. It was also starting to frustrate her because her feelings were bruised.

"Stop," she said and pulled away, separating them. She wiped at her eyes. "Look, I didn't mean to ruin dinner, but I suppose this was a conversation that was coming eventually. I know you feel something for me, but maybe it's not equal to what I feel for you."

"No, that's not it," he said quietly. "You're not alone in your feelings."

Hope dared to spark in her chest. "I'm not?"

"No."

"Then why do you pull away from me and then say things like, 'It's better this way,' as if you know that we don't have any kind of future together?" she asked, confused and hurt.

"Because I can't give you what you need and deserve," he admitted bitterly. "And I hate that I can't."

"What do you think I deserve? I don't need a fancy house or anything like that. Is it finances? Are you broke or something? I wouldn't care if you were. Finances can be fixed—but not if you walk away."

"I'm not broke," he answered, shocking her. "I—" He stopped short, leaving his statement unfinished. Shaking his head, he said, "I have more than enough to see to my needs but even if I didn't, I would never allow you to carry the financial burden of my care."

"It's not a burden if you're helping someone get back on their feet," she said, trying to be gentle. She sensed his pride was speaking. Men were so funny about money and where it came from. Her father had always ensured they all knew that no matter how much money Jenny brought in, he still made more.

"Frannie...please. I can't talk about this right now."

She had a choice—let it go and continue their evening as if it had never happened—or hold her ground and expect some answer.

Her heart hurt. For years she'd watched her mother swallow any grievance for peace in the house, and she swore she'd never be like that.

Yet, tears burned behind her eyes at the thought of ending things with Dante over his lack of equal communication. Was it a cultural difference? Or was she making excuses and dancing around the obvious that he was an emotionally unavailable man who'd been content to keep their relationship surface-deep, but he hadn't wanted to hurt her feelings, so he pretended there was more to it.

"Dante... I need more," she said as a tear snaked down her cheek. "And if you can't give that to me, I understand. But I can't allow myself to fall deeper for a man who's ultimately going to break my heart because he never promised me forever."

"What are you saying?" he asked.

"I'm saying, don't ask me to pretend that my needs don't matter because your needs are more important."

There. She'd said it—she'd essentially thrown a gauntlet.

Now, how he responded would reveal the depth of his true character.

Please, don't make me wrong about who I thought you were.

The truth burned his tongue. She deserved nothing less than honesty. How could he spill his guts about everything he was dealing with without putting her in more unnecessary danger?

Just tell her. You're already in the thick of things. More lies will only make it worse.

Dante turned away from her, needing to get his head on straight. He needed a minute to think. The smart decision would be to take the out—a clean break for reasons that would make sense without too much explanation.

He could easily say he was still torn up about his last breakup, and it wouldn't be fair to her to keep pretending otherwise. It would hurt, but she'd get over it. He would wear the "international asshole" badge for her safety.

But then he'd have to find a way to make peace with the knowledge that someone else would claim her heart, warm her bed and share her future—which made him want to smash things.

In a relatively short time, she'd become such an important part of his life, almost as if she were fused to him, and he didn't know how he'd survive without her.

He wasn't the romantic type—he didn't fall in love easily or frivolously—and he took matters of the heart seriously.

He would never pretend to love someone for sex or emotional warmth.

It was Frannie he wanted—even though the woman's gas could kill a moose when she ate too much dairy—because she was everything he never realized he needed in his life.

If it weren't for the threat of his uncle looming over his future, he would've proposed to the woman already.

"Dante?"

It was the tremulous tone that killed him. It was as if it was taking everything in her not to bawl her eyes out, and she was holding it together by a thread to get the answers she needed.

And he was doing this to her.

It was his fault that she was hurting.

He turned to face her. He needed more time. He would be honest with her soon. But not tonight. Tonight, he had to save what they had because he couldn't fathom letting her think he didn't care for her.

"My mother died in a car accident two years ago—a drunk driver—and I inherited a modest sum from her estate. Finances aren't a problem," he said, skirting around the truth. He had inherited money from his mother, but it was nothing compared to what he had inherited from his father's family trust—and what he'd banked as the family's premier attorney.

Lorenzo had secured Dante's inheritance the moment they returned to Italy—yet another reason he'd believed his uncle had been a good man.

Suffice it to say Dante would never have to worry about money.

Only his head.

Frannie blinked, unsure of how to process that information. "You're…rich?"

"Comfortable," he corrected, but he was obscenely wealthy, though he was less proud of how that money had been built.

His family's legacy was a patchwork quilt of vice that would turn a holy man's hair white.

"So, why are you so reluctant to take our relationship to the next level?"

"Because it isn't finances that keep me from taking that next step. Emotionally, I'm not ready," he lied. "And you deserve better."

Her expression crumpled, but she nodded. "I understand."

No, you couldn't possibly.

He needed more time to sort things out. "But I want to be in a position to be the man you need," he said. "I just need a little more time to sort things in my head."

"So, you're open to more, you're just asking for more time to get there?" she clarified, wiping at her eyes.

"Yes."

"I suppose that's fair," she said, though clearly that wasn't the answer she hoped for. He hated that she thought he was asking for more time to figure out if he loved her because he already knew the answer. He was head over heels about her. "I mean, I can't fault you for being honest from the start that you weren't ready for more. It's my fault for hoping for that to change."

"No, things happen," he said, unwilling to let her think it was one-sided. "I didn't plan on feeling this way about you either, but anything worth having is worth exploring slowly. There's no need to rush what is already beautiful."

It wasn't the romantic declaration she deserved, but it might keep her safe while he continued to find the answers he needed to move on.

Assuming he could move on.

That was the ugly truth lurking in the background of his thoughts. He was doing all this work, trying to piece together a puzzle, and he had no idea if it would help him. It was possible he'd finish the puzzle, discover how everything came together to create one messed-up picture, and then he'd have to be okay with the knowledge that he was right but couldn't change a damn thing.

Which wouldn't keep him or Frannie safe.

"I accept your offer. But, Dante...I won't wait forever."

Fair enough.

Hopefully, he wouldn't have to make her wait much longer. But he had a terrible feeling he was running out of time to solve anything, much less offer her the future she deserved.

Chapter 20

The following day Dante was running errands in town when his cell rang. Believing it was his PI, he answered without checking the caller ID.

"Dante, what are you doing? Running all over the place, making trouble…it's unnecessary. Come home."

Dante's blood chilled. He glanced at the caller ID, but Unknown Caller was all that showed. "Who is this?" He scanned the street, feeling exposed. "Who's calling?"

The caller ignored his question. The voice sounded altered to disguise identity and gender. Whoever it was didn't want to be recognized. "The family is worried. Such division, such pain. It doesn't have to be this way. People poking their noses in family business…" the person on the other line tsked like Dante was the problem child. "It's an ugly thing, unbecoming of a Santoro."

Was this his uncle calling him? No, if it were Lorenzo, he wouldn't waste time altering his voice; he'd want Dante to know that it was him. So, if not Lorenzo, who?

"Either you tell me who this is, or this conversation is over."

"Trust that I don't want to see you hurt," the caller said. "You're testing your uncle's patience. Come home and ask for his forgiveness. He will forgive you. He loves you like a son."

Unwelcome pain squeezed his heart. He didn't want his uncle's forgiveness, just as he didn't want his "love." He didn't have the proof yet, but he knew his uncle had had something to do with his father's death, possibly even his mother's. Lorenzo was willing to kill to keep the family secrets, which didn't make Dante feel safe or "loved."

But at one time, he'd loved Lorenzo like a father—and it was that pain that he didn't want to feel.

"Like he loved his brother?"

The silence on the other end was damning.

Dante's temper flared and took hold. "I know my father was killed and I'm going to find a way to prove that it was Lorenzo's doing. Cops paid off, alcohol *and* fentanyl in my dad's system when the man never drank, much less did drugs? I'm getting closer to the answers I need and when I find them—"

"Stop it," the caller hissed. "You're fighting a game you will lose. Don't risk everything for something in the past that can't be changed. You're acting like a child. Time to grow up, Dante. You're the heir to the Santoro empire. Don't throw that all away chasing ghosts."

Something about the caller reminded him of someone. Everyone in Lorenzo's inner circle was intensely loyal—out of fear or true admiration—but there was only one person near enough to Lorenzo to know his every move, scheduled his appointments and handled all details of his life.

"Pietro?"

Lorenzo's secretary and right-hand man, Pietro Romano, had been around the family for as long as he could remember. He handled Lorenzo's details and was as close as any family member to his uncle, possibly closer because he doubted Lorenzo would ever hire someone to take out Pietro like he had his brother.

"Did he kill my mother, too?" Dante asked point-blank. If anyone knew, it was likely Pietro. "Why?"

"From the beginning, he loved your mother. He would never hurt her."

Dante stilled at the unexpected information. For a moment, his tongue was tied, and the caller took advantage.

"You're angry, hotheaded, and set on what you believe is a righteous path. What if you're wrong? Your uncle is not a storybook villain."

"My father might disagree," he replied coolly.

"A rift between brothers you can never understand—and it's not your place to understand."

If that statement was meant to put Dante in his place, it had the opposite effect.

"I won't be lectured by a man who condones and supports my uncle's actions. You're just as bad."

"Everyone is a villain in someone's story, Dante," the caller reminded him.

He was done being schooled. "I won't stop until I have answers. He'll have to kill me."

"Dante, you're being foolish," the caller said, disappointed. "I thought you were smarter than this."

"And I thought my uncle was a good man. I guess we're both disappointed."

"Your answer is final? You will not come home?"

"No."

"Foolish boy." The heavy sigh on the other end sent a chill down his back. "Stubborn-headed like Matteo. And destined to end up in the same place."

The line clicked off before Dante could respond.

What did that mean? The same place? Did that mean Lorenzo planned to have him killed, too?

He always knew that was a possibility, and he'd been

willing to take that risk, but now he had Frannie's safety to worry about, too.

Somehow, he had to convince Frannie it was a good idea to leave Owl Creek for a few days.

A few days? Hell, he'd need to convince her to run away with him forever. Owl Creek was compromised at this point.

A sense of déjà vu washed over him. He was replaying his childhood. His father had scooped up his little family and run from the Santoro influence, never staying long in one place for fear of being found.

And eventually, that was exactly what had happened.

Was that his fate, too?

Would history replay itself with him and Frannie?

What if she got pregnant? Would Lorenzo wipe them out and take his child to start again with a fresh slate?

Lorenzo had never married and never had kids of his own.

But he remembered Lorenzo being solicitous and accommodating to his mother when they arrived in Italy. He'd been too young and grief-stricken to look beyond the surface values of their relationship to wonder why his mother had been so quick to return to Italy when his father had done everything in his power to keep them far away.

What was that bullshit about Lorenzo loving Dante's mother? But something was disturbing about that little nugget of information that he couldn't quite push away.

His mother, Georgia, had never remarried.

His uncle had never been far from her side.

He'd never seen them act inappropriately with each other but over the years, Georgia had become very familiar with Lorenzo, decorating his home as if it were her own, and Lorenzo had always ensured Georgia had whatever she wanted.

A sick feeling lodged in his gut. Had his mother been having an affair with Lorenzo all those years after his father's death? And had she known that Lorenzo had been responsible for Matteo's death?

No, impossible. His parents had loved each other. But love needed healthy soil to grow, and it was hard to imagine a life such as theirs as anything conducive to nurturing romance.

Perhaps Georgia had grown tired of running, and Lorenzo's offer of protection and wealth had been too much to refuse.

Lorenzo had been kind to Georgia, but was there more than he'd known? A story he hadn't been privy to that started behind locked bedroom doors?

The thought of his mother and uncle being intimate made him irrationally angry on behalf of his dead father. But did ghosts care about what happened after they died?

He pocketed his cell and hustled to his rental. He felt vulnerable out in the open. If Pietro had found him, chances were high that Lorenzo knew where he was, too.

Was he playing with him? A cat and mouse game?

Was Pietro trying to pull on his heartstrings at Lorenzo's bidding, or was it possible that Pietro truly cared and wanted Dante to be safe?

He hated all the mind games. It was one of the many reasons he'd realized being the Santoro attorney wasn't a good fit for him any longer. He loathed manipulating the law to benefit people who were controlling the system for their benefit, no matter who it hurt in the process.

Lorenzo was all about the end game—he didn't care at all about the pawns on the board.

And everyone was a pawn.

Including him.

* * *

Frannie was about to close the shop when Fletcher called her cell. She picked up, ready with a wisecrack about a fictitious book order, *Men Who Are Emotionally Constipated and the Women Who Love Them*, but Fletcher's news killed her good mood.

"Frannie, there's been an accident."

Immediately, her brothers and sisters jumped to mind, but when Fletcher said it was Dante, she almost couldn't process the information. Shaking her head, she repeated, "Dante? What do you mean?"

"He's okay, but his guardian angel must've been riding shotgun because his car went straight into the lake."

Frannie gasped, horrified. "Oh my God, are you sure he's okay? Where is he?"

"Ambulance took him to Connors to be checked out. He's got a bump on his head and the clinic doesn't have a CT machine. They want to make sure he doesn't have a concussion. But honestly, it's a damn miracle he's alive. I know you're not family or next of kin, but I knew you'd want to know."

Frannie was too stressed to appropriately thank Fletcher for breaking the rules for her, anxious to get to the hospital. "Thanks," she said hastily and hung up. She quickly shut down the store and practically ran to her car to drive forty-five minutes to the nearest hospital.

She might've broken several laws driving to Connors, but she didn't care. All that kept running through her head was how Dante could've been taken from her in a blink of an eye. She swallowed the lump in her throat, too terrified to think straight. She needed to see him, to see for herself that he was okay.

What if he had a concussion? What if his brain was swelling? What if when they did the CT scan, they found a tumor in his head that otherwise would've been lurking in his brain until it took him out on a Tuesday?

Whoa, settle down. A concussion was manageable. Fletcher said Dante was going to be okay. She screeched into a parking spot, not caring that she was parked like a blind monkey had been behind the wheel. Hurrying into the lobby and to the reception desk, she gave Dante's name and lied about her connection to him. "I'm his wife," she answered when the receptionist asked if she were family. It didn't feel weird or uncomfortable to claim either. She'd unpack that later.

She heard Dante's voice from behind the curtain in the emergency room bay, and relief flooded her to tears. Pushing aside the curtain, she smiled at Dante, his head bandaged but otherwise looking as healthy as ever and even a little sexy in his blue polka dot hospital gown.

"Are you okay, honey?" She asked, hoping Dante caught on so she didn't get tossed for being nonfamily.

"I'm fine. Just a little bump on the head," he answered. He introduced Frannie to the doctor. "This is my wife, Frannie."

She pushed away the thrill the tiny lie caused because now was not the time to get all fluttery about the future. "Give it to me straight…is he really okay?" She asked the doctor sternly.

The doctor chuckled, pocketing his pen. "Your husband is correct. The CT scan came back with no damage to the brain, though he might have a headache for a few days while that bump heals. I'd recommend light duty, plenty of rest, and no heavy equipment operating for a week or so. Other than that, he's one lucky guy. A car into the lake? That's a story to tell your grandkids someday."

Frannie chuckled and murmured thanks as the doctor left

to start Dante's discharge papers. As soon as the doctor was gone, Dante's easy smile disappeared. He started dressing immediately, shucking the hospital gown and pulling his sodden clothes from the personal bag left with him by paramedics.

Alarmed, Frannie stopped him. "What are you doing? You have to be discharged first. You can't just leave and your clothes are sopping wet. I can run over to Target or something and get you some sweats and a T-shirt to change into now that I know you're not going to die."

"A little wet clothes don't bother me. I'd rather leave now."

"Dante, that's not how the American healthcare system works. You have to finish your paperwork so the hospital knows where to send the bill. I know our healthcare system sucks in comparison to Italy's but it's what we have to work with."

"I'll send cash. We need to go. I didn't need a CT scan and told paramedics that but they insisted because I passed out when they pulled me from the water."

"Well, then it was the right call," Frannie agreed, confused why Dante was so hell-bent on leaving before being officially discharged. "You could've been seriously hurt. What happened?"

"I'll tell you in the car," he said, fully dressed. "Let's go."

Before she could stop him, he pulled her after him, and they slipped out the back door reserved for emergency personnel.

What is going on? "Dante…wait!"

But Dante was like a man being chased by the cops, and he wasn't interested in having a little chat while they sorted things out.

She swallowed, realizing that a giant red flag was flapping in her face, and she could do nothing but hope she was wrong.

Chapter 21

Dante couldn't afford to stick around for the discharge papers. His fake ID would only hold up to so much scrutiny. He hadn't planned on ending up in the hospital anytime soon. But if they'd tried to run his information, it would've returned as false, tripping authorities to his fake identity. Another reason why he'd tried to refuse a trip to the hospital.

Frannie was understandably confused. "Is there something you're not telling me? I don't understand why you were so freaked out about the hospital. Do you have some bad memories associated with a hospital stay? Does it have something to do with your dad?"

She was grasping at straws, trying to understand, *bless her heart*, but if he told her the truth, he would look like a criminal and ruin any chance of convincing her to leave Owl Creek with him.

As it was, his task was an uphill battle, but the minute his brakes failed and he landed in the lake, he'd known he was no longer safe in Owl Creek.

It also made his anonymous call—he assumed it was Pietro, but he couldn't be sure—seem much more of a last-ditch effort to get him to heel before more permanent measures were taken.

He felt terrible for soaking Frannie's car seats, but he'd

pay for a full detail later. "Yes, hospitals bring up bad memories," he said, stacking another lie on the pile he was racking between them.

"You'll need to call the hospital to make financial arrangements," she warned, trying to make sense of his actions. "I mean, I suppose as long as they get their money, it's fine, but it seems like it would've been a lot easier if you could've waited ten more minutes before running out—and you were literally *running*. I felt like I was being dragged down the hallway like a character in a movie being chased by bad guys."

"Sorry, I didn't mean to frighten you."

"It's okay, I guess, just weird," she admitted with a troubled frown before returning to the subject of the crash. "What happened? How'd you end up in the lake?"

Here was the real test—how much to share without tripping any internal alarm bells. He feigned confusion. "I have no idea. Maybe a faulty brake line? I took the turn and maybe I was going a little too fast, but when I pumped the brakes, nothing happened and I plunged over the side of the hill, crashing into the lake. I think I blacked out on impact."

"How'd anyone know you'd crashed?"

"A boater coming in saw the car go in and he called 911 on his cell."

"That boater is your true guardian angel," she said.

He nodded, but his mind was racing. There was no way that his new car had faulty brakes. He was sure that someone had cut the brake line, but he didn't want to scare Frannie.

"It seems so," he agreed, shifting in his wet jeans, hating how the damp fabric clung to his thighs, but he didn't want to return to his place. "Hey, I think I left some clothes at your place. Let's go straight there."

"I don't mind stopping," she assured him. "I think all you have at my house are a pair of pajama pants and a T-shirt."

"Honestly, I didn't want to admit it, but I do have a headache. I just want to relax for the night so pajama pants sound perfect."

Frannie softened immediately. "Of course. I'm sorry, I can't even imagine the horror of what you've been through tonight. It's one of my worst fears to drive into a lake. If you hadn't had your window open... I don't even like to think of what might've happened."

Yeah, same. "Too close for comfort," he agreed. "I'm grateful for getting through it."

Frannie sobered. "Dante, my heart just about stopped when Fletcher told me. Everything else seemed to fade to the background as unimportant in that moment. I was terrified that you were hurt."

"I'm sorry for worrying you," he said.

"It's not your fault. I'm not telling you to make you feel bad. I already knew how I felt about you, but this just made me realize that I can't fathom life without you. I hope I never have to experience that."

If his life were his own, he'd ask her to marry him right now, but he didn't have that luxury.

"I promise to never drive into a lake again," he said, trying to make her smile. "I confess, it wasn't ever on my bucket list, but I guess I can check it off anyway." Her strained chuckle hurt his heart. He reached over and squeezed her thigh. "They say statistically people are in one bad accident in their lifetime—looks like I just lived through mine. So there's a bright side to losing my rental car."

A tear tracked down her cheek, but she chuckled as she wiped it away. "And who is 'they'? Is that a legal term?"

It was his turn to laugh. "Definitely. I use it in court all the time. Judges love nebulous sources."

"I bet they do," Frannie said, rolling her eyes. They pulled up to Frannie's house, and Dante exited the vehicle so fast his head throbbed, but he ignored it. He couldn't help but scan the street, looking for anything that seemed out of place.

But Frannie noticed. "Are you sure you're okay?"

"Yeah, my head is pounding, though. My plans for the night include you, aspirin and a bed."

"I think I can make that happen," she said, brushing a tender kiss across his lips.

He didn't deserve a woman like Frannie. If he lived through this, he'd make sure she never went a day without knowing how he felt about her.

The only problem? His uncle seemed determined to snuff out his only nephew—and the heir to the Santoro legacy.

Frannie tried not to fret, but there seemed to be a lot of holes in Dante's story and his reaction to being in the hospital. Every time she thought they'd crossed a threshold and reached another level of trust, something made her question everything they shared.

And she hated that she couldn't take his word at face value.

She'd always told herself that she'd never put herself in a position where her partner didn't deserve her trust, because trust was the foundation of a solid relationship. The questions nagged at her brain, whirring in the background, creating noise that kept her grabbing her attention.

Was Dante lying to her?

He didn't seem all that shaken up about landing in the lake.

He hadn't said anything about contacting the rental agency or filing an insurance claim. For that matter, he hadn't said anything about filing a lawsuit against the car manufacturer for the alleged faulty brakes. Nor had he said anything about asking for an investigation into the accident.

It was like he climbed out of the lake with a nasty bump on his head, shook the water from his hair and decided to put it all behind him like a bout of food poisoning from a questionable restaurant.

But he'd landed in a *friggin'* lake!

If it'd been her, she'd still be wrapped in a blanket, shivering and possibly crying over the ordeal.

Wasn't almost drowning considered a traumatic event?

"I can almost hear your thoughts," Dante murmured, half-asleep beside her. "What's keeping you awake?"

She couldn't be honest, not with him recovering from a head injury, so she lied. Badly. "Inventory. I was supposed to get a new shipment and it didn't come, so I will have to check the tracking tomorrow."

"I'm sure it'll show up," he said. "Shipping has been backed up for a while. I think I read something about a strike on the docks or something like that. No one to unload the ships."

"Yeah, probably."

Dante turned to pull her into a snuggle. "You smell like home," he said with a sigh before dropping back off to sleep.

Was it an old wives' tale that you're not supposed to let someone fall asleep with a head injury? She wouldn't know because they'd left before the doctor could give them discharge instructions, including how to care for someone with a head injury.

But Dante was already asleep, dozing as if he hadn't nearly met his maker a few hours ago.

It was wild how people adapted to circumstances in their life, how things became part of their routine, even if it was anything but normal.

For years she'd suspected her dad wasn't faithful, but her mom had been brilliant at hiding any reaction to his infidelity, so as kids, they weren't subjected to screaming fights or relationship drama. Not that it was healthy, but it wasn't in their face.

But then her dad died, her aunt showed up, and all hell broke loose, shattering the illusion that their family was happy, healthy and well-adjusted.

Which made her think of her current situation with Dante.

Something wasn't right.

She was ignoring her intuition because she'd fallen in love with him, which wasn't a great endorsement for their future.

If they had a future.

He's hiding something, a voice whispered, and she couldn't look away from the facts staring her in the face.

She had this sense, a tingling in the back of her head, warning her that Dante was lying about something big, which should be all the evidence she needed to walk away and cut her losses.

But she couldn't bring herself to do it, which worried her.

A few years ago, she'd decided to purchase her first brand-new car. She'd been saving all year for the down payment, and she'd been ready to sign on the dotted line. She'd asked her cousin Max to go with her so she didn't get bamboozled by slick car salesmen.

Before they walked into the dealership, Max had imparted the best advice, saying, "Okay, the key to a successful negotiation is to be prepared to walk away at any moment—

even if they have the car of your dreams on the lot ready to go, make sure *they* know you can walk away. Desperation makes people sign bad deals and it's their job to make you feel desperate."

Max had been right. She had walked away from one dealership because the deal wasn't to her liking, but the next dealership had met all her terms, and she'd left the place with the car of her dreams—and the best percentage rate for her loan.

Knowing that you were willing to walk away—even if you were in love—was how people saved themselves from staying in a relationship that was bad for them.

A bad deal.

Was Dante a bad deal?

And by staying, was she signing on for something that ultimately was a bad emotional investment?

She didn't know the answer.

And that was the problem.

Chapter 22

Dante woke up to find Frannie had already left for the shop. His cleaned clothes were folded neatly on the dresser and there was a note on top that said she had breakfast scheduled with her sister Ruby before the clinic opened and that she'd see him for lunch. He was welcome to use her old pickup until he got a new rental.

Damn it, he must've slept like the dead not to realize Frannie was up and moving around this morning. His brain was still banging from yesterday's event, and it took a minute to shake the cobwebs free. Rising, he groaned against the fresh aches and pains that erupted throughout his body after being tossed about like a rag doll in a washing machine, and went to the shower.

Letting the water sluice down his face, he suffered a moment of panic and anxiety as the situation threatened to overwhelm him.

Too many questions, too many loose threads.

He'd paid cash for the car, stuck a rental agency sticker on it so anyone looking would assume it was a rental like any other, and paid for the cheapest insurance he could find on the internet using his fake identity, but he wasn't concerned about the car. He could get another without breaking a sweat, but it was more about the situation with Frannie.

If it weren't for his feelings for her, he would've bailed

on Owl Creek the second he started to feel twitchy, but he couldn't leave her behind, knowing he might've put her in danger.

Attachments were a liability, so he'd been careful not to have any until now.

He hadn't seen it coming. Frannie was the contingency he hadn't been able to foresee.

Losing his phone was inconvenient, but he had another burner back at his place, already preloaded with the important numbers he couldn't lose, including that of his PI.

Dressing quickly, he found the keys to the old truck parked out front and locked up before leaving. He needed to go to his place, pack and figure out how to get Frannie to leave with him.

Desperation had some crazy ideas percolating in his head, but short of kidnapping her, he didn't know how he'd convince Frannie to jump in the car and head into the unknown because it wasn't safe here anymore.

By the time he reached his place, he still didn't have the answers he needed, but he went straight for his hiding spot where he kept a thick stack of cash, his burner phones, and two more fake IDs in case his current identity got burned.

Booting up the phone, he sent a quick message to his PI, letting him know his number had changed.

Almost immediately, Nick called.

"I wondered why you weren't calling me back," he said.

"Yeah, my phone ended up in a lake."

"How's this?"

"It was in the car that also landed in the lake."

Nick whistled low. "Damn. Lucky to be alive. That's some *Final Destination* type stuff."

"Seems my uncle is upping the pressure. What you got for me?"

"Not much on your family yet but I do have some information on that person you asked me to look into."

Frannie's potential stalker. "Go ahead."

"Your guy graduated Boise State with average grades and then moved to Connors, not far from Owl Creek. Maybe about a forty-five-minute drive?"

"Yeah, about that," he confirmed. "What does he do for a living?"

"He's a gig driver for various companies—Uber, Door-Dash, you name it, he does them all."

"So he makes his own schedule."

"Pretty much."

Which would leave him plenty of time to drive to Owl Creek to mess with a former unrequited love. "Anything on his record?"

"Nothing criminal. Just a civil complaint from a neighbor that he failed to bring in his trash cans from the street for a week or so after pickup."

"Was it a recent complaint?"

"About a month ago. Nothing after that, though. Seems harmless."

Didn't feel harmless to Dante. No one right in the head snuck into another person's house to leave flowers uninvited. Especially if they hadn't seen or spoken to one another in years.

"Single? Married?"

"Not married but he might've had a girlfriend at some point. I hacked into his credit card and one of the transactions showed purchases at a lingerie store and a jewelry store a few months back. Nothing since, though."

He didn't like it. Dante had a sense about things. It was one of the reasons he'd been so good at negotiations—he could tell when someone was lying, hiding something, or otherwise off. Except he'd missed all the signs with his uncle until it was too late, and he'd been in waist-deep Santoro muck as his soul started to drown.

"Keep digging. I want to know everything."

But Nick had reservations. "Can I be honest?"

"Of course."

"I think you're barking up the wrong tree. This guy isn't anything but your run-of-the-mill awkward type. He doesn't exactly fit in with the usual social scene but that's not a crime. I think you're hypersensitive because of what you're going through with your family and that's making you see motive where it doesn't exist."

Nick made a solid point. Being chased was enough to make the most levelheaded person paranoid, but someone was messing with Frannie, and he needed to know why. If it wasn't this Allen guy, then who?

Dante grudgingly switched gears. "Right before my car ended up in the lake, I was contacted by someone using a voice disruptor. I think it was my uncle's man, Pietro Romano. He tried to convince me to come home and make peace with my uncle."

"Interesting. Did you get the number?"

"It wasn't a number I recognized but whatever it was, it's now gone because it was on the phone currently at the bottom of Blackbird Lake."

"What made you think it was your uncle's secretary?"

"Something in the way he was trying to get me to come home, to play nice for the sake of family. It reminded me of Pietro. Pietro is rigidly loyal to the family, my uncle in particular, but he was always kind to me. Not everyone attached to my uncle was a bad person."

"But he must've known something was coming because he tried to warn you."

"Yeah, it would seem so."

"What do you have in your possession that is dangerous enough for your uncle to kill to have back?"

"Something that would bring incredible shame to the Santoro name—a secret my uncle will do anything to keep hidden."

Frannie was still thinking about the situation with Dante's car as she shelved books and enjoyed the quiet of the empty store. She hadn't shared her concerns with Ruby at breakfast, but her sister had commented on her pensive mood, mistakenly attributing her uncharacteristic reserve to the family situation.

"It's going to be okay," Ruby assured her, reaching across the diner table to squeeze her hand in solidarity. "No matter what, we'll get through it as a family."

Frannie had smiled, appreciating her big sister's thoughtfulness, but felt guilty that her thoughts had been far from the family drama. Still, she'd said, "I know, it's just a lot to take in."

"Yeah, you're right about that. I talked to Chase yesterday and he said that Aunt Jessie is pushing for *half* of Dad's estate."

"Half? Is she serious?"

"I don't know serious, but greedy and self-centered comes to mind," Ruby said, sipping her coffee. "The nerve of that woman is beyond me. How are Mom and Aunt Jessie even related?"

"She's the evil twin, obviously," Frannie joked.

Ruby chuckled. "Amen, sister. But according to Chase, she has a snowball's chance in hell of getting what she's asking for. If anything, she might qualify for a small settlement, but honestly, I don't think she should get a single cent."

"Me either," Frannie murmured, playing with the handle of her coffee mug. "Mom seems to be handling things well."

"That's Mom in a nutshell," Ruby said dryly. "Allowing anyone to see what's really happening behind the curtain is beyond her capabilities. But then, I guess that was the consequence of living with Dad. He wasn't an easy man to love."

"Do you ever wonder why she didn't leave him?" Frannie asked.

"No. For all his faults, she loved him, and I don't know if that's an endorsement for unconditional love or toxic codependency. All I know is that I wish she could've fallen in love with someone better."

"The heart wants what the heart wants, I guess."

"Yeah, no matter how many red flags are flapping."

Ruby paid for breakfast, and they'd parted ways, but Ruby's last statement still echoed in Frannie's head.

Was she being blinded by love the same as her mom had been with her dad?

"Earth to Frannie, are you listening?"

Frannie was startled as Fletcher's voice abruptly popped into her thoughts. She had no idea Fletcher had even walked into the store, much less was calling her name. "I'm sorry, I didn't hear you come in. What's going on?" she asked, her concerned frown matching his dour expression. "Is everything okay?"

"No, it is definitely not okay," he said, gesturing to her office. "Let's go somewhere private to talk."

"I can't just leave the shop unattended, Fletcher," she said in a low tone, but she was worried about whatever was eating Fletcher to put that look on his face. She motioned for him to follow as she retreated deeper into the Self-Help aisle, which was sadly not the most popular book section. "What's going on?"

"You know how you asked me to look into your friend Dante?"

Her friend. She swallowed, embarrassed that she'd even asked, but now, given the circumstances, maybe it was wise. "Yeah, did you find something?" *Please say no.*

"He lied to you."

Oh, God.

Frannie stared, unable to process what Fletcher had just said. After a long moment, she asked in a strained tone, "What do you mean, he lied to me? About what?"

"His name, who he is…why he's here…the man can't be trusted. I don't want you around him anymore."

This was all happening too fast. "Hold up, what? I don't understand. What's his name and how do you know all this? Are you sure you have the right man?"

She knew she sounded desperate, but her world was collapsing, and she was grasping at straws.

Realizing she was sinking, Fletcher tried to soften the blow, but there was no easy way to deliver a crap sandwich. "I'm sorry, Frannie, but he's up to no good. Only people with something to hide lie about their identity. His name is Dante Santoro, not Sinclair, and he's part of a dangerous Italian family—the kind that gets away with shady behavior because they have enough money to make problems go away. You know what I'm talking about?"

Those red flags that she'd been ignoring…well, they were practically slapping her in the face now, but she couldn't reconcile what she knew about Dante with what Fletcher was saying. It was like he was describing a stranger.

"You have to have the wrong guy," she protested. "I know Dante. He's the kindest, most compassionate person I've ever met." She felt as if she couldn't breathe. "I'm sorry but you're wrong."

"Frannie, I know it's hard to accept but I asked Max for help because he has access to databases that I don't. The FBI has a file on the Santoro family a mile long but because they're Italian citizens, the FBI has no jurisdiction unless they commit a crime here in the States. They're too good to get caught doing something stupid here, so there's nothing they can tie back to the family, but their hands aren't clean. I'm telling you, Dante isn't safe to be around."

Is that why his car landed in a lake? Is someone after him?

Frannie drew a deep breath, trying to calm her racing heart. "Wait, wait, I need a minute to think," she said, fanning her face as tears crowded her sinuses. What nightmare was she in right now? Two days ago, she'd been wondering if she and Dante should put in an offer on a house together, and now Fletcher was telling her that the man she thought she knew—didn't exist!

"Are you saying he's part of the mob?" Frannie asked, trying to make sense of everything.

Fletcher exhaled a short breath, clearly hating to be the bearer of bad news but wasn't willing to back down. "Look, according to Max, the Santoro family isn't connected to the mafia but they're just as powerful. They're obscenely wealthy and that kind of money creates power. You've seen the movies about powerful families—they always manage to get what they want because enough money makes every problem go away. And sometimes that means people, too."

She couldn't make her brain connect the dots with what Fletcher was saying and what she thought she knew about Dante. "If he's part of this powerful family, why is he here in Owl Creek of all places? It's not as if our town is a hotbed of international intrigue. It's literally the most Mayberry of places on the map."

"Frannie, every place has its dark corners, you know that. Even Owl Creek. We have drugs, crime, you name it."

"Yeah, I know that," Frannie shot back, exasperated. "But Dante doesn't do any of those things. The man goes out of his way to make sure I have food in his fridge that won't send my stomach into a tizzy. He opens doors and is super protective. I didn't tell you because it didn't seem like a big deal, but I had a mysterious flower delivery two weeks ago that came from an anonymous buyer and then another flower placed on my bed a few days later... Dante has been my shadow making sure that I'm safe. Does that sound like a man who's dangerous?"

Fletcher stared. "What are you talking about...what flowers? And why didn't you report this?"

Frannie groaned, shaking her head. "Because it's not that important, more weird than anything else, and I didn't want to bother you with stupid stuff. I mean, it was flowers, not anything scary. But that's not the point. The point is, Dante's been by my side, determined to keep me safe, even if it was from imaginary threats."

"Frannie...did it ever occur to you that maybe he's acting like there's something dangerous out there because he knows exactly who sent those flowers and it spooked him?"

Frannie stilled. No, she hadn't thought of that possibility, but she did now. It made more sense than her random stranger theory. "I have to talk to Dante."

"No. I'll talk to him. I'll bring him in for questioning."

"For what? He hasn't committed a crime," Frannie balked. "You can't arrest someone for using a different name to rent a vacation house."

"We have no idea what he's doing here, or why. He might be an international criminal hiding out until the heat passes."

"That seems a little far-fetched," Frannie said, but her voice lacked conviction. *Helloooo, his car landed in a lake!* That internal voice was practically jumping up and down, gesturing emphatically.

The fact was…she didn't know what was true anymore.

Dante had lied to her.

That was the only indisputable fact.

And her stupid, gullible heart was broken.

Chapter 23

Dante walked into the bookstore and felt the unwelcome, hostile chill coming from the police officer standing beside Frannie. He knew something was up.

"Dante…" Frannie looked crushed, and he felt he was at the epicenter of that devastation. "I—"

"Is everything okay?" he asked, feigning confusion.

But the man cut in with a protective stance, his hand resting on his sidepiece as if Dante were a dangerous threat to Frannie. "I'm going to have to ask you to step outside for a minute, *Mr. Santoro.*"

They knew his real name.

Dante caught Frannie's wounded gaze, knowing this man must be one of her brothers. Had she asked her brother to look into his background? He'd never had to hide his identity before, and it was a foreign, uncomfortable feeling knowing they were judging him for being deceptive.

He couldn't blame them.

But he couldn't let Frannie think he was a bad person. He ignored the officer for a minute, directing his attention straight at the woman he loved more than anything. "Can we talk for a minute? I'll explain everything."

But the man wasn't having it. "Outside. Now."

Frannie asked him point-blank, "Is it true?"

The time for lies was over. "Yes." But he was oddly relieved. "And I'm glad you know. But you don't know everything. Let me tell you why."

"There's never a good reason for pretending to be someone you're not," the man replied, his tone hard. "Now, we can do this the easy way or the hard way. Your choice, Mr. Santoro."

Frannie held his stare. "How do I know you won't just keep lying to me?"

"Because now I have no reason to lie and when I tell you why I lied, you'll understand."

"Okay, hard way it is," Fletcher said, grabbing Dante's arm.

"Get your hands off me," Dante growled, stiffening against the man's grip. "I'm assuming you're one of her many brothers and I don't want to make things awkward but if you don't take your hands off me, you and I are going to have an issue."

The man seemed to find Dante's threat amusing. "I don't know how things work in Italy, but here in the United States, threatening an officer of the law is going to land your ass in hot water." He pulled Dante's arms behind his back and zip-tied his wrists together. "We'll finish this conversation down at the station."

But Frannie shocked him by intervening. "Fletcher… wait."

The man looked at his sister in frustration, shaking his head. "Frannie, you have no idea who this man is."

"As far as we know, he hasn't broken the law," Frannie murmured, still conflicted yet shooting dark looks Dante's way.

Dante saw his window, speaking directly to Frannie. "My name is Dante Santoro, I'm heir to one of the most influential and ruthless families in Italy. I changed my name because I didn't want to be found…by my family. I didn't tell you because I didn't want you to be involved with anything as ugly as what I'm dealing with. I haven't killed anyone or committed any kind of crime aside from using a fake name and I never would—which is another reason why I left Italy."

Fletcher quipped, "Great story, let's go."

They managed two steps to the door before Frannie said, "Fletcher, let him go."

"Excuse me?"

"Let me handle this. Dante isn't a threat. This is personal between him and me."

"The hell it is. This man is using an assumed identity. That's fraud."

Frannie couldn't argue that point, but he could tell she was weighing the morality of the situation against what he'd shared already, and she was wavering.

"All I need is a chance to explain," he said, pressing his advantage. He needed her to understand that he wasn't the villain he looked to be.

"Every criminal I know has a sob story—and usually, they're lying about that, too." Fletcher wasn't moved. "A trip to the station is all you're getting today."

This time it was Frannie who was exasperated. "Fletcher, you don't have to do that. He hasn't committed any *real* crime and he pretty much just came clean. Also, he's a lawyer, so he knows the law. Don't waste your time processing paperwork that's not going to go anywhere."

"Frannie…" Fletcher stared long and hard at his sister, but he was digesting her information. Finally, he glanced at Dante, exhaled and shook his head, muttering as he snipped the ties, "I swear to God, if you hurt my sister, I'll show you American justice with extreme prejudice."

Dante rubbed his wrists, nodding. "You're a good brother."

"Yes, I am," he growled, pointing to Frannie, "If he so much as blinks wrong, you better call me."

"I will," Frannie assured Fletcher. "I'll be okay. Thank you, though."

With one final stern glare Dante's way, he exited the bookstore slowly, as if reluctant to take his eyes off Dante. Finally, he climbed into his squad car and drove away.

"So that's Fletcher?" he supposed.

"Yes."

"He seems like a good guy."

"Stop it," she ordered, marching to her front door and locking it, flipping the sign to Closed. "You don't get to blow my world to bits and then try to chitchat about my family. I need you to spill your guts right now."

It was time to be honest—and he was ready for it. Lying to Frannie had become a bigger burden than he ever imagined, and he was relieved to finally be able to come clean.

"In the interest of saving time, what do you know?"

"I know enough. Your family is rich, connected and dangerous. My cousin Max works for the FBI, and they have a file a mile long on your family. But they don't have anything they can pin on the Santoro connection here in the States."

"Sounds accurate," he confirmed. "My family legacy is a checkered quilt of vice and infamy—and I wanted no more part of it once I realized the cost to my soul. I wanted out, Frannie. I swear to you, that's my reason for running away."

"Why'd you have to run away? Are you in danger from your own family?"

"Yes."

Her eyes widened as if she couldn't fathom such a thing, and he knew it was a lot to take in, especially for someone like Frannie, who'd never had to walk side by side with the devil.

She narrowed her gaze with dawning fear. "Your car... did your family have something to do with your car landing in the lake?"

"I don't have proof, but I believe so."

She gasped. "I don't understand...why?"

He sighed, levering himself into the oversize reading chair. "You're going to want to sit down," he said, preparing to tell her the whole sordid story. "There's no happy ending to this story."

Frannie's head was spinning, and she felt spun on her axis.

Dante's story was something out of a movie—these things didn't happen to actual people, did they?

Everything Dante had been through—from losing his father and mother to being drawn in by the uncle now trying to kill him—was more than she could process in one breath. She took a long minute to try and sort the facts into manageable cubes, but tears threatened to fall as she failed miserably.

"How are you handling this? My family has its problems, but they seem minuscule in comparison to what you're dealing with. Oh, God, you must think I'm so naive for going on about my family drama when it doesn't even compare to what you're faced with."

"I've never thought you were naive—kind and compassionate—but never naive," he said, trying to make her feel better. "That's why I think you're incredible. That generous heart of yours is a beautiful thing, and your love has made me realize what I needed most in my life."

Frannie wiped at a tear tracking down her cheek. "My biggest fear after my breakup with my ex was finding someone like him who would break my heart by cheating on me." A small bubble of laughter erupted as she realized there were much worse things. "Instead, I fell in love with an international fugitive with a murderous family. I think that's much worse, don't you?"

He fell silent.

She stared at her hands, slipping into a dark place as her heart wept. What was she supposed to do? Break up with him when he needed someone who wasn't trying to kill him? But then, what did that mean for her? Was she in danger, too? "Is that why you kept asking me to go away for the weekend?" she asked.

He looked miserable—and scared—as he admitted, "I'm not sure if either of us are safe here."

Frannie gasped. "What do you mean?"

"I never should've encouraged anything between us, but I did. And in doing so, I selfishly put your life in danger. I can't take back what I've done but I can do everything in my power to keep you safe. I have enough money to take us anywhere in the world and I have contacts that can create a new identity—"

"No!" She didn't want to be someone else. She liked her life here in Owl Creek. "You can't ask me to change everything about my life in the blink of an eye and expect me to skip after you. Honestly, do you really think that's fair?"

"It's not fair at all," he agreed, his eyes flashing. "And I hate having to ask but the thought of you being hurt because of me—it's more than I can handle! I won't have it happen again!"

Again? "What do you mean?"

Dante rose sharply from the chair, startling her with the sudden movement. Tension radiated from his solid frame. She'd never seen him so worked up, and it was a little jarring. She'd only ever seen the calm, cool-headed man who always seemed to have quiet wisdom to share. Not this man who seemed eaten up by an internal fire he couldn't escape.

"My ex—Belinda—the one I don't like to talk about… there's a reason I'm putting all my cards on the table so there's no more secrets between us. Are you ready for the full truth?"

"I think so," she answered, wary. *It gets worse?* In for a penny, in for a pound, as her grandmother used to say. "What happened to your ex?"

"Belinda was a top pediatric surgeon. Her skill was in her deft work on tiny babies. She had a gift that drew people from around the world to have her in the operating room. She could've handpicked any hospital on this planet as her primary residency, but she loved her home country and always wanted to remain in Italy."

"She sounds like a superstar," Frannie said, feeling insecure at an inappropriate moment. How could she possibly stack up against a résumé like that? Dante's ex probably looked like a supermodel, too.

Dante must've sensed her insecurity. He immediately soothed it in a way only he could. "She was incredible— but she wasn't you. Never forget that."

In that split second, Frannie felt a hot wave pass between them as if their chemistry couldn't be contained, even in moments such as this when the world seemed to be collapsing. A rush of powerful emotion nearly sent her to her knees.

As far as she knew, no one planned to fall in love—it just happened.

And sometimes, it happened with the person who seemed a lousy bet on paper. All the reasons to walk away were scrawled in big, bold letters, but she knew she wouldn't.

Couldn't.

She would stand by him. No matter what happened.

Even if that meant leaving behind everything she'd ever known.

"Tell me what happened to Belinda," she said bravely. "I need to know everything."

Dante nodded, understanding what was unspoken. His eyes watered, but he choked back the tears.

And then he held her hand and unloaded the most horrific story she'd ever heard. His voice broke at times as he recounted how he'd nursed Belinda back to health and then spirited her away when she could travel, leaving her in Switzerland to rebuild. How he'd been chased by the guilt he couldn't dodge.

She saw the pain in his eyes.

Felt the remorse.

And she knew that no matter who his family was, Dante was cut from a different cloth and would never do anything that led him down the same path. His only choice had been running, and she couldn't fault him for that.

Desperate times called for desperate measures, and it was easy to say but harder to follow through. Most people wouldn't have had the strength of character to do what Dante had done to protect himself and his loved ones, but Dante was one of a kind.

There was no way in hell she'd make him walk that path alone.

"I love you, Dante," she said, holding his gaze. "We'll figure this out together."

"Are you sure? Now is the time to cut your losses. I'll help you no matter what."

She heard the desperate note in his voice, battling a war she couldn't possibly understand, and it hurt her heart.

"I'm not going anywhere," she replied firmly. "But I think we should tell my brother and cousin Max. They might be able to help."

Dante shook his head, clearly opposed to that idea. "The fewer people I put in harm's way, the better. We need to keep our circle small. I know you're close to your family, but you have to trust me on this. Please keep this information between us."

Frannie didn't like it, but she agreed. *For the time being.* Everything was too new to start rocking the boat, but she knew Dante was too close to the situation to see that he couldn't do this alone.

Dante, relieved, pulled her close and sealed his mouth to hers in a passionate kiss that they usually reserved for private moments, away from public view.

But it was as if he wanted the world to know they belonged together. Frannie melted against him, loving how well they seemed to fit, but a chill slithered down her spine at the unpleasant sensation of being watched.

Maybe it was because they'd been so careful to keep their relationship private, or perhaps it was because a seed of paranoia had been planted about his family, but she couldn't escape the feeling that someone was watching.

And it scared her more than she wanted to admit.

Chapter 24

It took some doing, but Frannie talked Dante into not doing anything rash until they'd had time to make a plan. For one, she couldn't skip town without making arrangements for her shop and at least talking to her mom about an extended vacation as a cover story.

Dante conceded, but he was understandably jumpy.

Even though she promised to keep the situation between them, Franny knew she would at least have to talk to Darla. Someone in her circle had to understand what was truly going on just in case things went south in a bad way. Plus, Darla was getting married soon, and it didn't seem fair to not let her know what was happening in case her maid of honor disappeared.

Darla showed up at the shop the next day with a frown. "Okay, you're going to have to explain that very cryptic voice mail you left because I can't make head or tail of what you said."

"Sorry about that. I was nervous about leaving too much detail on the message."

"Yeah, see, when you say things like that my anxiety just gets worse. What is going on?"

Frannie drew a deep breath, still unable to believe she was in the middle of something this complicated. She tried to prepare Darla. "I'm going to need you to suspend your disbelief and listen to what I have to say because I can guarantee you, you aren't going to believe me at first."

Darla's eyes widened with interest. "You've got my attention. Shoot."

With something this big, it was probably best to throw it all out there and sort the details later. "Dante is part of a dangerous wealthy family—not the mob—but rich and powerful enough to bend the rules to their benefit, and they're after him. His name is Dante Santoro, and we'll probably leave town soon. I wanted to let you know so that you don't worry."

Frannie realized Darla couldn't process all of that as fact because who could? These kinds of things didn't happen to ordinary people. Particularly people who lived in Owl Creek, a town known for its pristine lake and quaint downtown. Darla proved she was right with her reply. "I'm sorry, what?"

Frannie tried again. "I told you it was a lot. Here's the thing. Dante changed his name so he could get away from his family, but they may have found him already. Dante thinks they're the reason he ended up in the lake. They tried to kill him by cutting the brakes on his car."

"That *actually* happens?" Darla said, incredulous. "I thought that only happened in spy movies. I wouldn't even know how to find a brake line, much less cut one."

"You barely know where to put the gas in your car," Frannie quipped. "But I had the same reaction as you. I'm still having a hard time wrapping my head around everything, but it's very real—and very dangerous."

Even though Dante had asked Frannie to keep details private, she couldn't keep that intel from her best friend.

Frannie shared what had happened to Belinda and how

she was starting a new life in Switzerland, but not as a pediatric surgeon any longer.

Darla stared for a long moment, then snapped out of it and declared, "You have to break up with him."

"I'm not going to do that," Frannie said, shaking her head. "I love him."

"And I love strawberries but I'm deathly allergic and if I eat one, I'll most certainly die a horrible death. Sometimes we have to give up things that are bad for our health."

"It's not Dante's fault that his family is awful. He's trying to do the right thing."

"Yeah, and brownie points for his moral victory. But if you end up dead as collateral damage, I could not care less about his emotional growth. Catch my drift? His ex-girlfriend was beaten almost to death and then maimed for life. Dante's got bigger problems than most people and you're too sweet and loving to see that he's going to get you killed—and then if that happens, I'm going to have to go to prison for killing Dante. See how all of that is bad?"

Frannie loved Darla's bold declaration, but she recognized it for what it was—fear. "Nothing is going to happen to me. Dante is determined to keep me safe, which is why we probably have to leave Owl Creek."

"This is ridiculous. What are you even saying? Leave town with a guy who has killers after him? No, let *him* leave and have him send you a postcard when the heat dies down and you don't have to worry about eating a bullet during dinner."

It was sensible, but she knew she couldn't let Dante deal with this alone.

"If Tom were in the same situation, you wouldn't hesitate to do whatever you could to help."

"Tom would never be in a situation like this," Darla

countered, shaking her head. "Tom lines up and color co-ordinates his socks. He would never end up on the run for any reason—and I like him that way. Come to think of it, your situation has me rethinking all the times I called him boring. I like boring."

"Yes, you love Tom. That's the point, Darla."

At that, Darla fell quiet.

"See? We do what we have to for the people we love—and I love Dante."

"Are you sure? You barely know him," Darla returned in a plaintive tone. "This is the premise of a true-crime documentary in the making. No one in their right mind would just leave everything behind for someone who's being chased by dangerous people. What can I do to change your mind?"

"Nothing."

Darla groaned. "This is a nightmare."

"It's not great," she agreed. "But I wanted someone in my circle to know in case things go south."

"Not to sound like a dick, but how are you going to be my maid of honor if you're fleeing the country? And what about your family? It's not like they're going to be fine with you disappearing. Hell, Max will have the FBI chasing after you and then your lover boy will have two people after him."

Frannie laughed, even though it wasn't funny, but it was because it was so Darla. "Yeah, about that… You might want to replace me in your wedding. As for my family, I'll think of something so they don't worry."

"You're irreplaceable."

Darla's deadpan answer was about more than the wedding, and Frannie's eyes teared up. "Nothing is going to happen to me." It was a promise she didn't have the right to offer because she didn't know what the future held, but

Darla needed some reassurance, or she might fall apart. "With any luck, the situation will resolve itself, and this will all be an unpleasant memory."

"Unpleasant is one word for it."

"I don't like what's happening either, but I can't ignore how I feel about him. This is the real deal—the kind of love that only comes once in a lifetime—and I'm not going to walk away. We need each other."

Darla sighed, giving up even though she didn't seem convinced. But at least she didn't keep pressing, and Frannie was grateful. She couldn't fight her best friend and still have the strength to be Dante's support.

The fact that Darla intuitively knew that was why they'd been best friends since the third grade.

They understood each other. They loved each other.

And that love was why Frannie had to tell her.

Dante felt lighter but no less anxious. He had hated lying to Frannie—each time he saw that questioning look in her eyes, knowing she was sensing his dishonesty, he'd wanted to break down and lay it all on the line, but he'd known he couldn't.

Now that part was done. He'd told her everything down to the grittiest detail—and she was determined to stand by his side, which humbled him in ways he couldn't even put into words.

No one had ever been so steadfast, so loyal, and he vowed to make sure she never had reason to question his integrity.

His phone rang, and he checked the caller ID this time before answering. It was Nick, his PI.

"Dante, I thought you might want to know...that guy you had me watching just got flagged on some suspicious purchases with his credit card. It could be nothing, but it was out of pocket enough to warrant a second look."

"Yeah? What kind of purchases?"

"Zip ties, chlorine bleach, ethanol and acetone, and an industrial-size bag of cloth towels. Purchased this morning."

He didn't like the sound of that. "Why would a gig driver need those chemicals?"

"He wouldn't. Unless he was planning to make homemade chloroform to knock out one of his passengers."

A warning bell went off in Dante's head, urging him to check on Frannie at the shop. "I have to go," he said abruptly, clicking off. He immediately rang Frannie. She picked up on the second ring, and relief followed. "Are you okay?"

"I'm fine," she said, chuckling quizzically. "You told me to act normal, so I'm just doing my usual shelving. Darla stopped by earlier but it's just me now."

"No customers in the shop?"

"No, it's nice and quiet. Gives me a chance to catch up on my paperwork. I was thinking of maybe asking Darla to cover the shop while we're gone on 'vacation.'"

"Yeah, sure, good idea," he said, distracted. He still had a bad feeling. "I think you should close early today."

"I can't do that. I have a shipment coming today."

"Frannie—"

"Oh! I gotta go, looks like someone's heading my way. I'll see you later. Let's have dinner with my mom tonight."

And then she clicked off like danger wasn't pressing in on them from all sides—and some danger she didn't even know was coming.

Frannie placed her cell phone on the counter just as the front door opened and a man walked through. There was a tingle of recognition, but it took a minute for her to realize she was staring at Allen Burns. However, he didn't look like the same guy she'd shared a few classes with in college.

The years had been rough.

His reedy frame had become soft and doughy, his complexion splotchy and uneven, but his vibe threw her off the most.

Where he'd once been shy and quiet, preferring his plants to people, now there was a disordered air of chaos around him, an anger that pulsated beneath the surface of his seemingly approachable veneer.

Don't be so judgy, a voice admonished. Allen had spent his life being bullied by people who made assumptions. She couldn't do that to him, too.

"Allen? Oh, gosh, I almost didn't recognize you! How are you?" she asked, trying to be polite and engaging as she would with anyone who entered her store. "I haven't seen you since graduation. What have you been up to?"

"Frannie…it's so good to see you," Allen said, licking his lips and glancing around the shop. "This…uh, your place?"

"Yep. Bought and paid for—well, not exactly paid for yet, but I'm doing my best, despite the economy."

"You always did love books," he said, stepping a little closer in a way that made her twitchy. "Anyone else here?"

During her freshman year at Boise State, the campus had hosted a women's safety course with the cooperation of the local police. During one class, the instructor had brought a convicted rapist to talk about how he would pick his victims. He'd look for a woman alone, with hair in a ponytail or a single braid because it was easier to grab and pull the victim off-balance, and he'd look for someone who didn't make eye contact because it suggested a level of humility that he could subdue. But going above and beyond those practical tips, most of his victims shared a commonality—they ignored their intuition because they didn't want to come off as rude.

Frannie stepped back as if heading to her counter to grab the short stack of books waiting for her to shelve, her mind moving quickly. *Keep him talking.* Someone was bound to walk in at some point, and likely he'd leave. "So, what's new with you? What brings you to Owl Creek?"

"Where you going? No hug? I haven't seen you in ages, and you're treating me like I got the plague." His tone was joking, but there was an odd gleam in his eye, and his left hand had moved to his jean pocket.

"Actually, I've got a little summer cold. I better keep my distance, or you'll end up with the sniffles, too."

His gaze narrowed with cold suspicion. "Oh, I get it. You're too good to say hello to an old friend now that you've got your fancy boyfriend."

Frannie stilled. How did he know about Dante? "Allen… how'd you know I was engaged?" she asked, stretching the truth a bit.

Allen ignored the question and slowly advanced toward her. "You know, I always thought you were better than most girls. Always so nice. You never made me feel like a freak like the other girls. I liked you."

"I liked you, too, Allen," she said, careful to keep her tone soft and calming, but her heart raced. "But I'm confused by how you knew I was engaged. I haven't seen you in years."

"I've seen you."

She swallowed. "Oh yeah? When?"

He ignored that question, too, but added something else that froze her blood. "I know what you like. More than he ever could. I know you, Frannie."

"Allen, you're starting to scare me. Tone it down, okay?"

"You like to sleep naked with the ceiling fan on medium and only a light sheet for when it gets too breezy."

"Allen!" She felt exposed. "Have you been watching me?"

"You like to eat dairy when you know you shouldn't because it hurts your stomach something awful, yet you do it anyway. I get it, I do things I shouldn't, too. But I can take care of you, make sure you stop doing things that aren't good for you."

"I don't need anyone to take care of me. I need you to get a hold of yourself and stop acting like this or I will call the police."

"I can't have you do that," he said, moving with a swiftness she hadn't realized possible to jerk her toward him. She slammed into him with an *ooof*, and something acrid and chemically pungent went over her mouth and nose as Allen held her with an iron grip.

Instinct made her scream, but she realized too late she should've held her breath and stomped on his instep instead. Her head started pounding as the chemical smell choked out her breath. No matter how she struggled, Allen's grip held her tight. Her fingernails dug into his arm, but he didn't waver. Within a few minutes, her muscles lost their strength, her vision started to blacken, and she slumped in his arms, passed out cold.

Chapter 25

Dante jumped out of the old truck and ran into the shop just in time to see a thick, doughy man grunting with the difficulty of dragging Frannie's inert body out the shop's back door. Sprinting toward them, he caught the man off guard and punched him hard, causing him to drop Frannie and stumble back.

He grabbed the man by his shirt and drove his fist into his face again, breaking his nose. Shaking him like a rag doll, he yelled, "What did you do to her?"

The man glared up at him through the blood, bubbles of red snot dribbling from his nose and mixing with the drool. "She was supposed to be mine," he said with hot resentment. "Not yours. You took her from me!"

"You're a nutjob," Dante said, shoving him with disgust. The man tried to roll away and scramble to his feet, but Dante drove his foot into the man's soft gut and sent him sprawling, gasping for air. "Don't move," he ordered in a thunderous roar, grabbing the first thing he could find to tie the man's hands together. He remembered seeing Frannie stash a roll of duct tape in a utility box beneath the counter. Winding the tape around the man's hands and legs so tight it probably cut the circulation off, he called 911 while checking on Frannie.

She was still breathing, slow and steady. Just as Nick had

surmised, the asshole had made his own chloroform. Dante could only imagine what he'd had in mind for Frannie once he got her loaded into his car. He had to stop thinking about the what-ifs, or else he might do something he regretted.

Picking her up gently, he carried her to the oversize reading chair that was her favorite and gently stroked her face, trying to wake her up.

Within a minute, Owl Creek PD showed up with lights and sirens. Frannie's brother was first on the scene. He quickly saw Frannie unconscious and started yelling, but Dante cut him off. "The man you want is behind the counter, near the back door. I've got him tied up with duct tape. I think he used chloroform on her."

"Get a medic in here!" Fletcher yelled before moving toward the back where Dante had left the man trussed up like a Christmas turkey.

Paramedics poured into the building, and Dante stepped out of their way while they checked her vitals.

"BP is stable, but her oxygen is low. Let's get her loaded up for transport," the paramedic instructed as he fixed an oxygen mask over her face.

Another officer bagged the cloth that the man had dropped on the ground when he tried to drag Frannie's body out the back door, and Fletcher confirmed it was chloroform. "Who the hell is this guy? Is he one of yours?" he asked Dante, glaring with accusation. "I told you if you hurt my sister—"

"He's a guy Frannie went to school with at Boise State," Dante barked to shut Fletcher up, following paramedics as they loaded her onto a stretcher. "His name is Allen Burns. Look him up. I'm heading to the hospital with Frannie."

He didn't explain to Fletcher how he knew. That wasn't his problem, and he sure as hell wasn't staying behind while the ambulance took Frannie away.

When she woke up, he wanted to be by her side.

But Fletcher wasn't finished. "Hold up, where the hell you think you're going? We're not done here."

"The hell we aren't. That ambulance is taking the woman I love, and I'll be damned if I'm going to sit around and wait for your permission to be there when she wakes up. If you want to talk later, fine, but for now, I'm following that ambulance."

The two men had a short stare-down, but Fletcher grudgingly backed down when he realized Dante wasn't playing chicken with him. "Fine, go. But there will be questions later."

"Fine," he growled back, jumped into the truck and chased after the ambulance. All he could say was that if that asshole had somehow hurt Frannie with his bathtub chemistry set, he'd break all the laws to make sure he never had use of his fingers again.

He pulled into the parking lot and sprinted into the lobby, bypassed the registration and went straight to the ER bay. A flabbergasted receptionist hurried after him, screeching about calling security, but Dante wouldn't let anyone stop him from seeing Frannie.

He found Frannie's bed just as her eyes were opening sluggishly. One nurse was finishing a blood draw and another was adjusting her oxygen flow. The doctor, startled by the commotion Dante had created, saw the concern on Dante's face and waved off the security team that had started piling in after him. "I'm assuming you know Frannie Colton," the doctor said.

"Yes, she's my girl," he answered, wishing he could say she was his wife. "Is she going to be okay?"

"Your name?"

"Dante Sinclair," he said, using his fake identity. The fewer people knowing his real name, the better.

Frannie weakly pulled at the oxygen mask so she could speak, and both men swiveled to protest, but she batted at both of them with a frown. "My head feels like it's full of rocks, and my mouth tastes like a stinky sock smells."

Dante's sudden relief was palpable as he leaned forward and kissed her forehead. "There's my brave girl. How are you feeling?"

"Not great," she answered, looking to the doctor. "Hi, Doc, am I going to live?"

The doctor chuckled, shaking his head. "It'll take more than a clumsy chemical attempt to drag you down. We're running some blood tests to check for any other possible toxins, but your oxygen levels are already returning to normal. I think you're going to be fine, aside from a monster headache. We'll get you some Tylenol for the pain."

But Frannie declined, saying, "I think I've had enough chemicals in my body for the day." To Dante, she said, "I'd rather just go home and lie down in a dark room, sleep it off."

"I will happily arrange that," he said, but then people he could only assume were more family anxiously burst into the room.

Two women who looked similar enough ignored Dante and went straight to Frannie.

"Oh my God, Fletcher group-texted us to let us know someone had attacked you in the store," the first one said, shocked. "What happened?"

Frannie sighed, clearly still processing what had happened, but she took a minute to make quick introductions. "Dante, these are my sisters, Ruby and Hannah, and yes,

I was attacked by a guy I used to know. If it weren't for Dante... I don't know what he had planned."

The women spun on their heels to rush Dante, crushing him in a surprise hug that startled him. "Thank you!" Ruby said, squeezing him hard. "You saved our baby sister. You're a freaking hero."

The one named Hannah wiped away tears. "I'm literally in shock right now. How does something like this happen in our little town?"

"He's been watching me for a while, I guess," Frannie said, swallowing. "He...he...ugh, he watched me sleep. I feel so damn violated right now and icky. Like my skin is crawling at the thought."

Dante wanted to punch the man all over again. Speaking of... "I should probably talk to your brother and give him an official statement. I didn't give him an option of holding me at the scene, but now that I know you're safe..."

Frannie understood immediately, nodding. "Yes, please go talk to my brother. Let him know what happened. Ruby or Hannah can take me home. I'll see you back at my place when you're done."

It was a solid plan, even though he hated the idea of leaving her side. However, seeing her with her sisters, he knew she was in good hands.

"All right, but only because I don't want your brother showing up at your place trying to put me in handcuffs for refusing to answer questions at the scene."

"Fletcher can be stubborn like that," Ruby agreed. "Don't worry, we'll get her home safely."

"Nice to meet you," Hannah said. "Though I wish it were under better circumstances."

"Yes, indeed," he murmured. Stealing another glance at Frannie as her sister smoothed the hair back from her crown with such love, he suffered a moment of envy for never knowing what that was like.

That's how a family is supposed to act with each other.

Backing away, he left Frannie in the able care of her sisters and headed to the police station.

Frannie loved her sisters, but she was bothered by the odd expression on Dante's face before he slipped out. Before she could dwell too deeply, Ruby was peppering her with questions.

"Okay, I need details. What the hell?"

Frannie knew they wouldn't rest until she spilled the beans, so she drew a deep breath and shared every detail, down to the weird tingle in her gut that warned her that something was wrong.

"It's so strange. At first I was really happy to see him because I haven't seen him since graduation and I thought we were pretty close, but there was just something weird about his vibe, the energy was off. I think it was something in his eyes. I don't know, but I definitely listened to my intuition, and I tried to put space between us. Unfortunately, I did not do so well at remembering to hold my breath when he put the cloth over my face. Within minutes I was blacking out. If Dante hadn't showed up when he did, I don't know what would've happened."

Ruby shuddered. "I don't even want to think about it, but obviously he was up to no good."

Hannah looked disturbed. "Why were you friends with him in the first place?"

Frannie frowned. "Because I don't like it when people are bullied just because they're different. He wasn't like this when we were in school. When I knew him, he was quiet and shy, and really sweet. I don't know what happened to him between graduation and now but he's definitely not the same person."

Hannah nodded but switched gears. "And who is your knight in shining armor? The chemistry between you is obviously not platonic, so…new boyfriend?"

"Um, yes," Frannie admitted. "We were taking it slow so I didn't want to prematurely share that I was seeing someone, but we've recently agreed to make it official." *Right before planning to skip town because his family is trying to kill him.* Better to leave that part out. "His name is Dante Sinclair and I'm crazy about him."

"Well, he saved your life so he's automatically my favorite person right now," Ruby said.

Frannie smiled, wishing they had more time to get to know Dante under better circumstances. "He's really great," she murmured.

"I definitely get a better vibe from him than your last guy," Hannah admitted. "I mean, I always wanted to be supportive but your ex…seemed smarmy from the start. Good riddance to that guy. Tell us more about Dante. That accent is so yummy."

"He's…um, from Italy." Maybe she shouldn't have shared that? It was hard to censor herself with her sisters but denying the obvious would've been a red flag. "And yes, that accent was the first thing to grab my attention. Followed by his obvious good looks," she added with a blush.

"Can't blame you. Who isn't a sucker for a good accent?" Ruby said. "Well, it's official, you have to bring him to family dinner soon. Mom is going to want to meet him, and it sounds like he and Fletcher have gotten off to a rocky start? So, sooner rather than later would be great so we can help smooth out any bumps."

Rocky wasn't the word for it, Frannie thought, shifting with discomfort. Fletcher knew the whole truth about Dante, and she hoped he kept that information private.

She was nervous about Fletcher and Dante talking without a buffer, but she could only hope her brother kept a level head and Dante didn't say or do anything to make Fletcher regret trusting him.

Chapter 26

Dante walked into the small police station, determined to resolve this without creating more problems between himself and Frannie's brother. She was so close to her family he didn't want to become a wedge, even though he knew it was probably inevitable.

They weren't going to be happy when he and Frannie split town. He would look like the bad guy, and there was no getting around that.

But he didn't have to hasten that opinion by creating friction with Fletcher.

He checked in at the front desk, but Fletcher saw him come in and waved him over to his desk.

"You showed up," Fletcher said with surprise, hitting him with the full measure of suspicion he probably deserved.

"I told you I would."

"Well, forgive me if I don't exactly trust your word right now," Fletcher said. "Have a seat."

Dante bit his tongue and levered himself into the uncomfortable metal chair opposite Fletcher. "I'll tell you everything I know."

"You're damn right you will," Fletcher said. "Start at the beginning. How'd you know that guy was at the shop?"

"I didn't." If he told Fletcher that his PI had been following the guy, he'd ask why and that would open a can of worms. Instead, he said, "I usually stop in to see Frannie at some point during the day. It's part of our routine."

Fletcher didn't seem to like any mention of Dante and Frannie's relationship, which made Dante wonder if he'd been this protective when her ex-boyfriend was out there cheating on her or if he was reserving this attitude just for Dante.

"Then what happened?"

"I saw a guy dragging Frannie down the short hallway to the back door and chased him down, punched him in the face and then subdued him. After I realized he wasn't going anywhere, I checked on Frannie while calling 911. Then you guys arrived. That's the long and short of it."

"How'd you know it was a guy from Frannie's college?"

"She'd mentioned him."

"Did you know him?"

"No."

"Then how'd you know it was him?"

My PI told me. "A hunch."

"Guess it was a pretty solid hunch."

"Guess so."

"Also pretty lucky."

Dante leaned forward, finished with the tough cop routine when he wasn't the enemy. "Look, we can be enemies if you want but it'll just make things harder on Frannie and I don't think either of us want that. I love your sister. Seeing that asshole try to drag her unconscious body down a hallway made me see red. I've never been a violent man, but in that moment, I was willing to go to hell if he hurt her. I'm just grateful that I caught him in time before he managed to get her into his car."

At Dante's blunt statement, Fletcher stilled, as if the

importance of what mattered just slammed him upside the temple. All this male posturing was immaterial after realizing they'd all come too close to losing the woman they all loved.

That was the thing, Frannie was a gem. She was kind, compassionate, funny and wise—it was hard to find anyone who didn't find her delightful—which made him feel ugly for selfishly needing her to leave with him.

Fletcher exhaled a heavy breath, frowning as he admitted, "I get that you care about my sister. That much I can see is true. But I can't wrap my head around the other stuff. I'm an officer of the law—integrity matters—and when someone's guilty of lying about something big, chances are, they'll lie about something small. And I make it a point to avoid entertaining liars in my life. But when my baby sister loves someone who's admitted to lying…it puts me in a bad spot. Do you get what I'm saying?"

It was the first honest dialogue between him and Fletcher, and Dante sensed taking advantage of the fragile moment was necessary. "I don't blame you. If I had a sister, I'd feel similarly protective. You already know my family is problematic and I was trying to distance myself from their influence. But it doesn't wipe away the fact that I did lie—to many people for many reasons—and I understand your knee-jerk reaction to keep Frannie away from me."

"Great. So at least we understand each other. But where does that leave the situation?"

The situation would resolve itself as soon as he and Frannie left town, but for now, he wanted justice. "How about we focus on the guy who tried to kidnap Frannie? We can figure out the rest later."

"The investigation is just starting but we've got a detective chasing down the man's background, etc. He's in custody and that's where he'll stay until he's arraigned."

"Unless he posts bail."

"Not likely. Frannie used to babysit for the judge's family. Once this case crosses his desk, he'll set the bail as high as possible and I doubt the guy is rolling in a family trust. He can cool his jets in a jail cell until then."

That was good news, at least. Small-town connections could be a blessing at times.

"If you're running from your family, my guess is you're not planning to stay in Owl Creek for long. What happens then? You gonna break my sister's heart when you bail? Or are you trying to talk my sister into bailing with you?"

The man was too clever. He saw more than he shared and used his "country cop" routine to create the illusion of a dull-minded man—which he was not.

When Dante remained silent, Fletcher shook his head. "Look, man, I'll level with you. Frannie is an adult and she's capable of making her own decisions. But her heart is soft, possibly too soft for what you've got planned and I don't want to see her get hurt. Understand? So, if you're planning to leave town…do it when she's at the shop and just go. Let her move on with her life if you can't offer her a real chance at happiness. Because my sister deserves more than scraps from a man who can't offer nothing but pain and heartache."

Dante swallowed, knowing that Fletcher was right. What was he offering Frannie? Asking her to leave everything she knew for an uncertain future as he ran from his family, leapfrogging from one town to another, only one step ahead of his uncle each day? Was that fair?

That was no life for a woman like her. She deserved the best kind of life where she was cherished *and* safe.

"I would never hurt her," Dante said, though the promise tasted hollow.

"Maybe not intentionally, but you already admitted you're on the run. I don't see how this ends any way but bad."

"I never meant to fall in love with her," he said as if that improved the situation. "I tried to keep some distance between us."

Fletcher seemed sympathetic, saying with a knowing glance, "Oh, I know Frannie can be persistent when she gets something in her head—trust me, I know—but sometimes she doesn't know what kind of trouble she's stepping into because she only sees the good in people. It's one of her best qualities but it sure keeps her family on their toes."

Dante chuckled, Fletcher's words giving him a rare glimpse into what may have been young Frannie's life—protected by a wall of siblings, all the while skipping right into trouble without a second thought. "That's probably what drew that creep straight to her," Dante murmured.

"Likely. Frannie always did love championing an underdog."

Was that what he was to Frannie? The underdog in her eyes? Someone she needed to champion?

He ought to be the one being the champion for her.

Again, he was struck by the fear that he was repeating a loop from his parents.

His father had dragged his mother down a path littered with thorns, not realizing how each step left his mother cut and bruised until she was willing to do anything to be safe again.

The desk phone rang, and Fletcher gestured for Dante to hold up a minute, then answered. His expression darkened as he listened, his jaw hardening. "You're kidding me," he said, shaking his head. Blowing a long breath, he said, "Thanks for letting me know, man. Keep me posted." He hung up and turned to Dante. "That was the detective assigned to Frannie's case."

Dante waited, instantly tense. "What did he find out?"

"That was one helluva hunch," he repeated, eyeing Dante with fresh speculation. "The detective just found a fortified room in Allen Burns's house. Looks like he was planning for a reluctant guest."

"What does that mean?" Dante asked.

"It means that man planned on kidnapping Frannie and holding her hostage for a long time. The sick bastard had shackles bolted into the wall and a bucket in the corner. Holy hell…"

Just like Fletcher, Dante reeled from that intel. He wouldn't have known to get to the shop if he'd missed Nick's call. A delay of even a few minutes could have doomed Frannie to a nightmarish hellscape.

"Tell me how you knew."

Dante didn't want to lie to Fletcher. He was walking the razor's edge with the truth, and it didn't matter that he had a good reason—because more lies just made him look more guilty than he already did in Fletcher's eyes.

"Take a walk with me," Dante said, rising.

Fletcher frowned but agreed, motioning toward the back door. He punched in the security code and stepped outside the building. Once alone in the vehicle yard, Fletcher asked, "Okay, what's with the field trip?"

"My dishonesty has only ever been grounded in necessity. The fewer people who know what's going on, the safer they'll be. You're Frannie's favorite brother. I didn't want to put you in a dangerous position, but it looks like there's no way to fully clear the air between us without the full truth."

"Seems about right," Fletcher agreed, waiting. "So what's the full truth?"

"I knew about Allen Burns because I had my PI looking into him when Frannie started getting weird flower deliveries."

"Go on."

"First, it was a bouquet delivered to her shop. She thought they were from me. When I told her I hadn't sent the flowers, we tried to find out who sent them, but they were sent anonymously through an internet company using a local florist. Frannie waved it off, thinking it was a harmless mistake or maybe even from one of her friends who thought it might be funny to prank her. I didn't find the humor and wanted her to report it, but she said she didn't want to put more on your plate given what your family has been going through."

"That's Frannie, always looking out for everyone else."

"Then, after spending the day on the lake, we got back to her place and there was a single flower laid on her pillow, deliberately placed there for her to find. That was the final straw for me. I didn't want her staying alone after that, but she still didn't want to make a report."

"Damn it, Frannie," Fletcher swore under his breath. "Yeah, those were definite red flags. I knew that was a mistake but Frannie can be real stubborn when she wants to be."

"Well, hindsight and all that. Now we know Allen was the one stalking her, waiting for the right moment to grab her."

Fletcher nodded. "So, why the secrecy? Why'd we have to come outside for you to tell me this?"

"There's more."

Fletcher braced himself. "All right, go ahead."

"The reason my PI was looking into Burns was to either confirm or rule him out. The thing is, Owl Creek isn't safe anymore—for me or Frannie. After my brake line was cut—"

"Hold up, there hasn't been a report completed yet about your car. How do you know it wasn't just a faulty manufacturer issue?"

"Because my PI got a hold of the mechanic shop contracted to go over the vehicle and there was a clear cut in the line. It was deliberately sabotaged. There's only one reason that could happen and it has everything to do with my family. They won't stop until they get what they want."

"What do they want, exactly?"

"Either I come home with my tail between my legs and agree to rejoin the Santoro family or die. There are no in-betweens with my uncle."

Fletcher whistled low. "And I thought *my* dad was a prick. Your uncle sounds like a peach."

"Yeah, that's one word for him. But my point is, he won't stop. Not until he gets what he wants."

"What's stopped him to this point?"

"Aside from the fact that I keep staying one step ahead? I have something of great value to him with the power to destroy the Santoro reputation. My uncle will do anything to get that piece of leverage back."

"I'm dying to know what it is that you've got but my sense of self-preservation keeps my curiosity in check. All I'm gonna say is, I hope you have it in a safe place."

"I do."

Fletcher sighed, shaking his head as if unsure what to do with all that information, but at least he'd lost that suspicion in his stare. That was something.

"Okay, here's the deal," Fletcher said after a pause. "I don't know why—and I hope it doesn't bite me in the ass—

but I'll take a chance and trust you're being truthful this time. I don't know how to solve your problem with your family. But I can tell you if you want to have a life with my sister, you'd better find a solution more solid than being on the run until the end of your days, because Frannie isn't cut out for that life."

Dante knew that. God, he knew.

All he could say was, "I'm working on it," because it was the truth, but even Dante knew that wasn't nearly good enough.

Chapter 27

Frannie finished getting dressed. She was folding her hospital gown neatly when her mother's voice nearly made all three Colton sisters jump like guilty schoolchildren caught sneaking candy from the teacher's desk.

"Francesca!"

"Mom!" Frannie's hand flew to her chest to keep it from plopping from her sternum. "You scared the crap out of me."

To her shock, Jenny pulled Frannie straight to her for a tight hug as if she were terrified to let go. "I just heard what happened." She released Frannie only to glare at her other two daughters. "And why did I have to hear about it from Hettie Long, the biggest gossip in town, while picking up a package at the post office? Hmm? Neither of you could've picked up the phone and let me know what happened to my youngest daughter? Honestly, shame on you both."

"Mom, it happened so fast... I was going to call but I thought maybe it was something Frannie should tell you in person," Ruby said, looking to her sisters for help. "It wasn't like we weren't going to tell you."

Frannie came to Ruby's rescue. "Beyond a nasty headache and the sudden urge to take some self-defense classes, I'm fine. Don't be mad at Ruby and Hannah."

"Yeah, don't be mad at us," Hannah piped in.

"I'm not mad, I'm just…gosh darn it, Francesca, don't you ever worry me like that again!"

And then Frannie saw the misplaced anger for what it truly was—fear. She swallowed, softening. "Mama, I'm okay and the guy responsible is sitting in jail. Don't worry, crisis averted."

A tear escaped Jenny's eye, and she wiped at it quickly, nodding. "Yes, of course. I'm just rattled, is all. Hettie made it sound so…" she huffed a short breath, looking for clarification "…well, dramatic."

"To be fair, it was kinda dramatic," Ruby said. "Some weirdo tried to kidnap Frannie by knocking her out with chloroform."

Frannie swallowed, flushing with the terrible memory. "Yeah, definitely in my top three most horrible experiences. Zero stars—I do not recommend."

"This isn't funny. Don't you dare make jokes," Jenny scolded with an appalled expression. "This kind of thing isn't a laughing matter. Who is this man who rescued you? I need to personally thánk him."

Oh, boy, she thought introducing Dante to her mom would go a lot differently, but there was no escaping the moment. "Mom, I would love for you to meet Dante. He's my, um, boyfriend."

Jenny's eyes widened. "Boyfriend? You're seeing someone?"

"That's what she just said," Hannah quipped.

"You pipe down. I'm not in the mood for any sass," Jenny returned sharply.

Hannah shared a look with Ruby and said, "Well, if there's no sass allowed, I'm out because that's pretty much what I'm made of." Despite her statement, she brushed Jenny's cheek with a quick kiss and made her exit. But not before making a telephone gesture to Frannie, mouthing, "Call me," and blowing her an air kiss.

"Good going, Mom, you chased off Hannah," Ruby said dryly. "Are you happy?"

Jenny waved off Ruby's comment, more concerned with Frannie. "Darling, are you sure you're okay?"

"I'm fine."

Ruby looked at her watch. "Mom, if you want to drive Frannie home, I'll go back to the clinic."

Jenny shook her head. "I wish I could but I'm filling in for a night-shift nurse tonight. I have a private patient in Connors."

"Travel nursing now?" Frannie asked, surprised.

"Only here and there. I'm only doing this as a personal favor for a friend. If I could cancel I would. I don't think you should be alone."

"I won't be alone," she assured her mom, returning to the subject of Dante. "My knight in shining armor will be with me and he won't let anything happen."

"He stays the night?" Jenny asked, mildly troubled, as if Frannie hadn't lived with her ex-boyfriend before he became a cheating turd. "Francesca, is that wise? How well do you know this man?"

"I know him well enough to know that he's the real deal and I think I'm going to marry him. Don't worry, Mom, you'll love him. He's terrific."

Jenny looked like she didn't know what to say—caught between gratitude for Dante saving her daughter's life and the discomfort of acknowledging her daughter had an adult sex life—but she accepted Frannie's decision. She looked at Ruby. "You've met this man?"

"Yes. Today, actually. He's really good-looking," Ruby said with an approving wink at Frannie.

"That's the least important thing," Jenny said, dismissing Ruby's assessment. "Character matters more than what's on the outside."

"Yes, because character was what you were most concerned with when you met Dad," Ruby retorted, calling Jenny out for her hypocrisy.

Jenny had the grace to blush as she settled her purse more securely on her shoulder, preparing to leave. "Please take it easy. You've been chemically assaulted. You need to rest."

"I will," Frannie promised.

"I'll expect to meet this knight at Sunday dinner, yes?"

"Can't wait."

Jenny kissed Frannie on the cheek, then Ruby, and left.

Ruby exhaled a long breath, shaking her head. "Will I ever understand our mother?"

"I don't think any of us will. It's part of her charm—the mystery."

"Is that what that's called?" Ruby pretended to consider Frannie's answer, then remarked, "No, I think it's called 'emotionally distant.'"

"Cut her some slack, Ruby. She's going through a lot. Hell, I think we're all going through a lot."

"Yeah, but you officially win with the 'almost kidnapped' thing. No one else had that on their Bingo card. You're so damn competitive," Ruby teased, poking at Frannie gently. "Okay, let's get out of here."

"Sounds good to me. Can we get a milkshake on the way home? I'm craving sugar."

"Anything you want, sissy."

Frannie smiled, refusing to let any bit of sadness pull at her knowing that she had no idea if Sunday dinner would happen. For all she knew, Dante would have them on the road before the weekend hit.

And she had mixed feelings about that.

She loved Dante—but she loved her family, too.

Fate was cruel to make her choose who she loved more.

Dante finished with Fletcher, still at odds at how easily the tables might've turned the opposite way, and the tension cording his shoulders made him want to punch something. The fact that Frannie had been in danger was more than he could stomach.

He loved her more than anyone.

It was an odd thing to love another human being more than yourself. He thought he'd known true love with Belinda, but now, he knew what he'd felt with Belinda had only been a test run for the real thing.

He'd always care for Belinda, but his feelings for Frannie made him want things he had no business daring to dream about.

Marriage. Kids. A home.

None of that was in his future—even with Frannie by his side, he couldn't give her those things.

It wouldn't be fair to any children they might bring into this world.

But Frannie as a mother? His heart stuttered as fresh longing made the pain of future loss worse.

If he weren't such a bastard, he'd walk away now, but he couldn't.

He'd do anything to make her happy, but it would always be temporary, with a life on the run.

What was he doing?

What was he asking of her?

To leave everything she knew? To go where?

He didn't have the goddamn answers, and it killed him that he couldn't offer much more than his body at night and a promise that he would love her forever, even if he couldn't provide the beautiful life she deserved.

Detouring sharply, he ran into the local florist shop and purchased their biggest bouquet. The last time Frannie had received flowers was from that lunatic. He wanted her to have something beautiful from him to wipe away the terrible memory.

His cell rang. He picked up as soon as he saw it was Nick.

"They have him in custody. Thank you," he said with gratitude. "If it weren't for your call…" He didn't like to finish the thought. It tortured him enough. "Anyway, I appreciate your diligence."

"I'm glad it all worked out," Nick said, switching gears quickly. "I got something you're going to want to know. It's about your parents."

"What is it?"

"On a hunch, I did a deep dive into your mother's finances before she died. I found something that you might find upsetting."

Dante braced himself. "Go on."

"I think your mother had a relationship with your uncle long before your father died."

"What do you mean?"

"I found deposits going back two years from an international bank account in an account only registered to your mother. I traced the deposits, and they are registered to an account owned by your uncle. Do you know of any reason why your uncle would be sending your mother money?"

He didn't, but he was beginning to realize his mother had many secrets.

Was there anything from his childhood that rang true anymore?

His father had been troubled, but he always assumed it was caused by the burden of staying on the run.

Now he wondered if his father had known that his wife regretted choosing a life with him.

Adult relationships were complex, but in his young heart, he'd just wanted his parents to love each other as they once had.

Too bad it didn't always work out that way.

With both of his parents gone, only one person could answer his questions—but even when he was on good terms with his uncle, Lorenzo had refused to answer anything about the past.

Particularly about his brother.

Dante didn't know how to think about any of this anymore.

"Thank you," he said, needing to think. "I'll be in touch."

He clicked off and headed to Frannie's.

But as he pulled onto the street, he saw a car he didn't recognize parked in the driveway.

Perhaps Ruby had stayed until he returned?

His gut tingled in warning. Something felt off.

The old truck rumbled to a stop, and he left the flowers behind until he could ensure that all was well.

His paranoia was on full alert.

He couldn't explain it, but each step closer to the front door filled him with cold dread.

It was probably one of her many family members, he tried to reason, but as he opened the front door, he realized his first instinct had been right.

His uncle's men had found him.

And they were screwed.

The situation had just escalated to panic, and he didn't know how to save Frannie.

Time to find a way.

Chapter 28

Frannie waved as Ruby pulled out of her driveway and disappeared. Her stomach was full of vanilla milkshake, and her headache had subsided slightly, but there remained a dull ache that she assumed sleep would take care of.

As she watched Ruby drive away, she noted how right Dante was about her neighborhood. It really was a ghost town of empty houses. She'd never noticed before, but now she felt suddenly insecure. Letting her blinds down, she went to lock the front door, hoping Dante would show up soon.

Don't be a ninny, she told herself when goose bumps rioted along her forearm for no good reason. Except…all those times when she'd talked herself down in the past and felt watched, it had been valid because Allen *had* been watching.

She still couldn't shake the heebie-jeebies knowing that Allen had watched her sleep, had seen her naked, peeping through her bedroom window while she slept.

Like she'd told her sisters, the man who'd walked into her shop hadn't been the man she'd befriended all those years ago. What had happened to curdle an otherwise nice man? Human psychology had always fascinated her, but she hadn't wanted to face a genuinely disturbed person like she had today.

Rubbing her arms briskly, suffering a chill even though it was warm outside, she couldn't shake her jumpiness. She headed to the kitchen for a glass of water, her mouth still tasting like she'd drunk a chemical martini. But before she got there, a large, square-shaped man stepped into view, shocking the sense out of her.

Before she could scream, an arm clamped around her throat and cut off her airway like an iron bar was pressing against her windpipe. "No screaming," a voice instructed in a thick Italian accent that left no room for misunderstanding. "I can snap your neck before you take another breath," he warned.

I'm having the worst day of my life, she thought desperately. Surely there was some universal rule that you couldn't face mortal peril twice in one day?

"Stop wriggling and I'll let you breathe."

Compelling offer. She stopped struggling, and the grip around her neck loosened, allowing her to draw a gasping breath.

The man from the kitchen gestured for his accomplice to bring Frannie to the dining room. She was forcibly shoved into a chair, her hands and feet tied tightly, while he roughly emptied her purse on the kitchen table, pawing through her belongings as if he had the right.

"I don't have any money," she said, pretending to be ignorant of who they were.

He ignored her, grabbing her cell phone and pulling the SIM card to snap it in half before tossing the remnants to the floor.

Frannie cried in outrage, "Hey! That phone is new!" but he didn't seem to care about personal property. As she started to call him out, he pulled a gun from his back waistband, and her rebuke died on her tongue.

He checked his watch as if he had more pressing things to do than terrorize small-town bookstore owners, and asked sharply, "When will Mr. Santoro arrive?"

"Um, who?" Frannie feigned confusion. It was a long shot, but Frannie wasn't above trying every angle she could think of to buy time or delay a truly awful end. "I don't know—"

"Your lover, Dante," the man cut in, annoyed with her clumsy attempt at deception. She'd make a terrible spy. It always looked so much easier in the movies. Also, she wished she'd paid better attention to how to escape a dangerous situation. "We know he stays with you every night. When will he be here?"

"And how would you know that?" she asked, wrinkling her nose. "Are you some kind of pervert? Were you peeping through the windows, too?"

"Answer the question."

"I don't know," she lied, wishing he hadn't broken her phone. Although she wasn't sure how she could warn Dante away, given her current situation.

"Have you ever experienced the exquisite agony of toothpicks shoved beneath the nail bed?"

She felt the blood drain from her face. "Um, can't say that I have. Doesn't sound like something I would be into. You do you, though. I try not to judge."

"You think you can joke your way out of this?" the man asked, unamused.

"Judging by the stone-cold look on your face, probably not," she admitted. "But you can't blame me for trying. Sometimes a good laugh can ease the tension." *And I tend to ramble when I'm nervous.*

"My patience is growing thin. When is Mr. Santoro coming?"

She could play stupid for a few more minutes or just

cut to the chase. "You're... Dante's family?" she pretend-guessed.

A dark brow went up. "Family? No. Hired by the family to bring Dante home. His family is quite concerned about his absence."

That's a crock of crap. "In my experience, family doesn't try to force members to come home if they don't want to."

The man shrugged. "Different kind of family."

Frannie bit her lip before asking, "Are you going to kill me?" Might as well end the suspense.

"Depends."

The simple answer belied the horror of the moment. Her life meant next to nothing to this man. She was no more significant than an ant beneath his shoe. *Well, screw him.* If she were going down, she'd go down without begging. Hopefully, the end was fast and didn't make a huge mess. Lifting her chin, she said, "I believe in reincarnation. I plan to come back as something with very sharp teeth and will hunt you down like a monster out of a horror movie. Just letting you know—so choose wisely."

"Either you are mentally unhinged, or you have a lot of spirit. I cannot decide which."

"And I can't decide if that's a compliment," she returned, refusing to be cowed, even though she was trembling inside. The thing about facing down your potential death twice in one day, it did something to you. Maybe she was still reeling from the chemicals in her system, but she felt oddly detached from everything, which gave her a different level of clarity bordering on recklessness. "Dante is a good man. He doesn't want any part of the Santoro legacy. Why can't you leave him alone?"

"Not my business. I was hired to bring him home. Nothing

was said about a plus-one, so either shut up or offer something useful."

"You're a bully," Frannie muttered but pressed her lips together when the man shot her a dangerous look. She sensed she'd end up in a ditch if she pushed her luck any further.

"I'm a businessman," he clarified, going to stand by the window to watch for Dante.

"So, you're in the business of terrorizing people?" she asked.

"I'm in the business of solutions."

"And Dante is a problem that needs solving?"

"Quiet," he ordered, stepping away from the blinds to stand closer to Frannie. "Your lover is here. If you're wise, you'll encourage Mr. Santoro to come quietly without trouble. I'd rather not make a mess that will require substantial cleanup."

Cleanup. She swallowed, imagining her insides painting her living room from the close-range impact of the bullet sending her soul into the hereafter. "Yeah, that would suck for you," she murmured caustically. "Or, you could just turn over a new leaf and walk away from a life of soul-stealing crime and spend the rest of your days atoning for all of the terrible things you've probably done under the guise of 'following orders.' Life is about choices—"

The sudden pain of her hair being ripped from her scalp as his associate buried his hand in her hair, yanking it hard, stole her breath. "You were told to be silent," the man reminded her in disgust. "American women do not know when to shut up."

Son of a bitch, that hurt. She blinked back tears as her scalp throbbed in time with the fresh pain in her skull. This had to be the worst day of her life.

And then the door opened—and Dante walked in.

"Hello, Mr. Santoro."

* * *

Dante froze, his blood turning instantly to ice as he took in the situation.

"Hi, honey, we have guests," Frannie said with a pained smile, her neck pulled at an uncomfortable angle.

Dante recognized Benito Ricci, the man holding the gun and watching his every move, as one of his uncle's hired men.

"You are a hard man to find," Benito said conversationally.

"Get your man's hand off my girl," he growled.

"You're not in a position to make demands," Benito said. "You've caused much trouble."

Dante held Benito's stare, promising violence without saying a word. After a long moment, Benito nodded to his associate, who released Frannie's hair. "What do you want?"

"It's very simple. Time to stop playing games and come home."

"My home is here."

"Your home is with your family."

"My family died."

Benito looked annoyed at this back-and-forth. "I'm tired of this ugly country—the language, the customs, the mouthy women, the terrible food—all trash. I cannot imagine what you find here more appealing than Italy."

"We're not exactly jumping for joy having you on American soil, either," Frannie muttered. "You're ruining Italian culture for me, buddy. Previously, I was a big fan."

Benito ignored Frannie, returning to Dante. "You will come with us with zero fuss. Your uncle has arranged for a private plane transport in Boise. He is most eager to put all this nastiness behind him, but first, I need you to procure what you stole."

"That's what he really wants, isn't it? Not me."

Benito shrugged as if that didn't matter to him either way. "The job is to bring you and the item you stole, home. That's what I intend to do."

"And if I don't want to return with you?"

"Then, things get *less* civilized," he answered, shifting his gaze pointedly to Frannie, and Dante knew how precarious Frannie's life was in that moment. "Aside from her constant yapping, she's not offensive to the eye. Perhaps with time, she could be trained to be a suitable Santoro wife, but my guess is that it's more efficient to start fresh with a good Italian woman."

"If anyone's offensive, it's you," Frannie shot back, mindless of the danger but making the situation much more difficult for Dante to save her life. "Also, you dress like a B-movie goon. I thought Italians had more style."

"I could cut out her tongue," Benito suggested as if he found that option more enticing by the minute. "Or perhaps a finger…"

Belinda's ruined hands flashed in his memory, and it took everything in Dante not to spring at the man's throat and rip it out with his bare hands.

Frannie's eyes widened as she swallowed, but she wisely remained quiet.

His options were slim for success. If his only play was to do what he could to keep Frannie safe, he'd take it.

He mentally calculated the odds of success if he rushed Benito for the gun in his hand and found them dismally small. He didn't want Frannie to get hurt, but he had a sinking suspicion that Frannie wouldn't leave this place alive if he didn't use his head to negotiate.

Purposefully relaxing his shoulders, he shoved his hands in his pockets as if casually discussing the latest stock news.

"Civilized, eh? Sure, let's discuss how this might enfold if I were open to negotiating terms. Perhaps I'm tired of running and I'm ready to put this all behind me, but not until I know the terms are beneficial."

"Negotiate?" Benito wagged the gun. "Does it look like you're in a position to negotiate? I hold all the cards."

The hell you do. "Call Pietro."

Benito narrowed his gaze with suspicion. "And why would I do that?"

"Because you have no authority to make deals—he does."

"No, you'll get your things, and we'll leave as planned or I'll put a bullet in your lover's annoying head."

Dante held his ground. "Call Pietro. Now."

"Or what?" Benito asked, looking bored.

"Just do it."

Benito's arrogant confidence faltered as he met Dante's unwavering stare. The Santoro stare was legendary—Dante had certainly perfected it before discovering how deep his family's corruption went and why the stare instilled fear in anyone on the receiving end. Benito swore under his breath before tucking his gun in his back waistband and punching a number on his cell. "He wants to speak to you," he said when Pietro picked up, then handed Dante the cell.

"Yes?"

"I'll come home on one condition—Frannie isn't harmed, not a single hair on her head, got it?"

"You'll bring the documents?"

The evidence in his safety-deposit box was his only ace and leverage, but he wouldn't let Frannie get hurt over this. "Yes," he answered tersely. "But I swear if anything happens to Frannie…"

"You have my word, she'll be unharmed—as long as

you hold up your end of the bargain. Your uncle is eager to end this."

"Yeah, I bet he is," he growled, hating that his uncle had won, no matter what. "Tell my uncle's men." He shoved the phone back at Benito.

Benito listened, clicking off with a curt, "Yes, sir," his annoyance probably marred with misgiving at leaving a loose end. That was not how things were done in his line of work. "Untie her," he said, shaking his head. "I'll be in the car. Make your goodbyes quick. I want to be on the road in five minutes."

Dante watched them leave, then went to Frannie as she rubbed her raw wrists, scowling even as she jumped into his arms, whispering, "Good thinking! We can slip out the back—"

"No, Frannie," he said firmly, pulling her free to stare into her beautiful eyes, memorizing the sight of her so he'd never forget he'd once been lucky enough to be loved by her. "I have to go with them."

"What? No! That was just a ruse, right? You can't go with them. You said your uncle wants you *dead*. I won't let you go. That's suicide!"

"I love you, Frannie," he said, ignoring her protests. "I always knew it would come down to this, but I never imagined I might fall in love with someone like you along the way. You deserved so much better—"

"No! Stop it, I won't listen to that crap," she whispered fiercely, her eyes tearing up. "I won't let you go. You're not thinking clearly. We can slip out the back…and… I don't know, run to the neighbor's house and call 911 or something."

"Listen to me," he said, gripping her arms and giving her a sharp shake to get her attention. "They will *kill* you and I'll still have to go with them. Don't you understand? I'm out of options. I'm purchasing your safety by leaving with them. It's the only thing I can do to ensure that you're not hurt. Let me do this for you. If something happened to you…I couldn't live with myself. Please, Frannie."

She crumpled at his pleading, wrapping her arms around him as she started to sob. "Please, Dante…please don't do this!"

He knew there was no other way. His uncle played by rules Frannie couldn't even fathom. She was part of a soft and kind world, whereas his was cruel and manipulative.

Dante felt the ticking clock. Gently disengaging Frannie's grip around his neck, he kissed her deeply, then cupped her face, leaving her with firm instructions. "Do not try to follow us, and do not give my uncle any reason to even think of you after this moment. Promise me."

"I can't," she cried, shaking her head.

"You must promise me, Frannie," he said, blinking back his tears. "I can't live with the thought of you being in danger. I need to know you'll be safe. Please do this for me."

Frannie didn't want to, but she slowly nodded with a choked, "I promise."

Walk away, the voice told him, and he dragged himself away from Frannie. Turning on his heel, he walked out the door, afraid to look back and see her crushed expression, knowing she might grow to hate him because of this moment, but she'd be alive.

And that had to be enough.

He was returning to Italy.

Time to put an end to all of this.

Once and for all.

Chapter 29

Frannie didn't know how long she sat in the dark of her living room, reliving the moment Dante had walked away, but her toes were numb from the cramped position, and the crusted salt from her dried tears made her face feel tight and gritty.

Rising with the stiff gait of an eighty-year-old woman with arthritis, she hobbled to the kitchen to rinse her face and drink a glass of water. Her brain wasn't working, but her heart was working overtime. Waves of pain and grief washed over her as she ran headlong into the realization that Dante wasn't coming back.

Worse, he'd sacrificed himself to save her.

Her head throbbed, reminding her she'd been attacked twice in one day, but the physical pain was nothing compared to the emotional anguish crushing her soul.

She didn't know what to do. Dante had made her promise, but she didn't care about promises made under duress. Except she knew next to nothing about Dante's family besides what he'd told her—and that had been as little as possible due to the circumstances.

She knew relatively little about Dante besides how he liked to sleep, how he brushed his teeth and loved to make her feel special and cherished.

A trapped sob threatened to burst from her chest as she

leaned over the sink, bracing herself as she tried to weather the pain.

She had to talk to someone. Damn it, her phone was in pieces, and she didn't have a landline. With shaking hands, she scooped up the spilled contents of her purse, slid them back into her bag, grabbed her keys and left the house.

She could not sleep in that bed tonight when it smelled like Dante. His absence would only remind her that he was truly gone.

Driving straight to Darla's house, she pounded on the front door, not caring that she was a mess and making a racket when everyone else in the neighborhood was trying to sleep.

Tom, Darla's fiancé, opened the door holding a bat, ready to use whoever's head to hit a home run, but when he saw Frannie, he immediately set the bat down and ushered her inside. "Darla!" he called out, adding with concern, "Frannie needs you!"

Darla came around the corner with an anxious frown, wearing a robe, her hair tucked in a silk hair wrap and a mint green face mask slathered on her face. "What's going on?" she asked, collecting Frannie in a hug as she sagged against her.

She smelled of coconut and pinto beans, which was an odd combination and made Frannie think of the time in junior high when they'd tried to tie-dye their shirts using all-natural ingredients instead of the actual dye. It had been a mess, and all they'd accomplished was a muddy mess that ruined two T-shirts.

"He's gone," Frannie sobbed, her body shaking as she let it all out. Tom left the room and silently returned with a washcloth so Darla could wipe away the gunk. There'd be no time for beauty rituals tonight.

"What do you mean?" she asked, casting Tom a grateful look as she quickly wiped her face. "Who's gone?"

"Dante," Frannie answered mournfully.

"Gone where?"

"Back to Italy."

"That jerk!"

"No," she said. "He was practically kidnapped, and there's nothing I can do about it because I promised I wouldn't."

"I'm sorry, run that by me again?"

Frannie didn't have the energy to go into details, so she gave the TL;DR version. "Dante was on the run from his big, scary family in Italy, but they found him and sent two awful goons to bring him back, using me as leverage." She sniffed back tears, which only made her head want to explode. She winced, adding, "Getting attacked twice in one day is overkill in the karma department. I swear I must've done something awful in a past life to be getting served up this plate of doo-doo in this one."

"*Attacked?* You were attacked?"

"Yeah, I was going to tell you tomorrow, but I never imagined that I might be ambushed when I got home. Allen Burns tried to kidnap me earlier today. Dante saved me, it was a whole thing...but in hindsight that was nothing in comparison to what was waiting for me when I got home."

"Are you kidding me right now? I can't wrap my head around any of this." Darla was visibly reeling, and Frannie didn't blame her, but she was too mentally strung out to soften the delivery.

"Me either, but it happened and let me tell you, stuff like this makes for great movies but it really sucks when it happens in real life!"

Tom, who usually left them to their conversations, had returned with a bottled water for Frannie and caught the tail end of her comment. He handed her the water and sat beside Darla. "Are you okay?" he asked tentatively. "Did they...hurt you?"

"No, nothing like that but the one guy nearly ripped the hair from my head and the other one threatened to cut my tongue out if I didn't stop talking. He, apparently, doesn't think much of our country and was really rude about it."

"And Dante just left with them?"

"He didn't have a choice. It was either leave with them, or they'd start breaking parts of me like they did to his ex-girlfriend."

"Geemini Christmas," Darla exclaimed in a horrified tone. "I can't believe this happened to you. Did you call Fletcher and make a report?"

"No, Dante made me promise not to," she said, feeling sheepish for not calling the police at the very least.

"Well, we can rectify that right now," Tom said, grabbing the phone. "How do you know they won't return and finish the job?"

"Because Dante talked to someone in charge and basically told them to stand down or else he wouldn't give his uncle something he wants really bad."

"Which is?"

"I have no idea."

"This is, like, spy shit," Darla said with the tiniest spark of wonder, as if she found it a little exhilarating even though she shouldn't, but Frannie didn't begrudge her fascination. She would've felt the same if she hadn't been living through it. "So, what happens now?"

"I don't know."

Darla grasped her hand and squeezed it. "No matter what, we're here for you."

"I know. I'm sorry I ruined your night. I couldn't stay at the house...not with Dante gone."

"You fell hook, line and sinker for him, didn't you?" Darla asked, shaking her head with sorrow at Frannie's suddenly watering eyes. She nodded, and Darla's expression melted with pure understanding and compassion. "Well, we just have to find a way to get him back."

"How?" Frannie asked plaintively. "Do you know anyone with the power to strong-arm one of the most dangerous families in Italy to return my boyfriend?"

"No, but you do have a cousin in the FBI. I'd start there. They might be interested in knowing what went down."

"But I promised Dante I wouldn't."

"Some promises aren't meant to be kept," Darla said, shrugging. "I know nothing would keep me from trying to rescue this guy," she said, reaching over to rub Tom's arm. "So, that's what you're going to do for your guy. Everything and anything. It might not work but it's worth a try. At least then you can say you did what you could."

Darla was right. She couldn't give up. Not yet.

"I'll call Max," she said, nodding firmly even though she couldn't quite see straight anymore. Fatigue, chemical warfare and emotional exhaustion had taken their toll, and the bill was due.

Darla took control, saying, "Absolutely—first thing tomorrow morning."

Tom rose. "I'll get the spare bedroom ready."

Frannie started to protest, but a yawn garbled her attempts, and all she could do was stare blearily at her best friend as her eyelids felt weighted with cement. "I suppose you're right," she conceded. "Tomorrow is a better plan."

Darla helped her up, and they walked together to the spare bedroom. Tom had just finished turning down the sheets like the most hospitable host at the most exclusive hotel, and she thanked Darla with a look.

And that was all that was needed.

Frannie crawled into the bed and dropped off before her head hit the pillow.

After a twelve-hour flight, Dante was back on home soil, and within the next hour, he was walking into his uncle's stately home.

Even though his eyes burned from lack of sleep, he went straight to his uncle's office, pushing open the door ahead of Benito and his accomplice, leaving them in his wake.

At one time, this had been his home—he'd had full run of the house—and it had been the first time he'd felt safe and secure.

He pushed away those memories and stared hard at his uncle Lorenzo, who, despite the circumstance, seemed pleased to see him.

"You're home."

"Don't," Dante warned.

Lorenzo's expression lost warmth, and he gestured for Benito and his accomplice to leave. Wordlessly, they exited the office and closed the double doors softly behind them.

"You've caused much trouble and strife, Dante," Lorenzo admonished as if he were lecturing an errant schoolboy caught breaking the rules. "I'm displeased with your lack of civility and loyalty to family. Your mother would be crushed to see what you've done."

At the mention of his mother, Dante stiffened, remembering the suspicious deposits over the years to his mother's account. "I need answers," he said coldly. "You wanted me home? Well, here I am. But this time, I want the truth."

"The truth about what?" Lorenzo asked, holding his stare unflinchingly.

"Did you have my father killed?"

"No."

Lorenzo didn't hesitate, nor did he react in a way that would suggest he was lying, but Dante had the evidence suggesting that someone had paid the investigating officer for a doctored investigation. "You're lying," he said to gauge his reaction.

"I'm not." Lorenzo sighed, leaning back in his soft leather chair as if resigned to the long overdue conversation. "Ask the question you're afraid to ask."

Fatigue burned behind his eyes, but he wouldn't leave his uncle's office until he had the answers to the questions eating him alive.

"If you didn't kill him...who did?"

"Your mother."

His world stopped turning. All he could do was stare, uncomprehending yet violently resisting the implication of his uncle's statement.

"No, she would never..."

"I'd hoped that you'd never ask this question. It's not something one should know about their parent. Your mother was a good woman but when pushed to the edge, even good people break."

"What would you know about good people?" Dante asked bitterly, reeling beneath the weight of the information.

"Just because I can't afford the luxury of goodness doesn't mean I don't know it in others," Lorenzo said quietly.

At that moment, Dante remembered how it felt to love this man, believe in him and wish he'd been his father instead of Matteo. After discovering the depth of Lorenzo's crimes, he'd been ashamed of ever wishing such a thing.

Now he didn't know what to think. He dropped heavily into the thick chair opposite his uncle, his brain swimming in a fog. "I don't understand," he said, trying to fit the pieces of this hellish puzzle together. "My mother loved my father."

"She did, but she'd wanted out long before your father's accident. He wouldn't let her. He threatened to take you and run, so that she never saw you again. She stayed for you. Not Matteo."

"My father ran because of you," he shot back, blaming Lorenzo. "He'd wanted a better life, a clean life for his family."

Lorenzo shrugged as if the reasons were immaterial to the outcome. "Whatever reasons he had, Georgia had lost any shared conviction, and soon after, her love for Matteo died. Behind closed doors, Matteo had become abusive—"

"My father wasn't a violent man," Dante retorted, refusing to believe it. Though a hazy memory of his mother crying behind closed doors and his father storming from the house returned to make him question what he thought he knew about his parents. He'd only been a kid—and a kid's memory was colored by the inexperience of their youth and a forgiving love for their parents.

"She wanted to get away from your father, but he kept you on the move so frequently that she couldn't save enough money to make it happen. She wrote me, asking for help."

"So you started sending her money," he surmised.

Lorenzo nodded.

"But why?"

"Isn't it obvious by now?" Lorenzo asked.

Yes, it was now. "You loved her," Dante said, closing his eyes, feeling sick. "You were in love with my mother."

"I could never refuse her anything."

"Did you conspire with her to kill my father?"

"No. There are some lines even I won't cross." He sighed.

"Your mother called me, told me what she'd done, and I helped take care of the problem."

That was the late-night phone call his mother received the night his father died—and why they were on a plane the following morning.

"Have I not given you everything Matteo should have?" Lorenzo asked stiffly, revealing a rare glimpse of his hidden wound. "I loved you as a son, and you betrayed me."

His uncle was right—he'd taken him in, treated him like a son, given him the best education and opportunity—but he'd hidden the true cost of that privilege until it was too late to refuse.

"You used my love for you as a weapon to keep me doing things that went against my conscience.'

To his surprise, Lorenzo conceded Dante's point. "Perhaps." He spread his hands in a conciliatory gesture, "I made mistakes in the moment that I wish I could take back."

It was the closest he would get to an apology from Lorenzo Santoro. Knowing what he knew now, there was no way Lorenzo had anything to do with his mother's accident. A cruel twist of fate had been responsible for the accident that had taken Georgia, or perhaps, karma had come for its due and delivered justice for her part in Matteo's death.

Either way, Lorenzo was guilty of many crimes, but neither Georgia's nor Matteo's death was one of them.

Dante pulled the envelope he'd taken from his uncle's vault and slid it over to him.

Lorenzo glanced at the envelope as if hating the contents but relieved to have it back in his possession, saying, "What happens now?"

Dante knew he couldn't stay. He didn't want the life Lorenzo had created for him, and he could never be like Lorenzo.

His uncle seemed to understand without Dante having to say the words.

Since Dante had left Italy, his uncle seemed to have aged ten years. Lorenzo had always been active and formidable, a robust man for his age. Now he appeared to be a shell of himself. Losing Georgia and now Dante was a blow he couldn't seem to recover from, and he'd lost the will to fight.

"I'm not cut out for the life you wanted for me," Dante said. "I'm not like you and I don't want to be."

"You're the Santoro heir," Lorenzo said as if that should matter to him. "You have an obligation—"

"No," Dante cut in, shaking his head. "Then, disown me. Cut me off. I don't care about the money. I will walk away from all of it, to be free of everything the Santoro name is attached to."

"You really mean that?" Lorenzo asked with a stiff upper lip. "You would walk away from your birthright?"

"Yes. If that's what it takes."

"What if I changed? Would that make you reconsider?"

Oddly, the offer hit Dante in a tender place, perhaps that place where fond memories of his uncle still lived. But he knew that even if Lorenzo's offer was sincere, his uncle was too set in his ways to make those kinds of changes in a meaningful way, and eventually, perhaps slowly, he'd revert to his old ways.

And he couldn't expose Frannie to this life.

"I've met someone. I want to make a life with her. A normal life, one where she doesn't have to look over her shoulder, wary of someone using her as leverage to get to you or me. She owns a bookstore and she's sweet and kind and compassionate—and not cut out for the cost of shouldering the Santoro legacy."

Lorenzo considered Dante's admission, and something

shifted in his expression. Perhaps he was thinking about how Georgia would've handled Dante's request, or maybe he was too tired to put up too much more of a fight to hold on to him.

"I will free you of your Santoro name so you can live your life as you choose," he said sighing heavily. "Your happiness is what your mother would've wanted. And if this is the only way I can give that to you...I will."

Dante swallowed, realizing what his uncle was sacrificing and why.

What may have begun as love for Georgia all those years ago had also changed into love for Dante.

Even if Lorenzo had shown it in ways that weren't all that loving.

Speaking of. "What you had done to Belinda..."

"Say no more." Lorenzo waved off any need to continue, shame in his eyes. "I'll ensure she's taken care of. She'll need for nothing. I swear it."

Dante believed him.

There was nothing more to say.

The rage that had lived in his heart for so long had burned away, leaving an empty hole that quickly filled with sadness and grief.

When he left Italy this time, he'd never return.

When he said his goodbyes this time, it was for good.

And they both understood what that meant.

"Thank you, *lo zio*."

Lorenzo gave an imperceptible nod, and Dante rose, walking away for one last time.

His uncle would never be a good man—but at one time, he'd been the best man in Dante's life.

And for that, there would always be a piece of Dante that loved Lorenzo like the father Matteo should've been.

Chapter 30

Frannie stared at Max, confused. "There has to be something you can do. Dante was practically kidnapped by his uncle's men, on American soil! Surely that's a crime? You said that the FBI had a file a mile long on the Santoro family. Here's your chance to bring them in, throw the book at them. Show them how America deals with international terrorists!"

"I'm not saying that a crime wasn't committed, but you said Dante went willingly with them. That doesn't sound like he was kidnapped."

Frannie glared. "They *forced* him to leave."

"At gunpoint?"

"No, but one of them *did* have a gun—and the other guy pulled my hair and threatened to cut out my tongue."

Max tried not to chuckle. It wasn't funny, but maybe in another situation, it would've been a little comical. However, there was nothing humorous about it in Frannie's eyes. "Look, you need to call the National Guard, the Army, or call the freaking president, for all I care. All I know is that I'm not going to sit here and do nothing while the future father of my children is being tortured by his awful, villainous uncle, okay? If I have to fly to Italy and find him myself, I will."

"I have no doubt you would try and in doing so, probably get yourself killed," Max said dryly. "Have you tried calling him?"

"I don't have his number and that stupid goon broke my SIM card." She perked up, remembering, "Hey, that's right, he broke my phone. That's a crime! Use that to extradite that jerk."

"Frannie… I can't deport a man for breaking your SIM card," Max said, trying to talk sense into her, but she had long since left rational behavior behind. She was frantic with worry and ready to hop on a plane to do something reckless if someone didn't help her rescue Dante.

"Please, Max…" she pleaded, needing something to calm her brain. "I'm losing it. I'm so worried."

Max relented, saying, "I'll make some calls, okay, but in the meantime, go home, take a long shower or a bath or something, and try to relax. You stewing isn't going to help Dante, okay?"

Of course, Max was right, but logic was not living in her head right now. She wanted action—she wanted the armed forces to storm the shores of Italy and rescue her beautiful Italian man. Yes, it was irrational and not grounded in reality, but she didn't care.

She just wanted Dante back.

"You don't understand. Dante told me what his uncle did to his ex-girlfriend and now she's living in Switzerland— no, *hiding* in Switzerland—trying to rebuild her life after she was maimed by Dante's uncle's goons! Now try and tell me that I'm overreacting."

Max sobered at this new information but was limited in what he could do. "Listen, I believe you. Dante is part of a dangerous family, but he willingly left the country. I can't just call up the Italian government and demand they hand over one of their citizens without a pretty big reason, and as much as I would love to help in any way possible, I don't know how."

"So that's it? I'm just supposed to sit back, hope for the best and basically move on with my life?"

Max tried a different perspective. "Maybe this is a blessing in disguise. Do you really want to be involved with someone who has ties to such dangerous people?"

It was solid advice—and if she were thinking straight, maybe it might've made a difference, but who could say they were thinking straight when they were in love? "Max... I love him, and I'm terrified. Please. Try and help him. I'll never ask another favor again if you do me this one solid."

Max took a long breath, shaking his head, but he agreed. "I'll make some calls, but I don't know if they'll go anywhere, okay?"

Frannie knew that when Max gave his word, he was good for it. She nodded. This was the best she could get. She had to hope it was enough.

Leaving Max's office, she headed back to Owl Creek to open the shop. The last thing she wanted to do was track inventory and smile with customers as if her world wasn't cracking apart, but it would provide a distraction, at the very least.

The practical side of her nature appeared, reminding her that she couldn't afford to let her business fold, no matter how her heart might be broken.

Just as she finished shelving her newest shipment—*How to Be a Boss Babe in 30 Days or Less*—her landline rang.

"Book Mark It," she answered, and smiled as she heard Darla's voice.

"Calling a landline is like being transported back to junior high before we had our cell phones and our parents insisted on keeping their old number for emergency services," Darla recalled with a nostalgic chuckle. "I kinda miss not being at everyone's beck and call. Anyway, any luck with Max?"

"It doesn't look promising. Max says the FBI can't just extradite from another country on the grounds of kidnapping if the kidnappee went willingly."

"Isn't coercion a thing?" Darla asked, incredulous. "Seems like that would be a thing."

"I thought so, but what do I know?"

"Well, if Max is on it, I feel confident he'll do his best." Frannie agreed, though it felt hopeless. "In the meantime, I'm trying to distract myself with work."

"How's that going?"

"Not great."

"Hang in there, something will work out."

"How?"

"I don't know but it seems like the right thing to say in a situation like this."

Leave it to Darla to coax a reluctant smile out of Frannie when she didn't want to laugh. "Thanks for letting me crash at your place last night. I slept like the dead."

"No problem. *Mi casa, su casa.*"

"Our senior Spanish teacher would be so proud you retained something from his class," Frannie quipped.

"Hey, I also retained a love of chile relleno, so I call that an educational win."

"Stop trying to cheer me up. It won't work."

"It's kinda working. I know you're trying not to laugh."

Caught. Darla knew her too well. "Okay, fine. But it feels wrong to laugh or feel any kind of joy right now when my boyfriend could be suffering unimaginable torment at the hands of his villainous uncle."

"Right, of course, but sometimes inappropriate laughter is the only thing that keeps us from running screaming into the streets when all hell breaks loose."

Fair point. "What would I do without you?"

"Aside from collapse into a dramatic heap, weeping and wailing, cursing the heavens for the cruel twist of fate? I haven't a clue. Thankfully, you'll never have to figure that out because you're stuck with me—and there is a bright side to all this drama…"

"Which is?"

"Since you're not skipping town and going on the run… you're back on maid-of-honor detail."

Frannie burst into laughter, realizing this was very true. "And what an honor it is," she replied with a roll of her eyes, but Darla was right. Life wasn't going to stop just because her heart was in pieces.

And it wasn't fair of her to ask Darla to put her life on hold because Frannie had fallen in love with a man who'd never been in a position to offer his heart.

Frannie ended the call and sat for a long moment, just trying to find her center again. *Breathe in, breathe out.* Calm and rational was her jam.

But one thought kept jamming her chill frequency.

Please be okay, Dante. Please find a way back to me.

It took several days for Pietro to finalize details of Dante's disownment, and in that time, he and his father's secretary had long talks about how things would work once he returned to the States.

"You're sure about this?" Pietro asked with a disapproving frown. "There's no turning back once this is done."

Dante knew what he was doing, and he was ready. "I am."

Pietro shook his head but finished putting the paperwork in order. "You will forfeit your inheritance aside from what your mother has already bequeathed, which is substantial but not enough for a lifetime. You'll have to go back to work."

"I don't have a problem with that. I hate being idle."

"Yes, you've always been industrious," Pietro said approvingly. "But why this dramatic move? Your uncle has agreed to change his ways...be the man you want him to be."

"Because it wouldn't last. He is who he is and he's too old to change his stripes—and it's not right of me to ask. Besides, the life I want to build with Frannie...is incompatible with my former life, and I choose her."

"What will you do in this new life?"

"Get my law degree to practice in the States, and maybe go into family law. Something that actually helps people instead of tearing them apart. I'm looking forward to being on the right side for once."

"A little idealistic but then, I suppose, that fits you."

Dante chuckled, but the lingering sadness at leaving everything he knew tugged at him. "You were good to me, growing up," he said. "I'll miss our talks."

"You were easy to be good to," Pietro said, pushing a manila envelope toward him across the desk. "Your new identity, fully vetted and legal. Unlike the documents you created, these should hold up against any search."

Dante opened the envelope and saw a large wad of cash as well. "What is this?" he asked, confused.

Pietro shrugged. "A little seed money for your new adventures."

"That's not necessary—"

"Please, let him do this one last thing," Pietro said. "You're the son he never had and he's allowing you to walk away. You have no idea how much this is costing him but he's willing to honor your request. The old Lorenzo would've found a way to force you to his will, no matter the cost. He is changing, bit by bit."

Dante closed the envelope, accepting the gift. He knew exactly how he'd put the money to good use. "Thank him for me."

Pietro nodded. "I will," he said, shaking Dante's hand. "It's been a pleasure watching you grow up to be a good man. Your plane leaves in two hours. A car is waiting to take you to the airport. I've arranged your final travel ticket. Flying economy…as is appropriate for your new identity."

Dante met Pietro's stare and saw the banked amusement. He grinned. *Cheeky bastard.* A sixteen-hour flight with multiple layovers and zero legroom. He'd done that on purpose. "Can't wait," Dante said.

And then he walked out, leaving behind everything he'd known since he was ten, to make a new life with the woman who'd changed his path forever.

Sixteen hours until he felt Frannie in his arms and vowed never to let her go again.

Maybe he'd see if he could upgrade his flight when he got to the airport—because sixteen hours was too long.

Chapter 31

Frannie did a final wipe-down of the counters at the café, shut down the machines, set the alarm on the bookstore and locked up. It was a week since Dante had been kidnapped—yes, she was still calling it a kidnapping—and Max had not received news.

Either no news was good news, or Dante was in a ditch somewhere.

She'd returned to some routine, but only by pretending that everything would work out somehow, no matter how unlikely that scenario was.

She spent a lot of time visualizing Dante walking through the bookstore door with a smile and a promise that he would never leave her again and that his family wouldn't keep trying to terrorize them.

What if—

"Ciao, bella."

Frannie's heart stopped at the familiar voice behind her. She squeezed her eyes shut as her heart leaped into her throat. Had she manifested so hard that she was hallucinating Dante's voice?

"Frannie?"

No, that was definitely Dante. She whirled around, afraid that no one would be standing behind her and that she was losing her mind to grief.

But it was her beloved Dante, standing there as if nothing had happened, as if he hadn't been carted off by those gangsters, breaking her heart into a million pieces, scrambling her thoughts into porridge as the miles stretched between them.

"Dante?" Her voice broke as she ran full tilt into his arms, squeezing so hard she might've cracked a rib or two, but she was afraid to let go as if he might be a figment of her imagination. "Is it really you? Am I losing my mind? How are you here? Did you escape?" Her eyes widened as she rushed to add, "I kept a bag packed in the car with some cash and clothes in preparation of this very scenario—"

"Frannie," he laughed, swinging her around before setting her on her feet to meet her astonished gaze. "I'm not going anywhere. I'm here to stay. There's no need to run."

"I don't understand...what happened?" she asked, confused. "The last I saw, you were being kidnapped—and I don't care what my cousin says, they coerced you into leaving—and you said...well, your uncle wanted you dead! How are you alive?"

"It's a long, sad story and I will tell you every detail but first, just let me taste you." He brushed his mouth across hers in a tender kiss that stole the strength from her knees, reminding her that she was putty in his capable hands and always would be. "God, I missed you so much. A week was an eternity without you."

She felt the same. "Don't ever do that to me again," she said tearfully with a happy smile. "I don't care what happens in the future, you're not leaving without me."

"My love, you will never have cause to worry about that happening. I am yours and you are mine. And now I can offer you what I couldn't before. My uncle and I came to an agreement and I'm free from my Santoro ties. I'm going to get my law degree to practice in the States and we're going to do it right. I want to marry you, Frannie. Now, if possible, but if not, I'll wait until you're ready. I have some money burning a hole in my pocket and I want to buy the home we'll raise our kids in."

"Did you just propose?" Frannie asked, tears welling in her eyes again.

"In a very clumsy and inarticulate way, but yes," he said, laughing. "Please don't hold that against me. I just can't wait to make a life with you."

"I would never hold that against you," she murmured, rising on her toes to kiss him again. "My answer is yes. I will absolutely marry the hell out of you, Dante. I will marry you so hard it leaves a mark on your soul."

"Perfect," he murmured with hunger in his eyes as he lifted her off her feet, deepening the kiss between them as if they weren't in the middle of the sidewalk, putting on a show for everyone to see, but Frannie didn't care. She wanted everyone to know that Dante was her knight in shining armor—no matter what the world threw at them.

And she couldn't wait to start her new life as Mrs. Dante Sinclair.

Or whatever new name identity he'd traded for his Santoro legacy.

As long as her hand was in his…nothing else mattered.

They'd figure it out.

Chapter 32

Dante held Frannie in his arms, stroking the smooth flesh of her side as she cuddled against him. The darkness around them was a private blanket of security as he shared everything that had happened when he returned to Italy.

He left nothing out—even revealing the sordid secret that he'd stolen from his uncle. The papers Lorenzo had been desperate to keep hidden.

"I'd always known about the aunt who took her life when she was very young, but when I discovered it was to hide the shame of her child's paternity, I was sick to my stomach. My grandfather was a terrible man. To father a child with his own daughter...well, it was a shameful secret my uncle wanted to hide from the world."

Frannie was understandably shaken but compassionate, as always.

"Family secrets are a cancer," she said. "Discovering my dad had a big secret has made me realize that no one is immune to temptation."

Dante held her more tightly, determined to ensure the Santoro legacy never touched their children. He wanted them to know only love and happiness.

"I'm not legally allowed to practice law in the States yet,

but I'll do whatever I can to help you with your family's situation," he said.

Frannie sighed, her fingers tracing small circles on his chest as she said, "Thank you. We can certainly use any insight you can share. My mom and Chase are heading to court next week to deal with Aunt Jessie's claim. I don't know how that's going to shake out, but I know Mom would appreciate the support. Oh, about that, my family wants to officially meet you this Sunday at family dinner. Are you okay with that? My family can be a lot."

"I can't wait."

And he wasn't just saying that. He wanted the whole experience of what it meant to have a big family, and since he was officially an orphan…he was ready to adopt the Coltons as his new family.

He was all in—and couldn't wait to start.

A mischievous smile curved his lips as he murmured against the crown of her head. "How do you feel about being a pregnant bride?"

Frannie gasped in fake outrage, "Dante Sinclair, are you trying to give my poor mother a heart attack?" She rolled on top, staring at him with an equally flirty smile, looking like a goddess in the moonlight. "However, accidents happen…"

And he knew at that moment his heart would forever be safe with Frannie as his partner in love, life and laughter.

In all things. Just as it should be.

* * * * *